EVALD FLISAR (b. 1945) is a novelist, playwright, essayist and editor and one of the most prolific authors in Slovenia today. After a long period abroad – three years in Australia, seventeen years in London – Flisar has been resident in Ljubljana, Slovenia, since 1990. Between 1995 and 2002 he was president of the Slovene Writers' Association, and since 1998 he has been the chief editor of the oldest Slovenian literary journal *Sodobnost* (*Contemporary Review*). He is the author of fourteen novels (ten of them shortlisted for the Kresnik Prize, the Slovenian 'Booker'), two collections of short stories, three travelogues, two books for children and fifteen stage plays (seven nominated for Best Play of the Year Award, with three winners). He is also the recipient of the Prešeren Foundation Prize, the highest state award for prose and drama, and the prestigious Župančič Award for lifetime achievement. His works have been translated into forty languages (including an English-language edition of *My Father's Dreams*, published by Istros Books in 2015) and his stage plays are regularly performed all over the world, most recently in Austria, Egypt, India, Indonesia, Japan, Taiwan, Serbia, Bosnia and Belarus. In 2014 his novel *On the Gold Coast* (published in English by Sampark, Kolkata, India) was nominated for the most prestigious European literary prize, the Dublin IMPAC International Literary Award.

DAVID LIMON is an Englishman in Ljubljana, a translator, university teacher and researcher of intercultural communication. His literary translations include novels by Andrej Skubic, Boris Kolar and Evald Flisar as well as short stories and other works by a broad range of writers, including Fran Levstik, Ivan Cankar, Janez Trdina, Vitomil Zupan, Mirana Likar Bajželj, Tadej Golob, Nina Kokelj and Janja Vidmar.

OTHER TITLES IN
THE WORLD SERIES
SLOVENIAN SEASON

Dušan Šarotar, *Panorama* (translated by Rawley Grau)
Jela Krečič, *None Like Her* (treanslated by Olivia Hellewell)

PETER OWEN WORLD SERIES

'*The world is a book, and those who do not travel read only one page,*' wrote St Augustine. Journey with us to explore outstanding contemporary literature translated into English for the first time. Read a single book in each season – which will focus on a different country or region every time – or try all three and experience the range and diversity to be found in contemporary literature from across the globe.

Read the world – three books at a time

3 works of literature in
2 seasons each year from
1 country each season

For information on forthcoming seasons go to www.peterowen.com.

THREE LOVES,
ONE DEATH

Also by Evald Flisar and published by Istros Books

My Father's Dreams

1

It all began some years after the war for independence, when my family decided to move from the town to the country. The enthusiasm was indescribable. The faces of even the gloomiest among us shone, while my grandmother, who after her stroke could not move the lower part of her face, managed to stretch the right corner of her mouth. My mother was convinced that this was the most reliable sign that in our new home renewal and health awaited us.

The house was nothing special. It was near a wood on the edge of a village. It was most reminiscent of a neglected country inn, and it had a cellar in which the previous owner had left three barrels of wine. There were also some outbuildings, the functions of which we could only guess at.

One of them had definitely been a pigsty. This was established by my cousin Elizabeta, Mara's illegitimate daughter, born when my aunt was forty. Because of this, whenever Granny had a glass of wine on festive days, she liked to say that Elizabeta had been conceived immaculately or fathered by a malign demon. Elizabeta could discern not only smells that most people did not know existed but the history of spaces and the colours of feelings that hung in the air.

'I smell pigs,' she said when she entered the outbuilding, which Aunt Mara, an amateur painter with ambition but no talent, had decided to convert into a studio. Fortunately, only my mother and I heard her.

When Elizabeta sniffed again and added that she could also smell the mortal fear of the pigs that had been dragged into the yard to be slaughtered, my mother shouted for her to be quiet, for God's sake. After all, Aunt Mara had chosen the outbuilding as a studio because of the view of the river down below and the surrounding hills; besides which, it would all be aired and repainted and immediately impregnated with a mixture of Mara's paints and perfumes. And even reputable English families were known to live in converted stables.

Elizabeta calmly offered to keep quiet for the price of three large boxes of chocolates. 'Two,' bargained my mother. 'Two of the biggest' was Elizabeta's compromise solution. 'But for the last time,' said my mother.

Aunt Mara never suspected what sounds were supplanted by the baroque arias that accompanied her in the new space when, brush in hand and cigarette in mouth, she started to realize her 'renewed vision'. When Elizabeta commented loudly at dinner that these arias reminded her of the squealing of pigs, she immediately became agitated, but my mother's swift praise of her new artistic style softened her sufficiently that she forgot to call Elizabeta a little bastard and began to discuss at length the difference between watercolours and oils – to the delight of the rest of the family who one after the other offered improbable reasons why they couldn't finish their meal and quickly left the table.

Next morning Elizabeta got another box of chocolates from my mother.

Nevertheless, it seemed at first that everyone would get from village life what they most wanted; Granny the smell of freshly ploughed earth and the mooing of cows, as well as other smells and sounds that reminded her of her childhood. 'Carnations,' she scrawled on a sheet of paper, when the stroke robbed her of her speech, 'there will be carnations everywhere, and I'll sleep with the window open so that I can carry their scent with me when I take my last breath and go to the other side.'

Mum hoped that in the new house she could set up a private centre for meditation and healthy living and at the same time find enough room for at least two thousand books on Zen Buddhism, yoga, reiki, Rolfing and other aspects of the Age of Aquarius. As a retired secondary-school teacher, this seemed to her the only thing worthy of her time.

But, above all, she was enthusiastic about the paths that gently wound their way towards the valley and up towards the woods, just right for her daily morning run – or that extreme form of masochism the 'mini-marathon', as it was referred to by the psychiatrist that my parents visited as part of a healthy-living programme they engaged in to help with Dad's alcoholism.

After several years of stubbornly resisting the psychiatrist's interventions, Dad suddenly lost interest not only in drinking but also in all of life's other pleasures, including those that Mum was not yet ready to forgo. Thus a morning marathon was the only way to neutralize the energy that built up inside her daily because of Dad's indifference. Dad, who realized this, carefully set the alarm every evening so that she would never oversleep.

Immediately after quitting the programme at his own request he went to the head teacher of the school where he had taught history for thirty years and asked to take early retirement.

'History is over,' he announced, 'not because of what Fukuyama said but because of the success that our small nation has finally achieved. Freedom, that most mixed blessing of all, has completely ruined this land from which could spring tragic conflicts or big ideas and sowed the seeds of petty division, devious business dealings and the banality of the public media.' His subject, history, had ceased to be academic and become esoteric, and he had no intention of dealing with it further. He would like to withdraw, with appropriate severance pay, of course.

The head teacher, who was Mum's cousin and a good friend of the family, immediately agreed. The severance money contributed the vital missing amount that allowed Dad to buy the house where 'all his family', as he referred to us, would be able to find – better late than never – that genuine freedom which is the source of true happiness.

'At the end of the day, being free is our duty,' he said. 'A free country needs free people.'

Dad saw happiness in inertia. In contrast to Mum, who wanted to stay for ever young – and who was prepared to die for the idea – he decided to listen to Jung's advice that at the age of sixty a man must bid farewell to the things more suited to younger years and turn inwards, shaping from his memories a mosaic of life that will give meaning to his time on this earth and also provide a bridge that will, at the required moment, connect him to God. He emphasized that he would still be accessible but most of the time he would be sunk in thought, and he expected us to respect his need to retreat from the external world to the internal one, where a great deal of work awaited him.

Ultimately, everyone got what they wanted: Peter an ideal location for his telescope and star-gazing; me the perfect opportunity for aimless wandering through the woods and fruitless speculation about the future, which, it seemed likely, would be no different from my past; Mum's brother Vinko

– an accountant by profession but for years in the grip of an ambition to grow the biggest head of cabbage in the world and find his way into the *Guinness World Records* – fertile soil; Dad's cousin Vladimir the time as well as the peace and quiet in which to complete his memoirs of his heroic Partisan days; and his wife Eva, thirty years younger than him, a smooth enough road to allow her to disappear in his Alfa Romeo every day to have a good time with friends and leave him in peace.

After his speech, my father withdrew to his part of the house and left us wondering whether some of us were worthy of the saintly glow he emanated. For the first time in our lives, we felt as one that Dad had until now cultivated his best qualities in secret and that in his vicinity nothing bad could happen to any of us.

Renovation work on the house and its six outbuildings proceeded with such *élan* and solidarity that we soon shortened the envisaged completion date for our new home from two years to one.

2

The only one who failed to blend in with the homogenous familial whole that took shape in the glow of Dad's wisdom and the rays of Mum's energy was – inevitably – Elizabeta, partly, no doubt, because Mum stopped giving her boxes of chocolates but mainly because of her new school, where in most subjects, or so she claimed, she surpassed not only her fellow pupils but also the teachers.

'Boredom is Lucifer's favourite son,' Granny would say when she could still speak, but at that point no one suspected how prophetic her words would prove to be in connection with Elizabeta.

One Sunday during lunch the young troublemaker announced that the house and its outbuildings lay on a dangerous intersection of electromagnetic currents and so all our efforts to create an ideal family were doomed to failure. 'We're dealing with forces that themselves don't know what they want and are acting like mischievous gremlins who just do whatever comes into their heads at that moment.'

Mum was the only one to show any sign of being startled by this announcement; the rest of us merely shrugged, muttered something and then carried on eating.

Elizabeta hated lukewarm responses to her provocations. She went into full attack mode. She said that strange things were happening in the house; that for some time Aunt Mara had been filling the clearings and meadows in her watercolours with pigs rather than sheep; that Granny was arguing with someone in her room almost the whole night; that the books Mum had carefully arranged on the shelves in alphabetical order by author name had twice been jumbled up, each time according to some unknown and probably diabolical alphabet; that there emerged from my room at night guttural gasping and panting as if someone were being throttled. And twice she had seen Uncle Vladimir, stripped to the waist, standing in a wild storm in the middle of the neighbour's wheat field with his arms raised, begging the thunder to strike him.

On the table in Peter's room she had found some notes from which it was evident that through his telescope he had been watching a giant meteorite which was just two weeks from earth and would scatter its remains through space. Uncle Vinko wasn't digging in the garden to plant cabbages but was excavating three grave-like holes in which he was planning to bury our bodies when the spirit that ruled the place strangled each of us in turn.

The only solution was to sell the house and move back to town.

Her words were followed by silence. Some members of the family gave each other furtive glances; others stared stubbornly at their plates. Then simultaneously we turned and looked at Dad. It was clear he was the only one capable of passing judgement.

He popped the last piece of steak into his mouth and chewed it thoroughly. He carefully, contemplatively wiped his mouth and chin. Finally, he got up slowly and, without looking at anyone, went to his room. His door seemed to close somewhat more decisively than usual.

Mum had to take on the role of judge.

She said that in addition to pigs Aunt Mara could also paint giraffes, walruses or five-headed monsters if her artistic imagination so dictated; that Granny wasn't arguing with anyone in her room but listening to the radio because she couldn't sleep; that the books had not been rearranged by a goblin according to some diabolical alphabet but they had done so of their own accord when the shelves collapsed under their weight; that the gasping and panting coming from my room were the result of the terrible nightmares that had plagued me since I was five, certainly nothing to do with the obsessive masturbation often characteristic of boys my age.

As for Vladimir, we had to understand that he had a very young, flighty wife, who was sometimes too much for a hero in possession of ten Partisan decorations. Peter's notes on meteorites and so on were, of course, a matter for discussion between him and the professor under whose supervision he should long ago have finished his degree in cosmology. Certainly the earth would not crumble to dust merely because a naughty girl wanted to frighten her nearest and dearest.

'And Vinko himself', said Mum in conclusion, 'can explain who he is burying in the garden.'

Without prevarication, Uncle Vinko acknowledged that the holes really did look like graves, but his hobby was so important to him that he didn't have the time to think about killing any of us in passing. He merely wanted to bury the remains of the dusty farm equipment that was filling the shed in the orchard. He wanted to do it up and turn it into a seed store. What use were broken pickaxes, hoes, forks, scythes, sickles, ploughshares, harrows and so on? We hadn't returned to the village to start farming again after two generations of urban living. Everything superfluous that reminded us too clearly of other times, other places, other stories should be buried away out of sight. This needed to be done in order to distance ourselves from the mistakes of the past that had been hindering our efforts ever since we moved into the new house.

Mum was the first to applaud these words; the others followed her example. All except for Elizabeta, who stuck out her tongue and ran outside.

3

Since I had nothing to do I offered to help Uncle Vinko. Some of the things in the shed were so heavy that he couldn't easily get them to their graves on his own. Overflowing with gratitude, he left for me the dustiest and most decaying pieces of equipment. With the larger items that called for two pairs of hands, I always ended up, miraculously, with the heaviest or most awkward end.

I was extremely pleased when Peter joined us and started to pester Uncle. He asked him what were the philosophical implications of the fact that he needed a hoe if he wanted to bury a hoe and a spade to bury a spade; and, above all, whether he didn't see in his burying of old tools with new ones a symbolic re-enactment of the Sisyphean fruitlessness of all human striving.

Uncle Vinko replied that he normally left school-level philosophizing to fourth-year physics pupils, especially those who had already failed philosophy. He saw his actions as the decisive phase in the healing of the family spirit, which, for more than a hundred generations, had produced an endless succession of exploiters of every possible ilk, from counts through big landowners to the members of the Church and agricultural cooperatives, who had never ploughed and sown seeds in the earth out of love. The suffering of the family spirit could be sensed so strongly in these old tools that it positively radiated from them, he maintained; but together with the tools themselves it would be interred for ever. Only then would we be truly free – if it was freedom that we really needed. And wanted. From now on every tool that we used – be it a spade, an axe, a coffee-grinder or a computer – would be accompanied by a feeling arising from joy at life not fear of poverty or imprisonment.

He said these words more in celebration than in anger. Then he asked Peter to help us carry from the shed a piece of equipment so big and awkward it would need three of us to shift it. We each took a corner and with difficulty manoeuvred the thing from the gloomy interior into the daylight. We laid it on the grass and examined it, first with surprise – and then astonishment.

For it was like nothing we had ever seen before. Above all, it had no flat surface on which to stand it. From the central mass, which had no discernible shape or function, there protruded, without order or symmetry, many disparate steel, aluminium and even wooden excrescences. With some imagination it was possible to recognize among them the cubist forms of spades, picks, hoes, perhaps sickles and scythes, perhaps rakes and other tools, but these two were just the ends or beginnings of what they were supposed to be. In between, conjoined with other pieces, it was possible to discern the links of a chain, half a cogwheel, a toilet bowl, the workings of a wall clock, two weights and blackened frying-pan handles.

If these parts or fragments had been bound together with wire or welded together into a whole then the whole thing could be ascribed to the imagination of a modernist sculptor, and by relocating it to the domain of art, where everything is possible and everything permitted, it could be deprived of the aggressive concreteness before which we squatted like helpless children.

Making a visible effort, Uncle Vinko gathered himself and declared that this unfortunate joke by a drunken blacksmith should be thrown in a hole, covered over and forgotten. Peter was strongly against this: it could be part of a spaceship that had crashed near by. In any case, every unknown thing should first be researched, given a name and a meaning, so that later it did not leap forth from our subconscious in the form of neurosis.

But Vinko stubbornly insisted. I think he would have dragged the chained monster to the hole himself if my mother hadn't happened past at that moment, returning from her afternoon marathon (the morning one had been cancelled because of a downpour). She stopped and looked at the thing from every possible angle. She pressed here, pulled there, shook it to the left and to the right. Then, in a voice trembling with agitation, she told me to call my father.

In five minutes the whole family had gathered around the discovery, including Vladimir's wife, who had just returned from one of her escapades. With water from a hosepipe we washed the grime from the object. We wanted to see whether beneath the layer of compacted soil there might be evidence of joints and welds. Peter brought a magnifying glass to investigate. But all in vain.

We all waited to see what Dad would say. He was silent for quite some time. When he finally opened his mouth he did not offer a solution but merely asked what *we* thought about the thing.

Elizabeta said that it was an evil device made by spirits under cover of night in order to bring conflict and confusion to our family and to drive us away, since it was obvious that we would never find peace or happiness here.

'Nonsense,' Mum said angrily. 'We'll talk about spirits only when the last – and I mean the last – attempt to explain it rationally has failed.'

But she could not come up with a suitable explanation herself, so she fell into embarrassed silence.

It soon became obvious that, in trying to find a solution to the puzzle that lay before us, we were not searching through memory banks of appropriate knowledge but rather competing in imagination. In this regard the most creative suggestion came from Vladimir's wife, who ascribed the origin of the object to a crash between a sports car and a tractor full of farming tools: through the extreme pressure and the explosion of fuel everything had shattered and fused into this thing we were now unnecessarily scratching our heads about and wasting time that could be spent more pleasantly (in her case, on dates in town – and she immediately drove off to one).

Vladimir said that for him, as a scientific materialist, there were no mysteries on this earth that could not be resolved through a historical-dialectical approach. We should look into the past and ask the previous owner as well as his predecessor, for the object had not fallen from the sky. It had come from somewhere; someone had left or assembled it there; someone was responsible, someone was guilty. We needed to establish who, for freedom is only possible when blame has been fairly distributed, even for the most trivial things.

Aunt Mara brought her easel and began to paint the unidentified object. She said that it had definitely fallen from the sky, but that wasn't important; everything in the world was first and foremost an artistic challenge.

Dad turned to me. Since I didn't want to give the impression of indifference I swiftly contributed the idea that it must have been – because of the wires and clock wheels – a bomb, which when detonated hadn't exploded but rather imploded and sunk into itself.

Peter agreed that my suggestion was not such a stupid one but that the wheel in the centre was not from a clock, it was from a shortwave radio. He fetched three batteries, put them into the slot at the centre of the wheel and the strange creation began to screech and to broadcast a programme in which a man, in an unknown language that sounded like Arabic, shouted out a news item or something.

With lowered eyes and hands we stood around the diabolical device and listened to the voice coming from God knows where, maybe from space, maybe from the interior of the thing itself or from our defeated imaginations, which had, beneath the weight of the incident – like the object before us – become stuck together in a mass of uncertainty and unease.

It began to rain. We covered the thing with a tarpaulin and retreated to our rooms.

Renovation of the house began to falter; finally it stopped. Peter started to neglect his studies and then pulled out of his final examination, postponing it for a year. The unidentified object lay in the middle of the orchard, visible to all. It calmly accepted heatwaves, downpours, hailstorms, kicks, sampling, chemical analysis, photographic sessions and, above all, curiosity, for our house became a tourist attraction for both domestic and foreign visitors.

An American offered Dad a quarter of a million dollars for the mysterious object. Dad said he could have it for nothing if he told him what it was, where it had appeared from and what it was for.

Eventually the attentions of the curious and of journalists began to stifle us. Mum started running around the outside of the house, doing two hundred circuits a day. Dad submerged himself up to the eyeballs in the study of engineering, chemistry, agronomy, physics and related disciplines. He borrowed some books from Peter, others he collected from libraries and bookshops and brought them home in a minibus. He was getting ever thinner; his eyes burned as if inside he was slowly being consumed by the flames of hell. The method employed by Cousin Vladimir also failed to bear fruit. He compiled a report on the history of the house and of its previous owners, but none of them, including the one from whom we had bought it, could recall ever seeing the object in the shed. Although he had thrown some unwanted tools in there, most had been there since time immemorial.

4

After a few months the only ones still searching for an answer were Dad and Peter. The rest of us had grown weary of the mystery and gradually returned to our old habits and chores. It became bothersome, even somehow funny, especially when, in the middle of the night, we looked out of the window and saw Dad and Peter in the middle of the orchard measuring distances and angles between parts of the object and writing them down by torchlight. Then we would hear them below us in the living-room debating and arguing until dawn.

One day, in front of us all, Mum asked Dad to desist from his activities, which could lead only to ruin; if not for his own sake, then for that of his son, a student who had been a star of the faculty but who was now on the verge of losing his mind.

'I'm asking both of you,' she said, 'I'm asking you in the name of the family to stop.'

Peter said nothing.

For the first time in ages Dad addressed the entire family, as he was wont to do before the discovery of the mystery object. He said that the family had not been struck by an accident, as some liked to think. Quite the opposite. Everything on this earth had its purpose and meaning: nothing made by God or man was without its origin. And if we put God to one side there was still evolution, quantum theory and chaos theory – even they did not allow for the possibility that something could come from nowhere, find itself somewhere for no reason and be of no use to anyone.

Let us face the truth, he continued. We were a family that had gone off the rails because of the stresses of the modern world and, fearing disaster, we had returned to the countryside to seek our roots, to find fresh blood, a new energy for life. But it was more than obvious that relying on flight

Evald Flisar

THREE LOVES, ONE DEATH

Translated from the Slovene by David Limon

PETER OWEN
WORLD SERIES

WORLD SERIES SEASON 1: SLOVENIA

THE WORLD SERIES IS A JOINT INITIATIVE BETWEEN

PETER OWEN PUBLISHERS AND ISTROS BOOKS

Peter Owen Publishers/Istros Books
81 Ridge Road, London N8 9NP, UK

Peter Owen and Istros Books are distributed in the USA and Canada by
Independent Publishers Group/Trafalgar Square
814 North Franklin Street, Chicago, IL 60610, USA

Originally published in Slovene as *Ljubezni tri in ena smrt* by
Vodnikova založba, Ljubljana
First English language edition published by Peter Owen/Istros Books 2016

Paperback ISBN   978-0-7206-1930-0
Epub ISBN   978-0-7206-1919-5
Mobipocket ISBN   978-0-7206-1920-1
PDF ISBN   978-0-7206-1921-8

A catalogue record for this book is available from the British Library.

Printed and bound in Great Britain by
CPI Group (UK) Ltd, Croydon, CR0 4YY

This publication has been made possible with the financial assistance of the
Trubar Foundation, Ljubljana, Slovenia.

was an illusion. In whatever direction you flee you encounter a sphinx that blocks your path. Often the sphinx is a puzzle you have to solve if you don't want to get stuck where you are or run back to where you came from. In our family we have always fled: from poverty to the town, from urban poverty to America, from abroad back home, from disappointment to alcohol, from alcohol to treatment, from the effort required to live a healthy life to mysticism and from there back to the embrace of almighty Reason.

'In the past three hundred years not one member of our family has dared to confront that great, central obstacle on our path, the puzzle that cannot be circumvented or jumped over. Now the moment of decision has come for us, too. Are we going to flee, or are we going to face the challenge?'

With these words Dad turned and went to his room. He hadn't touched the food on his plate.

Mum began to cry silently. Large tears dripped on to the pieces of cauli-flower that she was absentmindedly putting in her mouth. Peter tried to add something, perhaps to clarify what Dad had left incomplete or not stated clearly enough. His eyes seemed to take in each one of us in turn, as if looking for encouragement or reassurance that we would understand what he was about to say. But, thanks to the dullness he detected in our eyes, he said not a word.

And thus silence became the tone and the colour of life in the half-finished house; guilt-laden silence that resembled consideration taken to extremes was merely the last defence against the despair that was waiting for an opportunity to erupt and overwhelm us.

Dad and Peter began to invite so-called experts to the house. They drank plenty of wine and spoke a lot. One of them used a special program on Peter's computer to analyse the shapes and relationship between the parts of the device. The result surprised him more than anyone: after each attempt there appeared on the screen the message 'Object of unknown origin'.

It was soon after this that a farmer from a village at the other end of the country wrote to Dad that the mystery object, as far as he could judge from the pictures in the newspaper, was nothing more or less than a plough. Without waiting for a reply, three days later he appeared on our doorstep, apologizing for turning up unannounced but saying that the matter wouldn't give him a moment's peace. If we had a field that needed ploughing, he would swiftly show us that common sense could solve any mystery.

The field and an ox were lent by our nearest neighbour, who also helped us to carry the device down the hill and attach it to an ox harness with two outgrowths – one reminiscent of part of a spade and the other of a link in a chain.

Then the farmer took hold with his left hand of the protruding part reminiscent of a hoe and with his right the handle of the frying-pan. He turned the object so that the wavy blade was on the ground, cracked the whip and the ox began to pull and the blade to plough. Behind the device there were deep, nicely levelled furrows.

'Plough,' repeated the farmer when he had gone over the whole field.

But the radio in the centre of the 'plough', even during the ploughing, had continued to broadcast the shortwave programme that had not changed since we first heard it. The male voice, still the same one, was without pause rather brusquely and didactically reporting, preaching or explaining.

Dad asked the farmer whether the radio had disturbed him while he had been ploughing. The man replied that he would have preferred a lively tune and then – embarrassed and none too pleased with himself – he took his leave.

Autumn arrived and a time of melancholy. Mum had abandoned her marathon-running in the summer; she had bought some cookery books and started to bake *potica* cake to compete with Mara, who was convinced that hers was the best. At school Elizabeta had bitten her mathematics teacher and drawn blood; she had then fled into the woods where we had found her after a few days with the help of the police, all cried out and chilled through. Vladimir completed his memoirs but was so dissatisfied with them that he threw them into the fire and swore he would never write another word.

This was not entirely unconnected with the fact that his Eva had not returned from one of her assignations. Instead, a letter arrived in which she informed him that she was leaving him – if she ever wanted to write her own memoirs, she must make an effort to have something to write about.

Uncle Vinko changed jobs and was working so much that he was completely neglecting his cabbages.

Then, just before the first snow, Granny died. On the notepad beside her bed she had scrawled her last word: 'lightning'. Three weeks after her funeral a debate blew up about what she'd been thinking of. Mum thought that as death approached she had felt as if she had been struck by lightning, but

Aunt Mara claimed that she had been trying to tell us something completely different: let lightning strike every one of us.

Elizabeta, who had been less irritating of late, said that the word lightning referred to the thing still lying in the orchard, although we had all forgotten about it because it was hidden by snow. She maintained that the shed, which had at one time contained a confusion of tools, a redundant radio and a toilet bowl, had been struck by lightning, and the extreme heat had welded the various items into the 'mysterious device'. That's what Granny had been trying to tell us before she went to the other world.

To the question as to why the shed had not burned down when the lightning struck, Elizabeta had no answer. She said that was another story, another mystery that we didn't need to concern ourselves with.

We looked at Dad and waited for him to choose a side. But he said nothing. No one dared to encourage him to speak; we knew that he had been drinking again for some time and that there was slowly building within him, undiscernibly yet inexorably, the old exasperation. We quietly hoped that he and Mum would return to the psychiatrist's programme, which perhaps hadn't worked the first time around because it had robbed them of their ability to face the unpredictable and had cultivated within them an over-rigid self-belief, excessive self-confidence. Perhaps the second time around, with the experience they had, it would have a benign influence on the psychologist and through him on themselves and other patients.

When the snow had melted we carried the unknown object back inside the shed. Mum bought a heavy padlock and asked me to secure the door with it. When I had done so, she locked it and threw the key in the well.

'There,' she said.

She and Dad began to take long walks in the surrounding hills. Spring awoke. We guessed that Mum was trying to bring Dad back into contact with nature, with the breath of living and understandable things, with the smell of earth, in which he had once seen the only possible cure for the melancholy that arises from the helplessness of the human intellect.

But his posture became ever more bent, reflecting the weight of a defeat from which he could not recover in merely a month or so. It was only in his eyes that we saw a gentle gleam that suggested that perhaps in a year or two he might be able to accept that the world was no less perfect because it contained things and events that could not be explained.

5

Over the next few months no one went near the shed, so we gradually forgot about the Great Mystery. But, before we could breathe normally again, there arose a new one, at first sight less puzzling but in some ways even more strange, for it had legs, arms, eyes and even a bald patch from which the sun's rays reflected as from a pane of glass.

It also had a name, although at first no one could believe it was real: Jaroslav Švejk.

This middle-aged and slightly clumsy-looking gentleman appeared in our dining-room one day after Sunday lunch at the end of June, when we were about to start on the cake that Aunt Mara had baked in honour of the sale of her first picture. He looked like a Sunday day-tripper who had got lost and wanted to ask how to find his way back to the path through the woods. This assumption was immediately undermined by Mum's expression, which quickly turned from a grimace of astonishment to great hostility.

She leaped up from the table, knocking over a cup of coffee, and dashed towards the newcomer, shrieking, 'No, no, no, please, no!'

She grabbed the clumsy man's arm and half pushed, half pulled him through the open door into the orchard, where she leaned him against an apple tree and began to rebuke him as if he were a child who had done something extremely mischievous.

We realized that the visitor was not a walker gone astray. It was evident that Mum knew him but that she did not want us to do so. As she waved her arms beneath the apple tree, hurling heaven knows what curses at his surprised but calm face, we began to speculate, as was our family custom, who he might be and what might have caused this lapse in Mum's usually calm demeanour.

Aunt Mara, still slightly inflated with pride because the neighbouring farmer had bought a picture of his favourite cow, which liked grazing beneath the window of her studio, suggested that the man had evidently come to look at her paintings. Word soon spreads, and she had obviously found a subject from which she would be drawing inspiration for her art for years to come. Mum's animosity towards the potential admirer of her work was a clear sign of the lack of respect for her talent, which nobody in the family seemed to believe in, particularly those from whom she would have expected the most support and understanding.

She began to wipe her eyes with a napkin, even though there was not the slightest trace of moisture in them.

We all knew that the most provocative speculation about the man's identity would be contributed by Elizabeta. 'It's your mum's former lover,' she said looking at me. 'He has come to lure her into his web once more. But your dad, in spite of his lukewarmness in recent years, still has his male pride and will not allow it, which means that in a few minutes' time we will witness a gladiatorial struggle in the orchard between two ageing but still determined men for your mum's favours. And what a nice conclusion to Sunday that will be.'

Thinking of the young wife who had left him, Cousin Vladimir remarked that as a rule former lovers do not return to revive relationships that did not suit them and that the whole thing was plainly something much more serious. The stranger was one of those figures that history could never find the right drawer for, and every so often, in line with some bizarre centrifugal law, returned to continue the process of causing grief which they had failed to finish before.

This meant that by definition the newcomer was a dangerous person from whom we had to protect Mum, for she would never have become so worked up if the man in question had not committed a great wrong against her in the past. We should sit him at a table, shine a strong light in his eyes and subject him to a thorough interrogation. Sooner or later he would confess not only the mischief he had committed in the past but also what he was planning for the future.

We looked at Dad, the retired teacher of history, who would certainly have something apposite to say about this suggestion. But before he could rouse himself from the strange torpor into which he had sunk Uncle Vinko, Mum's brother, shoved back his chair with such force that it crashed into the wall behind him. As swift as a weasel, he rushed through the door and charged towards Mum and the mystery visitor beneath the apple tree.

He was too far away for us to be able to hear what he was saying, although to judge from his gestures Uncle Vinko was talking with an energy that we had never seen before. But he appeared to be on the side of the stranger in the way he was trying to protect him from Mum's onslaught.

'I'm going to start a family chronicle,' Elizabeta stated.

My older brother Peter, who had so far remained quiet, frowned and said, 'This is all so stupid. The only important things are happening deep in space. That's where our fates are decided.'

Before I could ask him who decided, Uncle Vinko, Mum and the stranger came into the dining-room and looked at us as if they had an important announcement to make. The new arrival was extremely embarrassed; Mum had her head down and was defiantly biting her lip while Uncle Vinko was trying, not very successfully, to give the impression that he had things under control.

He said that God, moving in his mysterious way, had just enlarged the family by giving us an additional uncle, the supposed long-lost brother of him and my mother, who had fallen on hard times and who was looking for a roof over his head – temporarily, of course.

Unexpectedly, Dad invited the additional uncle to join us at the table.

In the ensuing conversation, which quickly became friendly, in spite of Mum stubbornly continuing to sulk, it emerged that Jaroslav Švejk was entangled in the branches of our family tree almost by chance, thanks to an indiscretion on the part of my maternal grandmother during a visit to Prague. The indiscretion was not in itself scandalous, but the excursion organized by the women's section of the Socialist Alliance had lasted only two days. In addition to this, Granny was already married with a three-year-old son – who became Uncle Vinko.

But it was the time of the hippies and free love, so no one got too excited except, understandably, my granddad, until Granny managed to shut him up with threats of some kind.

This was explained to us by Uncle Vinko, who had taken on the duty of introducing his lost half-brother to the family circle. Mum didn't utter a word, preferring to focus on Mara's cake: she was stuffing piece after piece into her mouth as if seized by terrible hunger. It was clear that she would have preferred it if certain details about her family, about which she had managed to remain eloquently silent, were to stay hidden, almost as if she was ashamed not only of her newly sprung half-brother but also her parents – particularly her mother who, Vinko said, had been obsessed with the idea of her children succeeding in life. As soon as she realized that he and Mum would not make much of themselves she had loaded her dreams on to the shoulders of the 'Czech bastard', as my granddad had evidently labelled this foreign acquisition.

Uncle Švejk had no desire to become a 'historical personage'. Even in school he had realized that he could only cope with this burden by trying to remain 'ordinary, absolutely ordinary'. Of course, the fact that he bore the surname of one of the greatest literary heroes of the twentieth century did not help and neither did Granny's decision to add to it the Christian name of Švejk's author.

She had done so in the hope that this resonant name would make his path towards 'historical significance' that much easier, but 'Little Švejk', as they called him, felt increasingly burdened by his mother's ambitions for his future; no one knew whether this was because of contrariness or because he identified with the eponymous hero of Hašek's book.

Whatever the reason, the more his malicious schoolmates ran after him shouting '*Ich melde gehorsamst!*' the less inclined Švejk was to make an effort at anything in life. And because it never rains but pours, his life was so dogged by bad luck that he was incapable of taking a step without causing a catastrophe of some kind – indisputable evidence, emphasized Vinko, that God prefers to take it out on those who strive hardest to live according to his rules.

'Will this story go on much longer?' asked Elizabeta with a yawn, trying to interrupt Vinko's flow.

Mum said nothing because she was choking on a large piece of cake, so Dad came to the rescue, giving Elizabeta a harsh look and saying, 'I doubt it will end before dinner, so you go and do whatever you have to do.'

'In that case, I won't,' said Elizabeta. 'I'd rather wait and see what I find out about my idiotic relatives.'

Aunt Mara tapped her on the head with the handle of her fork and told her to stop giving the impression that we were an uncouth family. And that

Mr Švejk had an interesting face, slightly reminiscent of an angular football. It would be a pleasant challenge to paint his portrait, she added.

Then Dad spoke. He said that no one was behaving as they should towards our guest, considering he was our long-lost relative. How he had become lost or why, he would not say – it didn't interest him at that moment; the story would emerge when the time was ripe and certain members of the family had found sufficient courage – and here he gave Mum a sideways glance. In any case, he was welcome and could move into our guest room, the purpose of which was precisely to give refuge to mysteries from the family's past.

As a family we were used to mysteries, whether they fell from the sky or arose from our subconscious, but it was the duty of the head of the family, which we acknowledged him to be, to protect us from the unforeseen. So he hoped Uncle Švejk would not take it amiss if he said openly that expressions like 'extreme bad luck' or 'catastrophe of some kind' filled him, to put it mildly, with great apprehension. A short clarification would help us to accept our new family member without undue concern and without fear that God was sending yet another trial.

The unexpected guest, who during Dad's intervention was discreetly touching his face as if to check whether his head really did resemble an angular football, said nothing.

Uncle Vinko, who had evidently become Švejk's protector and biographer – and with a sense of obligation that was visibly transforming into a kind of delight – broke in once more. He acknowledged that Dad's caution, so characteristic of him, was, of course, an honour for the family, but in the case of Švejk such concern was unnecessary. He had maintained regular contact with his half-brother the whole time of his supposed non-existence – although, naturally, in secret so as not to upset his sister.

A red-faced Mum rose from the table and left the dining-room.

6

Uncle Vinko felt that the moment had come when a more detailed version of Švejk's past might be received by the family with the right degree of understanding. With pauses and emphases, as if he were telling children a bedtime fairy story, he presented Švejk in all his lack of orthodoxy. Above all, he stressed his ability to stay calm in the midst of the worst catastrophes, something that had stunned most people who witnessed it. For example, once when he was getting out of a car and opened the door at the precise moment that a lorry was driving past, which removed the door and carried on for fifty metres with it attached, Švejk's main concern was for the driver's safety. He asked him at least ten times if he was all right. He would have asked him more if the driver had not succumbed to a fit of rage and punched Švejk in the face. 'He had every right to do it,' Švejk explained to the police officers, who wanted to know if he was going to press charges against his assailant.

Švejk's frequent mishaps soon became a popular topic of conversation in pubs and workplaces, especially at the bus company where he worked as a driver. It was no surprise that they soon began to invite him to appear on popular television shows. He accepted the invitations as something self-evident, but, in general, he disappointed people. Not only did he not recognize the mocking tone of the interviewer and thus deprived the viewers of their expected laughs, he was totally unwilling to admit that he had been at all affected by the long list of calamities that were enumerated for him.

His reply was always the same. 'We are sent to this world to learn patience and tranquillity. In this way we prepare ourselves for the next world, which won't be as kind to us as this one, which we try to blacken the name of at every opportunity.'

Each time an interviewer tried to get him to acknowledge the most infamous instances of his clumsiness – how one day, when picking up a pencil from the floor, he had managed to put his back out; then the boiler had exploded in his bathroom because, when repairing it, he had connected up the wrong wires; and, finally, he forgot to turn the tap off, causing a flood not just in his apartment but also in all those below.

And how did he manage to trap more passengers in the closing doors of his bus in a single week than other drivers managed in a year? Not to mention the ship that he spent painstakingly constructing inside a bottle only to accidentally destroy it with acid. And, while we're at it, how many times had he received a terrible electric shock when trying to repair the iron without unplugging it first?

In each case Uncle Švejk calmly murmured, 'Oh, I don't worry about such things. In fact, I don't worry about anything. I became a bus driver because I enjoy getting people where they want to go. Of course, it's of no historical importance, but it brings me enough satisfaction to be able to say that I'm happy.'

We realized that Vinko's frankness did not bother Švejk at all – on the contrary, he was enjoying it along with the rest of us.

'What about women?' asked Elizabeta. 'Has there been any love in Uncle's life?'

'How old are you?' protested Uncle Vinko.

'Old enough to start being terribly interested in such things,' replied Elizabeta cheekily, only to be rewarded with another tap on the head from Aunt Mara's fork.

Uncle Vinko looked at Dad, who indicated with a barely noticeable movement of his head that he should steer the story in the requested direction. But Vinko began to waver; he wasn't keen on the idea. Nor was Uncle Švejk, who was alternately blushing and going pale.

'There are no reliable data about that,' said Vinko. 'All that is known is that once, when asked by a female clerk filling out a loan form whether he was married, he replied so loudly that even those at the end of the queue heard him, "I would be, but I've never been asked, and I'm too scared to do so myself." So in that area things are somewhat hazy,' concluded Uncle Vinko.

'Ooooaaah,' yawned Elizabeta. 'This uncle is so boring.'

'Wait till I've finished,' said Vinko quickly, as if concerned that the annoying girl was going to undermine the others' interest.

He continued. One day, to widespread astonishment, Uncle Švejk was offered some contract work at the national television station. This was no doubt because his ambitious mother had knocked on some key doors in the hope that her son could climb to the position of director general, from where he could launch a political career. She was convinced he was, at the very least, capable of becoming mayor. After all, he had appeared on enough shows for his inner peace and relaxed attitude to problems to be widely known.

The health unit of the television station hired him to prepare a brochure with advice on how to avoid stress so that the exhausted directors, producers and other members of staff could learn to relax.

Uncle Švejk thought the request a reasonable one and not beyond his capabilities. And so a few months later there appeared a glossy eighty-page brochure, paid for out of the licence fee, in which the burned-out television staff were advised 'always to sit on the soft part of their behinds' and to relax by staring at a picture of the Alps and daydreaming that they were walking along a green mountain valley with their favourite aunt, or, if that didn't suit them, to take up origami. The publication included a 21-step diagram showing how to make an origami bird.

If none of these recommendations did the trick, employees were advised to rub lavender or sandalwood into their scalps.

Švejk's advice wasn't to everyone's taste – some were annoyed by the directions on how to pass through a revolving door. 'Immediately enter the available space. The door will automatically rotate – don't push it. Step out as soon as you are able. If you do not do this in time you will have to return to where you started and repeat the whole process.'

The newspapers noted that when the publication was presented the reaction of some of the staff so upset Švejk that after the press conference he spent ten minutes in the revolving door before he managed to exit from the building.

7

Following these events there was no demand for Švejk's talents for some time, Uncle Vinko continued, nor for his statements, which one of the serious newspapers labelled as a mixture of banality and cryptic wisdom. His final offering was 'For each of us, the only true destination is a sense of inner peace.'

Švejk achieved his inner peace by driving bus number 7 and delivering people to their workplaces, shops, the dentist's, school, the mortuary and back.

His own destination was no longer so unquestionable. He began to be assailed by dark thoughts, as if the business with the brochure had left a deep wound. His smiling face began to be reminiscent of a disguise for his pain, which, to his more perceptive passengers, was all too clear. One day a serious, soft-spoken man – who it later turned out was a regular on the number 7 – before alighting patted him on the shoulder and said, 'The most thankless thing in this world is being good.'

'Is it really?' shouted Uncle Švejk so loudly that the other passengers jumped. 'Get off my bus and fuck off.'

'Now *that* I like,' commented Elizabeta, earning another tap with the fork.

'I am merely quoting,' said Uncle Vinko, looking at Dad, 'for the sake of authenticity.'

Dad nodded, and Vinko continued with his narrative. We noticed that he was enjoying himself, for the family was charmed by his storytelling gift. Uncle Švejk, who was blushing more and more, was enjoying it less and less.

Uncle Vinko spotted this, but he was too carried away with his narrative fervour to stop.

The kindly man was so completely astonished by Švejk's words that he literally fell out the vehicle. The remaining passengers put their heads down so that they resembled a collection of sitting tortoises. A few found enough strength to turn their heads and follow the efforts of the insulted passenger to elbow his way through the crowd on the pavement.

Even fewer saw Uncle Švejk running after him or heard him shouting, 'I'm sorry, I'm sorry, I'm sorry!' This was witnessed primarily by Uncle Vinko, who rode to work on the same bus.

'Why are you only telling us this now?' Dad demanded.

'All in good time,' said Vinko and continued.

When Uncle Švejk, with head bowed, returned and got back behind the wheel, everyone on the bus understood that this was no longer the same man who had driven them for so many years. He had undergone a sinister change – and not only him but them, their lives, their town, the villages in the mountains.

It was the mountains that Švejk saw as the new source of inner peace – the shimmering snowy peaks that on a clear day he could see through the windscreen of the bus. By staring at them (in line with his advice to the television people) he gradually regained his former calm, and his regular passengers stopped lowering their eyes when getting on and off. One day even the gently spoken man appeared and behaved as if nothing had happened. Things were back to normal; people knew they would get to their destination on time, and Uncle Švejk once more enjoyed helping them do so.

Once or twice those who were sitting directly behind him even heard him whistle a jolly tune and sway slightly to its rhythm.

But the feeling of tension remained. This wasn't tension between Švejk and his passengers but a collective intuition that something could intervene and change their destinies to such an extent that they would no longer be recognizable. No one could tell whether Švejk knew this any better than his passengers or not. The only thing that witnesses could later describe with any reliability was Švejk's surprise when a tank appeared on the road in front of the bus.

But the incident did not come completely out of the blue. For quite some time there had been talk that the federal army would try to occupy the international border crossings of the Alpine republic, which had declared independence. However, between rumours and tanks actually moving towards the city centre there was quite a difference, and so Uncle Švejk did not hesitate. With a sudden turn of the wheel he positioned the bus across the road, forcing the tank, which was at the front of the column, to come to a rattling halt.

Reports on what followed differed in just one detail: whether Uncle Švejk *ran* or *marched* towards the machine that represented the power of the dying federal state. Some insisted that he swaggered rather like John Wayne heading for a showdown with the bad guy. Others claimed that he rushed towards the tank and climbed on to it like a large, clumsy squirrel. Uncle Vinko was of the opinion that he went into battle in a dignified way, head held high, although not excessively so but in just the right manner, like a samurai.

But all agreed that the young soldier standing behind the machine-gun on top of the tank didn't have much time to react and what time he did have he wasted in trying to work out what was happening. Then Uncle Švejk stabbed him in the heart with a long screwdriver that he kept beneath the seat in case he had to tighten a screw, for he wanted his bus to run smoothly, without any unnecessary noises.

When the young soldier let go of the machine-gun that he had been gripping tightly – more out of fear than deathly intent – Uncle Švejk lifted his limp body and threw it on to the road, where it landed with a dull thud and, after a brief shudder, lay motionless. He slid down from the tank and jumped up and down on the body until he grew weary of it. Only then did he remove the screwdriver from the heart of the first victim of the coming war.

'What have you done?' yelled the soft-spoken man when Švejk returned to the bus. 'You murdered my son!'

'Jesus Maria,' breathed Aunt Mara.

'The family now has a killer. Well done,' said Elizabeta.

'Be quiet,' said Dad.

Uncle Vinko continued.

The soft-spoken passenger rushed towards the corpse, kneeled beside it and lifted the head of the young soldier on to his lap. He removed the boy's helmet and ran his fingers through the damp hair of the Slovene recruit, who had been ordered by his officer in the federal army to climb on to the tank and go into battle without telling him who he was fighting against or why.

At the sight of what had happened the bus passengers and the soldiers on the tanks in the column, which had stopped, knew that there was no going back. Jaroslav Švejk also realized this.

'We must remain calm,' he said absently, as if sending the words somewhere into space. When he regarded the consequences of his intervention in history, he somehow did not feel as if he had created the scene he was now witnessing.

When the father of the dead soldier headed towards him Uncle Švejk received him with the words, 'I've done something terrible. Do what you want with me.'

But the man passed him by without a word, without even a glance. He went past the bus without looking up or meeting the eyes of his fellow passengers, with whom for more than twenty years he had ridden to work and home again. He set off across the field next to the road, not towards the town but straight towards the distant villages, towards the mountains, with slow but decisive steps, without once turning around, not even when one of the soldiers on a tank, who had misinterpreted the incident, sent a hail of bullets after him. He simply collapsed and lay inert in the middle of the field, on his back, less than five hundred metres from his son, without either of them having done anything wrong, for sometimes wars erupt, Vinko said pointedly, in which the innocent die and the guilty survive, and then they try to work out what went wrong, not only for them but for their victims.

Then the tank moved and pushed the bus off the road. The wish of Švejk's ambitious mother had been realized: he had left his mark in history, but only by not being able to stop its flow.

'On the contrary,' said Dad. 'History is over, nothing more can happen. From now on we shall only be assailed by greater or lesser mysteries, conundrums more suited to solvers of crossword puzzles than heroes. That's just how it is. We should be satisfied with helping each other get to where we want to be. Our lost uncle has brought us an excellent recipe for life, and I, for one, shall try to abide by it. I recommend that you all follow my example.'

He turned to Mum, who had just reappeared and reached for the last piece of Mara's cake.

We looked at Švejk, who during Vinko's story of his heroics had been shifting awkwardly in his seat. We all now felt a desire to listen to him. I don't think there was anyone at the table who had not sensed in one way or another that Uncle Švejk had brought something new into our lives, perhaps benignly funny or perhaps not, perhaps circus-like or scarily unpredictable, perhaps of short-lived interest or life-changing. And so we all felt that his words, when he finally spoke, would have particular weight.

'A bus,' was the first thing he said. 'All my life, for as long as I could, I drove a bus. If you take me in I'd like to continue doing that. It could be a school bus, a work bus, as long as it has stops where people who have to be at a certain place at a certain time get on and off. I get most pleasure from delivering people to their destination neither too early nor too late. If that's not possible, I don't know what I'll do. Then, it seems to me, I'll have to give my life some serious consideration and maybe move in with the gypsies.'

'Why the gypsies?' asked Mum.

'On the way through the woods I came across their village. They were all very friendly towards me. Particularly the children, who especially enjoyed it when I slipped on the wet ground in front of one of the houses and fell on a rotten egg that one of the less friendly ones had put there.'

'Jaro, stop it,' yelled Mum, wiping her mouth, messy with cake, with a paper serviette. 'We'll put you in the guest room. You can stay a month, more than enough to get your thoughts together and make plans. But, for God's sake, stop playing the clown in front of my family, because here for entertainment we usually watch television – and only a few of us do that. And those hardly at all, because entertainment holds practically no interest for us. And don't think you can stay here for good, because that's not possible.'

Uncle Švejk gave a friendly nod and said, 'The most beautiful thing in the world is relatives you can rely on in good times or bad. I promise I'll entertain you only when you want me to. The rest of the time I'll invest all my energy in being boring.'

8

But our 'freedom fighter', as Dad called him, began to entertain us soon after moving into the guest room. After unpacking his few belongings from his rucksack, he went to lean out of the window on the first floor to enjoy the view of the valley and hills.

His anticipated enjoyment was marred by a terrible shattering noise unleashed by his movement and probably by his astonishment when his forehead met the windowpane which was, he later explained, 'so clean that I simply didn't see it'.

Mum claimed that the window in the guest room was the dirtiest, since we hadn't had any guests and so never cleaned it, but with regard to the circumstances it didn't really matter who was right.

One of the pieces of glass fell on to the head of Dad's cousin Vladimir, who was, at precisely that moment, walking around the house and wondering whether he should once more try writing his Partisan memoirs. He received a cut to his bald patch so deep that Dad had to drive him to hospital.

He almost had to take Uncle Švejk as well, for when the 'hero of the war for independence' was about to rush downstairs to apologize, he tripped on the top step and tumbled to the bottom, hitting each step with his coccyx, his backbone, his shoulder-blades and finally his head. We heard thud, thud, thud, thud and, finally, thump as he landed in front of the members of the family that had been drawn into the hallway by the sound of breaking glass and the noise from the stairs.

'Now he really does have an angular head,' commented Elizabeta.

To which Aunt Mara, in a rare moment of agreement with her daughter, added, 'If I did a painting of him now I could title it *A Hard Landing*.'

To which Mum commented, 'Jaro would have to kill himself before he recognized a hard landing.' Then she turned to her silent brother and said, 'I hope you've broken every bone in your body and are fit only for a home for the disabled.'

But Švejk collected himself very calmly, as if falling downstairs was his regular morning exercise. 'Don't worry,' he said, 'I feel on top of the world.'

That certainly wasn't true, since the next few days he moved as if he had dislocated about five joints, and when he thought no one was looking his friendly smile twisted into an expression of agony that charmed Aunt Mara.

'That's what men should be like,' she said. 'Made of steel. But they don't make them like that any more. They died out with Wild West films. Such a shame that this Švejk looks as if he had been moulded from clay by Picasso. Otherwise I would ask him to pose nude for me.' At that she stared into the distance and sighed longingly.

Clearly the idea gave her no peace, for two days later at dinner Elizabeta reported how she had heard her mother persuading Švejk to 'reveal himself to her brush' and how Švejk promised he would as soon as he achieved certain goals.

Mum and Uncle Vinko were shocked to hear this, but Švejk and Aunt Mara both began to explain at once that such a conversation had never taken place, and Mara added that the 'malicious little hussy' had thought the whole thing up. The malicious hussy then received a tap on the head with a fork.

Vladimir, who was brought home by Dad with ten stitches on his crown, added, 'I'm afraid that from here on in everything is going to go downhill in this family. But I won't say anything because I am also a guest here.'

Perhaps because both of them felt they had to watch their words, Vladimir and Uncle Švejk became the best of friends. But that didn't happen overnight. When Švejk was settling in and we were becoming accustomed to his foibles, Vladimir was full of sarcastic comments at his expense, especially in connection with his clumsiness, which Vladimir claimed could be deadly as it could lead to the house burning down and the destruction everything we possessed.

Once, during dinner, he even recommended that someone should follow Švejk and keep an eye on him, as he himself bore a scar on his head – which had never stopped hurting since the accident – that showed how dangerous it was to leave him on his own.

'There's nothing wrong with your head,' said Dad, 'except perhaps that it's full of resentment towards a life that has in your later years brought you a young wife who has driven off with your hard-earned Alfa Romeo. You've only yourself to blame, so stop taking it out on our innocent guests who have, while they are living under our roof, the same rights as others.'

Mum agreed, even though she didn't waste any opportunity to accuse Švejk of laziness, stupidity or worse, but she evidently thought that this right belonged to her alone. She even began to defend Švejk whenever a particularly caustic comment was made at his expense.

It wasn't long before we all quietly knew what no one dared to acknowledge: that we would miss Švejk if he decided to leave.

But he showed no sign of doing that. Even Mum warned him less and less often that his month under our roof had almost expired. And when it actually did run out, and Uncle Švejk still hadn't found a job or anywhere to move to, it became crystal clear that we had acquired a permanent member of the family. In fact, Uncle Švejk had been unobtrusively preparing himself for that role since his arrival. He had somehow known he would be allowed to stay.

Since he had arrived in summer shirt and trousers and his rucksack contained only a box of tools, five pocket handkerchiefs, a broken alarm clock, a brochure about coping with stress and a bunch of newspaper cuttings about his 'heroism', Dad decided he had to supply him with a wardrobe.

To begin with, he tried on some old shirts, trousers and jackets from the three men in the house. He felt most comfortable in the clothes of Cousin Vladimir, but Vladimir said that, thanks to the profligacy of his errant wife, he had such a modest wardrobe that he felt disinclined to share it with anyone.

In the end Dad suggested the establishment of a 'Švejk fund' into which all the members of the family would contribute part of their savings, each according to his abilities and goodwill. I contributed a tenth of my pocket money. The only one reluctant to contribute anything at all, as we all expected, was Elizabeta, who said that Aunt Mara gave her too little to survive on. The largest contributions came from Dad, Mum and Vinko. And so Švejk acquired enough clothes so as not to embarrass us when he went into the village.

That didn't happen very often. In the beginning he was more interested in the family than in the wider surroundings. He felt an unusual need to win over each one of us individually and acquire an ally in case Mum should try to get rid of him. He would come into our rooms, often when it was obviously inconvenient, although he always politely knocked. He would ask questions, some of them too personal, alternately bothering and amusing us but at the same time creating the impression that he had no idea what he was doing. His excessive friendliness seemed to force us to be friendly to him in return.

And so he gradually winkled out of us things that were nothing to do with him and created a database with which he could, in Vladimir's opinion, 'send every last one of us to the gallows'.

Dad rejected Vladimir's concerns as the delusions of an old paranoiac who, in the days of communism, had had his snout in the trough for too long. 'Who are we, after all, and what have we done that an unexpected new family member can harm us?'

After the end of history, claimed Dad, the only dangerous ones were those who had money and, in particular, those who had more represented a danger to those who had less. In that regard we posed a greater threat to Švejk than he did to us. Instead of fearing him we should learn something from him, for his simplicity concealed a kind of wisdom that would benefit the younger generation in particular – those who, since the introduction of the internet, were exposed to much worse manipulation and were at risk of much greater malformation than ever before.

'It would also', added Dad, 'benefit old Partisans who are unable to accept the fact that they no longer have absolute power and that even the women who previously clung to them in the desire to share their unearned privileges might now abandon them.'

Jaroslav Švejk had been among those who had removed the trough from in front of Vladimir and those like him, opined Dad, but that should not be a reason to distrust a man who had found his moment in history, even though his action was such an obvious symptom of the human stupidity that had overtaken this part of Europe at the end of the century that it would be impossible to find a worse one. Vladimir actually nodded in agreement, but he did not believe Dad's assurance that Švejk posed no threat to the family.

More unusual was that for the first time I doubted the validity of Dad's evaluation – me, his most loyal ally. The reason for this was my chronic curiosity, which flared to unheard-of levels soon after Švejk penetrated our family circle. My curiosity followed his and was more intense, although his must have had a specific goal, whereas mine served no purpose but my own obsession.

9

Whenever Švejk knocked on a door and amiably intruded into the personal space of some family member or other, I cunningly got myself into a position where I could hear most of what was being said behind the closed doors. In the case of my older brother Peter, I held a funnel to the wall of his room and didn't miss a word. And thus, thanks to curiosity about the reasons for Švejk's curiosity, I got an insight into the nature of the family into which fate had delivered me.

'What are you thinking about when you're hidden away here for hours on end?' Švejk asked Peter during his first investigative visit to his room.

'I'm usually not even thinking,' replied Peter, 'or at least not about anything specific, but more floating in a kind of mist of half-formed impressions that from year to year accumulate into an ever-growing mountain of indigestible material. I feel like this because of a kind of drunkenness, an intoxication with ideas and plans that greatly outweigh my willpower and ability to solve them, and so they ferment inside me like alcohol.'

'I see,' said Uncle Švejk. 'But from time to time you probably think in a more normal way, more soberly.'

'Of course,' replied Peter. 'Sober or drunk I think about many things but, above all, about how to find my way into the world. How to experience it so that it doesn't remain only as ink on newsprint or flickering characters on a computer screen. I studied philosophy and gave up just before graduating because it was becoming like a woman who studies only herself and the premature lines on her face in the mirror. Now I'm in the fourth year of physics and cosmology. But I'm wondering whether to abandon that as well, because, in truth, it is determinedly pushing me in the direction of religion and the search for God. And that again is philosophy.

'I'm contemplating', he continued, 'abandoning reflection on important things and becoming a cynic like the rest of my generation, obnoxious and arrogant in a way that will appear both sincere and spontaneous. Almost everyone my age knows how to do that. Then, it seems to me, I'd know all the answers before the questions were even asked. I'm tired of posing questions without finding answers. After all, that's no longer fashionable. Today, it's fashionable to have answers ready and the simpler the better – a mouse click, and there you have it. On the one hand, I feel disconnected here in the village, but, on the other, I like living among people who believe that the world is how it appears on television. Simplicity in others promotes in me a desire to simplify myself, and for some time that desire has been the only light at the end of the tunnel. Do you have any idea what I'm on about?'

'I'm trying to understand,' said Švejk. 'That's the most we can do. To try. The only nobility is in having good intentions.'

'Well,' replied Peter with a laugh, 'then that's the noblest pathway to the hell in which we are all in one way or another living. The path to heaven is always out of reach because of our fear that we will be left without illusions about the future. Hell becomes heaven the moment we accept that it is the only thing there is. I looked through the brochure on how to deal with stress that you prepared for the TV people. Quite simple, but in a profound, philosophical sense truly wise, requiring no further evidence or clarification. For a bus driver you are quite unusual.'

'No, I'm not,' replied Švejk, 'I'm quite ordinary. Although sadly not as normal as I would like to be. Your grandmother tried to make something exceptional out of me. Fortunately, I realized in time what her intention was and sabotaged it without her realizing. I see that as the greatest success of my life. I am talented at playing the fool, but at the same time my personality is a product in which I have invested no little thought and effort. Now I must go.'

'Wait,' said Peter quickly. 'I haven't told you everything. Especially what weighs on me most heavily. I don't need simple wisdom, I need specific advice.'

'I see,' said Švejk.

'I think I'm falling in love with my cousin Elizabeta. There are ten years between us. In fact, she's not my real cousin. She's not the daughter of my father's deceased brother, Mara's husband, but a later product. In terms of relationships this is not incestuous yearning. It's a natural feeling of attraction towards a fifteen-year-old whose sexuality is awakening. You can report me if you wish, but I have to tell you. What can I do? You must have some experience.'

'I made a promise,' said Švejk, 'that I would not talk about my experiences in this area. That cautious approach has saved me a great deal of unpleasantness. I particularly want to avoid any difficulties within the family that has taken me for its own. Someone who has been shipwrecked does not cause problems on the boat that rescued him from drowning.'

'Dear Uncle,' said Peter with a laugh, 'you were rescued by a boat that is rapidly letting in water. The worst thing is that we all know this but none of us wants to admit it let alone talk about it. It cannot have escaped your notice that playing dumb is the main method of communication in this family. And now you are going to do the same. Wittgenstein said, "Whereof one cannot speak, thereof one must be silent." That could be our motto. We watch, silent and scared, as water floods our vessel, loosening joints and washing away bolts, and we do nothing. Save us, Uncle. Be the first one who dares to speak. Save the ship that saved you. Don't let it sink with you on board.'

Almost a minute of silence followed. Then Švejk gave a deep sigh. 'Such catastrophic reflections are no doubt the result of years of dabbling in philosophical and similar waters. It seems to me that this family, which you compare to a sinking ship, is a very robust construction. Any doubt about its solidity can only harm it. I see no signs that it is threatened in any way.'

'Because you don't know the secret,' said Peter. 'Because you don't know that a sphinx has appeared among us and that the head of the family has lost all faith in himself as well as his potency and authority. Without a firm hand on the tiller the ship is without direction. What is more, the sphinx has affected not only my father but all those who have confronted it. It has posed a question to us all that cannot be answered. All except you. But my father has decided that we should no longer talk about it, so I cannot tell you where that sphinx is or where you can see it. In fact, I am breaking a family agreement even mentioning it. So, please, say nothing to anyone about this.'

'No problem,' replied Švejk. 'I will pretend I know nothing. In fact, I really don't know anything. Now I'm going.'

And he went.

10

The next conversation I managed to overhear was that between Uncle Švejk and Elizabeta. Her room was in the loft, so I had to crawl into the roof space next to the thin wall of her room. I had to be extremely careful not to give myself away by making any noise. This took quite some time, and I missed the beginning of the conversation. The first words I heard were Elizabeta's.

'Of course I'm happy with myself,' she was saying. 'I think I'm the most happy-with-myself girl in the northern hemisphere. Why are you even interested?'

'I just am,' said Švejk.

'Everything has a reason,' said the adolescent sage in a maternal manner, 'especially in connection with you. You must have a hidden agenda. I've suspected you from the word go. I'm almost certain you would like to rape me. You've probably spent half your life in prison because of attacks on adolescent girls.'

'I've never done anything as attention-seeking as that,' replied Švejk without embarrassment, 'and I've no hidden agenda. I'm just interested in what kind of person you are. What are you like inside? Because it seems I'm going to stay here, I'd like to know as much as possible about my relatives so I can offer my help if any of them are in need of it.'

'First of all, we are not related,' said Elizabeta. 'Second, you'd die of horror if you knew what I'm like inside. A malicious young hussy, as Mum calls me, is only a fraction of what I really am. I am an extremely clever, exceptionally beautiful and hot fifteen-year-old girl, my body and soul full to the brim with only one thing: wickedness.'

'Really?' said Švejk.

'Really,' replied Elizabeta.

'Well,' continued Švejk, 'tell me about this wickedness.'

'There's no point,' said Elizabeta, 'because you are not well read and have no idea what wickedness really means. Have you read de Sade's *Juliette* and *La Nouvelle Justine*? You haven't. So how can I explain to you why I decided to follow the path of wickedness in my life and nothing but? And, in any case, how can I be sure you won't betray me?'

'I'm not a traitor,' said Švejk.

'"I'm not a traitor," said Judas, kissing Christ,' responded Elizabeta with a laugh. 'If the family finds out about my plans they will lock me in the cellar or send me to a psychiatric hospital.'

'I doubt,' said Švejk, 'that you're really like that inside.'

'You haven't the slightest idea what I'm really like,' said Elizabeta. 'Although I'm proud that I'm different, at times I'm scared by my plans and desires. It's good that I haven't yet found the courage to begin. I need something, or someone, to push me over the edge. For now, I'm merely recording what I'm going to do. I'd like to be selfish, sinful and a terrible villain, just like de Sade's Juliette. Let me read you something.'

I heard pages being turned and then Elizabeta reading, '"It is certainly the case, madam, that debauchery leads to murder; every weary person must renew his strength through what fools refer to as a crime . . . Murder is thus one of the sweetest spurs of debauchery." And, listen to this. "I adore your cruelty. Swear to me that one day I, too, will be your victim; since my fifteenth year I have cultivated only the idea that I shall one day die as the victim of the cruel passions of debauchery."'

'So,' continued Elizabeta, 'what do you say to that?'

'I think,' said Švejk, 'that you are terrified of being bored, which is normal for someone your age who has fallen under the influence of a book that you at best half understand and which is not a book of specific instructions, like my brochure on stress avoidance, but a novel, something completely made up, which does not oblige anybody, least of all someone as nice as you, to allow herself to develop in that direction. I'm convinced that soon you will see things completely differently. Certainly, when you fall in love for the first time.'

'You really are a total idiot,' replied Elizabeta, 'and you look it as well. Do you really believe that there can be a bond of affection between two people that can be anything less than a sign of weakness? I'll never fall in love because there is no one and nothing I could fall in love with. In any case, it would only be an obstacle on my path. I'm interested in crime, murder, incest, torture, robbery. For now I master only scheming and hypocrisy. For other things I need a partner. Sadly, all the boys hereabouts are dumb peasants on mopeds who are proud that they smoke on the sly. And you are too stupid, too rectangular and too clumsy to be considered, so don't delude yourself that we might embark on a path of wrongdoing together.'

'No danger of that,' said Švejk. 'It's characteristic of idiots that in spite of their best intentions they remain good; they avoid evil like money avoids a pauper; although they are capable of doing wrong through clumsiness, which is true of me as well. But I seek no excuse for all I've done wrong in the certainty that I was doing good. To err is human, said one of the popes, or I think it was . . . But to intentionally devote your life to evil, and at an age when you should be blossoming with pure goodness, seems to me like tearing up a cheque for a million dollars the minute someone gives it to you. That cheque should be wisely invested, for growth is the natural order of things.'

'No,' said Elizabeta decisively, 'according to de Sade the law of nature is destruction, for that is the only thing enabling new growth. I want growth through the destruction of everything and everyone, including myself. And, I'm sorry to tell you this, you as well. Although you last of all because I want you to see what I am capable of.'

'When did all this begin?' asked Švejk. 'You probably didn't start thinking like this in the cradle.'

'No,' replied Elizabeta. 'I've been thinking like this since the moment I realized the kind of family I belonged to. I sometimes think about sinking the family ship with a torpedo or two. To seduce first Uncle Vinko and then Vladimir and then tell everyone what they have done. Are you shocked? Are you afraid of me?'

'A little,' admitted Uncle Švejk.

'I'm glad,' said Elizabeta, 'because that's my goal. To shock, break commandments, spread fear. Shock therapy for a world of pretence and polite manners. Excuse me, if I may, how nice, that's so kind of you, I like you, I love you, I respect you and all those other repulsive phrases fill me with the desire to assemble a massive bomb and blow everything sky high. I mean this shitty family I live with and into which you've stepped as if clumsily treading in dog shit – which is just like you.'

'You know what,' said Švejk, 'you've finally convinced me that everything you say is just a pubescent teenage girl's attempts at being provocative – a joke in not very good taste. I'm not as naïve as you think, and there's no need to make fun of me. In spite of that, thanks for your time and goodbye.'

'Wait,' said Elizabeta and then fell silent for a moment. I heard Švejk move towards the door. 'Will you tell Mara what I've been saying?'

'I take it as a great insult that you could even ask something like that,' replied Švejk.

'Right,' she said. 'If you really promise that this is just between the two of us, I'll tell you something that I shouldn't even be thinking about.'

'Go on, then.'

'The device,' said Elizabeta. 'It's all the fault of the monstrous device that Vinko found in the shed at the end of the orchard and that Peter's dad, the family *capo di banda*, declared to be the Great Mystery. I call it a devilish machine created by spirits to bring discord to the family and to drive us away, for we are not fated to find happiness and peace in this house.'

'Where is this thing?' asked Švejk, after a pause.

'Mara painted it,' said Elizabeta. 'You could have seen the painting in her studio, but on the orders of the boss of the family she had to destroy it. And I'm not allowed to tell you where the thing itself is; I could receive a lot worse punishment than I already have. The desires that I talked to you about appeared after it was removed and we were sworn to secrecy. To be honest, I'm frightened by what is happening to me. Sometimes in the middle of the night I wake up crying. I never felt I was a bad person – I was naughty but never wicked. I think I need help. But who can I turn to, who would understand?'

She began to cry heartbreakingly.

11

For almost a minute I heard no other sound. Then Švejk cleared his throat as if indicating that he was about to say something important. The rhythm of Elizabeta's sobbing slowed. I think she wanted to hear what he had to say.

'You can turn to me,' he said. 'I'll do whatever is in my power to help. And perhaps there's more in my power than you realize. Chance always takes me where I am most needed. Even on the way here I had a feeling that a task awaited me which I could not avoid. And that what awaited me was something more even than my intervention in history. I really have thought long and hard about driving a bus again and helping people arrive safely and punctually at their destinations. Now I see that you are my passengers, the members of the family that has taken me as its own. It's my duty to rescue you from the ambush that has befallen you and to save you from the delusions that are obsessing you. Don't worry, Elizabeta. The good soldier Švejk will find a way.'

'Then come and give me a hug,' said Elizabeta and stopped sobbing.

'Is that what you really want?' asked Švejk cautiously.

'It is,' she said. 'Hold me tight. In this house no one hugs me – I sometimes hug myself just to feel the warmth.'

'But . . .' Švejk began then stopped.

'But what?'

'I've never embraced such a beautiful young girl. I've no idea how to do it.'

'Who have you embraced before – old dears?' asked Elizabeta with a laugh, her mood recovered.

'Not exactly old dears,' he replied, 'but embracing such a young girl seems almost a sin.'

'So, sin a little,' said Elizabeta. 'Are you afraid?'

'I know it sounds boring, but I don't know how to be anything but good. That's my only talent. I don't really know what I'm doing in this world. My story has already been written.'

'That's another story,' said Elizabeta. 'You are a different Švejk. And I'm Elizabeta, who has not been in any story yet. I'm creating my own. Be one of the characters in it. Come and give me a hug.'

'I can't,' said Švejk. 'Something tells me I'd lose control of the bus and drive my passengers into an abyss. Too many unhappy people have entrusted their fate to me, including you.'

'You really are dumb,' said Elizabeta. 'Do you have any idea what awaits you in this house? The power of the thing is so horrific that it cannot be resisted. It changes you into the opposite of what you are. You can outwit it in only one way: to be the opposite of what you want to be. Then it forces you to be what you really want to be. I've worked it all out very carefully. If I want to be good, I must be wicked. If I want to be honest, I must lie. If I want to be virtuous, I must behave like a little slut. Then the device, which has great power but is at the same time very stupid, will make sure that what I do is changed into pure goodness. You, meanwhile, will end up as a murderer and a source of misery for everyone you meet between here and the grave.'

'I doubt this device has such power. I know I'm pretty clumsy, but I know how to deal with machines and so on, however unusual. Of course, it would be easier if I could see it, but if that's not possible . . .'

'Shall I show it to you?' asked Elizabeta.

'You said you weren't allowed.'

'I can still do it. If you promise not to tell anyone.'

After a brief silence Švejk said quietly, 'I promise.'

'You won't get scared? You won't close your eyes?' she asked.

'It's not in my nature to close my eyes to things.'

'Right,' she said.

For some time I heard nothing but rustling and movement.

Then Švejk asked, 'What are you doing?'

'I'm getting undressed. Can't you see?' said Elizabeta with a laugh.

'But you said you'd show me the secret device,' Švejk protested.

'That's why I'm getting undressed,' she said, 'so that you can see what beautiful, firm tits I have. I'm actually grown up, ripe for any kind of sin, even the worst. And look at my thighs, aren't they seductively rounded? Who could resist them?'

'Me,' said Švejk, his voice tight. 'I will resist, and I won't look at this.'

'You said you wouldn't close your eyes.'

'Before the device,' Švejk gasped, 'not you.'

'But you are closing your eyes to the device,' she replied. 'That's where its power lies, don't you see? It is compelling me to do something that I wouldn't think of doing even in my wildest dreams. That I reveal myself to the family fool and show him what some would crawl around the world on their hands and knees to see. It's forcing you to do the opposite of what you want to do. Instead of licking your lips and reaching for me you close your eyes. You're helpless before the device. We all are. It will destroy us all.'

'No', gasped Švejk, 'it won't.'

I heard his large body turn and bump into the door, which then opened, the wooden floor at the top of the stairs creaking and then something extremely heavy tumbling down. I heard something breaking, wood cracking and something hard banging against something harder – and then silence.

Finally I heard Elizabeta's voice at the door. 'So, this time he really has managed to kill himself. My first crime.'

And then Mum's voice on the stairs. 'Jaro, what were you doing in the loft? Jesus, who's going to pay for all this damage?'

12

The malicious young hussy celebrated her entry into the kingdom of evil in vain, for Uncle Švejk survived his terrible fall downstairs as if he had nine lives. It's true that while rolling down he sustained such injuries that he had to stay in bed for ten days, but his good humour did not fail him, and every suggestion that he should go to the doctor's was rejected as unnecessary.

'I feel fine,' he insisted, 'but I do feel extremely tired, so I'm going to rest for a few days if no one objects.'

'You go ahead,' said Mum. 'After a month's rest a few more days won't do you any harm.'

As school was over I offered to take food, water and two glasses of wine a day (Mum thought that any more than that would delay his recovery until late autumn) to Uncle Švejk's room.

Of course, my offer did not mean that self-sacrifice was a prominent feature of my character – at least, not at the age of seventeen, as I was then. I offered because in the village where we lived Švejk was the most interesting thing by far. Besides which I knew that his research tour, temporarily suspended, would sooner or later reach me, and I wanted to be next in line. His curiosity aroused my curiosity as to what he might ask me and how I might reply.

The first day he asked me only whether there were any painkillers in the house and, if not, whether I would pop to the chemist's in the next village on my bike. But since Mum had a comprehensive pharmaceutical collection in the bathroom I didn't need to leave the house. Uncle Švejk must have been in worse pain than he was prepared to admit, for on the first day he polished off a whole box of aspirin and immediately requested another.

'Don't tell anyone you are bringing me tablets,' he said. 'I don't want anyone getting unnecessarily upset. I'm not actually in pain; I'm taking them instead of lozenges. I like sucking bitter things.'

'And you,' he finally asked the next day, with a quick glance, 'have you thought of your future, what you want to become?'

'Nothing,' I replied, grasping the opportunity. 'I don't want to become anything. I have no goals, no plans, no wishes. Except for one.'

A tactical silence followed that Uncle Švejk managed to ignore for a while. But then he couldn't help himself and asked if I would confide in him what this wish was.

'Perhaps I'd like to be a writer,' I said.

'Oh,' he said in surprise, 'like Jaroslav Hašek, who created me?'

'You weren't created by a writer,' I said. 'You were the result of a mistake by my grandmother. That's what Uncle Vinko says, and he's not in the habit of lying. I want to become a writer so that I can earn something from the stories that are constantly being woven in my head.'

'It's the first I've heard of this,' replied Švejk. 'You like making up stories?'

'Very much,' I admitted. 'So much so that at the end of the day I don't know what's real and what's made up.'

'That's not very nice for others,' he chided me.

'I know,' I acknowledged, 'but everyone has their faults, and that is mine.'

'So, what story did you make up last?'

'A story about a mysterious object that fell from the sky and ended up in the shed at the bottom of the orchard and changed a family of ordinary people into lunatics and neurotics who have convinced themselves that there is a power greater than them which has to be ignored because it can't be resisted.'

'Oh,' said Švejk, suddenly showing interest, 'that's a story and not real? I mean, your imagination is so fertile you can think up something like that?'

'I can think up whatever I want,' I said. 'Even Dad says that at my birth God gave me two gifts: laziness and imagination. Dad doesn't realize that the one encourages the other and that the two combined really are a gift, for which I'm grateful.'

'But if the power of this object is so great,' said Švejk, 'it would touch you as well, wouldn't it? So you, too, would be one of the lunatics and neurotics. How do you know you're not?'

I gave a contemplative frown and asked, 'Do I seem mad to you?'

'Not particularly,' he replied. 'You do seem quite lazy, but that doesn't bother me too much – you may have noticed that I'm inclined towards laziness myself. But I'm interested how you can avoid the power of the device while all the others are unable to resist it.'

'How do you know they can't?' I asked.

This put him in a slightly embarrassing position. I was offering him the opportunity to make unflattering statements about the rest of the family. I saw a brief struggle taking place within him, but in the end principle won.

'I assume,' he said, looking for a way out, 'I assume they can't. At least not all of them, not completely.'

'Actually, even you have been unable to resist its power.'

'Really?' he sounded alarmed. 'How did you arrive at that conclusion?'

'By the fact that you can't tell fact from fiction,' I replied. 'I made up the story of the mysterious device. I created it in my head. How can its power have any influence on real people in a real family if even the family in the story merely assumes that it has a power they cannot resist?'

'Hang on a moment,' said Švejk, even more embarrassed. He was frowning as if he had been asked the million-dollar question.

'On the other hand,' I said, 'it is precisely you who is demonstrating that it is possible. As soon as you believe a story it becomes real and so does its power. You believed and so you speak of the device as if it were real. But that's also the way I speak about it in my story. My mysterious object, although made up, works in the same way. So, you're right, it can influence all those who know the story in the same way, and thus it is possible that this really is a family of lunatics and neurotics.'

His torment lasted for some time.

'You know what,' he finally said, 'my back has suddenly begun to hurt. I think I'd like to be alone for a while.'

Uncle Švejk would have been more honest if he'd said he had a headache. Because I left him wrestling with a dilemma such as he had probably never experienced before. I had offered him two models of reality: the empirical and the literary. Does only that which can be touched exist, or can that which merely pretends to be real also exist? Can both exist at the same time? And, if so, which has the most influence, the greater presence?

(That I offered him two models to choose from I realize only now, as I write. At that point I didn't have the words to express this; then I just felt he had to choose between two realities and that his next step would depend on the choice he made.)

I came up with the story of the made-up story in order to stop Uncle Švejk poking his nose into the family secret. When Dad had decided we were not going to talk about it any more it was not without good reason. I thought that Peter and Elizabeta blabbing about it was a big mistake, although I half believed what they were saying. Lately they really had been behaving as if they were under the influence of an unknown force – and, above all, they had confirmed it with their words.

But why, as Švejk had asked, was the mysterious object not influencing me? Or was it, and I did not realize it? I waited impatiently for Švejk to recover and to continue his enquiries with the older members of the family. If they also confessed that they were behaving differently and that they suspected the influence of the device, then that would be proof that something unusual really was happening.

On the other hand, I would never find out if Uncle believed my story that the device was a fabrication. So I felt torn. On the one hand, in the hope that I could protect the family secret, I wanted him to believe that story; on the other, I wanted to hear what Mara, Dad, Mum, Vinko and Vladimir would have to say about the object.

13

When, two days after our talk, Švejk crept downstairs to join us at dinner, it seemed that he had forgotten about the events of the previous week and was interested in other things. Once again, he was in a good mood and seemed full of energy.

'Although when I came here I promised to bore you,' he said, 'I realize that most of all I am boring myself.'

'Except for me,' responded Elizabeta quickly, 'who is bored by all of you but especially myself.'

'Be quiet, silly girl,' said Aunt Mara, hitting her daughter's hand with a fork. 'It's you who is boring.'

'So,' continued Švejk, 'I've decided to look for a job as a bus driver.'

'Excellent, Jaro,' said Uncle Vinko. 'Well done.'

'About time,' added Mum.

'A wise decision in every way,' agreed Dad.

'Except as far as passengers are concerned,' said Elizabeta, 'for, of course, there aren't any.'

'Forget passengers,' said Vladimir. 'He'll manage to find the occasional one. The problem is that there are no buses.'

'He'll find a bus as well,' said Dad.

'They've all been done away with,' said Vladimir hotly. 'Even farmers race around in Audis. I don't know where the world is heading.'

'Maybe I could buy or hire an old bus for special journeys,' said Uncle Švejk. 'For school outings, pensioners' trips and so on.'

'I didn't know you had any money,' said Mum, with a palpable air of surprise.

'I don't,' admitted Švejk. 'I have a little, but more for a bike, certainly not for a minibus, let alone a bus. I thought that . . .' And he fell silent.

'That we could help you,' said Dad. 'Of course we will.'

'Since when were you so generous?' snapped Mum. 'You've never shown any signs before.'

'You're right,' replied Dad, almost with surprise. 'But I wasn't mean. More prudent. And because of my prudence we are living in this house today. That's why my generosity is all the more surprising. As if something is happening to me over which I have no control.'

'I know what's happening,' said Elizabeta meaningfully.

'Me, too,' added Peter.

'But I don't,' said Mum, 'so please tell me.'

'Something is happening that only the blind fail to see,' said Elizabeta.

'Are you saying I'm blind,' said Mum in annoyance. 'Are things happening you are concealing from me?'

'Whatever,' said Dad, trying to calm things down. 'We shall help Švejk buy or hire a minibus or a bus, and then he can do what he wants with it. He could even transport bags of cement. Why not? I'm sure he'll find a way.'

'I'm sure he will,' added Mum acidly. 'Jaro is well known for finding his way – now out of one mess, now another.'

'Since when did you become such a cynic?' Dad asked her. 'You never were before.'

'It's true,' acknowledged Mum with surprise. 'Evidently something is happening to me, too, over which I have no control.'

'And only the malicious young hussy knows *what* is happening,' added Elizabeta. 'You lot have no idea. If idiot Švejk manages to hire or buy a bus with your money, we could turn it into a mobile brothel for Italian hunters and German tourists, and I'd get a job there.'

'Jesus,' yawned Aunt Mara. 'What's happening to you?'

'Nothing that my mother doesn't deserve,' said Elizabeta, putting out her tongue, which shocked Mara so much she couldn't even lift her fork let alone tap her daughter on the head with it.

'Anyway,' said Švejk in a placatory voice, 'in the coming days I'll extend my enquiries to the whole village and then the neighbouring ones. I'll be moving about quite a lot and may even sleep elsewhere so that I don't come bursting into the house in the middle of the night.'

'Sleep elsewhere?' said Mum in surprise. 'When you've hardly left the house for a month?'

'You go ahead, Jaro,' said Uncle Vinko. 'You're a grown man, responsible for yourself. You have every right to sleep elsewhere, even in a ditch if you can't find anything better.'

'Then dress well,' said Mum, 'because you'll have trouble finding anything better than a ditch.'

Švejk felt a need to redirect the conversation. 'I'm surprised,' he said, 'that here in the village, where you could do so, you have no pigs, ducks, chickens – not even a cat or a dog.'

'We have no animals because we are not farmers,' said Dad. 'We are an educated urban family which has moved to the countryside to avoid the waves triggered by an earthquake that registered nine on the Richter scale – more often known as the "change of system". We are a family that has left the town to re-establish contact with our historical roots. But that doesn't necessarily include animals, to which we are allergic – some of us to cats, some to dogs, others to bees and others to everything that walks and crawls. In any case, our neighbours have enough animals, as is apparent from the pictures in Mara's studio, where you can see more cows than are actually grazing in ten surrounding villages.'

This was, of course, untrue. There were no more than ten cow portraits in Mara's studio and Dad was being sarcastic, which was unusual for him. Uncle Vinko looked at him with unconcealed surprise, but most surprised of all was Dad himself.

Similarly, it was not true that our neighbours had all that many animals or that we had all that many neighbours. On one side, the first one had long ago demolished his house, and the only surviving son had ended up in a home for chronic alcoholics. The next one had tried raising pigs for city butchers, but the neighbours hounded him because he was unable or unwilling to reduce the stench that arose from his pigsties and enshrouded half the village. The one next to him abandoned his farm to weeds and, after his wife left him, became a building worker. The last neighbour before the woods hanged himself, leaving behind a wife and a son who supported both of them and his grandmother on his modest wage as a waiter in the former primary school, now converted into a bar. On the other side, at the top of the rise, we had more successful neighbours – one of them even had some cows, which wandered as far as the window of Mara's studio (he was the person who first bought one of her paintings). The second had a tourist farm, and there was a marked path leading to his place that joined the road below our house and then ran along a narrow strip of grass between cultivated fields.

'I'm sorry, Mara,' said Dad.

We were all stunned, even Mara. This was the first time that Dad had ever apologized to anyone in front of the whole family.

'One way or another,' he concluded, 'as soon as Uncle Švejk finds a suitable vehicle we'll buy it, lease it or hire it. Then he can do with it as he sees fit.'

Having said this he rose, carefully wiped his mouth with his napkin, smiled, immediately looked deadly serious again and, with head held high, walked to the door and almost slammed it behind him.

There followed a minute's silence.

Then Elizabeta turned to Švejk and asked, 'Can I come with you on your investigations?'

'Actually,' said Švejk evasively, 'I'd prefer to do it on my own. Later I can take you on trips as a conductor if you like.'

'She won't like,' Mara reassured him.

'I'd like to do that,' said Vladimir, surprising us all, particularly Švejk.

'Everything is possible,' he said diplomatically, although it was clear that the proposal did not appeal to him at all.

14

The next day Švejk went into the village. Vinko had advised him to visit the bus company in the town where there was the greatest chance of getting a job as a driver, but Švejk had decided he would rather be self-employed, a private contractor able to decide who he transported and when and why and for what price. In any case, he made the point that he would never transport anything other than people, so a lorry or tractor with a trailer was out of the question; only a vehicle, whether large or small, with seats would do. Secondhand, of course, and cheap. For a start, he could take the whole family to the seaside if we felt like a short holiday, and then he'd see; he was sure he would drum up some business. 'Faith in the future is the foundation of inner peace,' he added.

Because, as usual, I had nothing particular to do I secretly followed him, at a discreet distance, so he wouldn't see me. Whenever the opportunity arose, I sneaked closer in the hope that I might catch the odd word or two, but that didn't happen very often.

On the first day Švejk spent quite a few hours in the garden of the village inn. He introduced himself to each new customer and paid for a beer, wine, juice or whatever they wanted to drink. Then he sat with them until the next person appeared, and so on. In each case, after a few words he broke through their mistrust and got them on his side. I was disappointed that I could observe his interpersonal skills only from a distance, from the corner of a nearby house. I couldn't get closer because I might get attacked by the dog that was on a long chain in the yard next door.

When Švejk headed home in the evening he was staggering a little – at one point ending up in a roadside ditch, out of which he crawled with as much dignity as he could muster before continuing on his way, not looking left or right, as if he didn't care whether anyone had seen him.

So as not to return at the same time as him, I lingered until dusk at the edge of the woods and then in the orchard at the back of the house. In passing, I peeped into the shed where we had locked the mysterious object that we were pretending didn't exist. Even the grass had not been cut up to a distance of two metres from the locked and bolted door. Without being aware of it, we were no doubt hoping that the shed would as quickly as possible be overgrown by bushes, brambles and grass, so that it became invisible.

When I pressed my face to the dirty windowpane I couldn't see anything inside other than vague shapes. For a moment I thought that the object was no longer there, that it had vanished as suddenly as it had appeared. But, when my eyes got accustomed to the gloom, I saw that it was still crouching there like some strange beast in the hope that someone would carelessly stray near enough for it to leap on them. Although I couldn't swear to it, it seemed that every so often individual parts of the device were glowing like the coils of an electric ring. And, if I listened closely, I was sure I could hear the shortwave radio broadcasting news in an unrecognizable language. Evidently Peter had forgotten to remove the batteries.

However, it seemed impossible that after all the time that had passed the batteries would not be flat. Most likely I wasn't actually hearing anything other than the memory in my brain, which did not want to be expunged.

When I got home there was no sign of Uncle Švejk anywhere. Mum said that he had gone to sleep as soon as he returned because he wasn't feeling too good. And where, for that matter, had I been?

'In the woods, as usual,' I replied and added that I didn't feel too good either. The idea of dinner with the family seemed so unappealing that I locked myself in my room and until midnight thought about Švejk and his intentions.

Was he really interested in buying a vehicle? Was he telling the truth?

I don't know why, but I was becoming increasingly convinced that Elizabeta was right when she said he had a hidden agenda. So, the next day, when straight after breakfast he again went to pursue his investigations, I followed him once more.

To my surprise he went to the nearest neighbours. It was Sunday, so they were at home. I was unable to establish what he talked to them about or what he asked them. I was prevented by their two dogs, who began to kick up a fuss as soon as they saw me (although, curiously, when Švejk arrived they had merely whimpered). And at the top of the hill, at the tourist farm, I was unable to sneak up to the window without being observed by one of the neighbours.

Then Švejk headed for the village fire station. I followed at a safe distance. On the grass in front of the building they were having a meeting of the local volunteer fire brigade. Hidden behind some bushes, it was not difficult to follow what was happening, although I was slightly too far away to be able to hear exactly what was being said. Švejk went straight up to them, boldly introduced himself, shook hands with the nearest ones as if they were acquaintances he had not seen for a long time and waved to those who were slightly further away, like a king greeting his subjects.

For the first time I began to think that Švejk's homilies about inner peace were not entirely without foundation and that he really was in possession of some secret that invested him with careless self-confidence. I could only dream about appearing among strangers with such nonchalance and within a minute get them to pay attention to me.

What was more, after a few minutes it became clear that it was Švejk who was leading the meeting. Soon after, the men got up, unbolted and opened wide the doors to the fire station, and some of them disappeared inside with Švejk. I heard the rumbling and rattling of an engine. Then the fire engine, with Švejk at the wheel, appeared from inside the building, its siren wailing, which can't have been much fun for those living close by. For a while he manoeuvred around the space between the woods and the road, and then he reversed into the fire station as adeptly as if he had driven in front first.

The impressed fire-fighters gave a round of applause. A few minutes later a much older fire engine appeared. As it moved forward it shuddered and jumped, and its rattling exhaust pipe belched greyish black smoke. As soon as it had emerged fully, the engine coughed a number of times and then fell silent. Whatever its driver, Švejk, tried, nothing would bring the antique vehicle back to life.

Švejk climbed out of the cabin with a large screwdriver in his hand. He opened the bonnet and leaned inside so that only his large behind was visible, rhythmically moving this way and that in time with his unsuccessful efforts to coax the uncooperative engine to life. This lasted a minute or more. The village fire-fighters shuffled impatiently, awaiting the outcome of the unequal struggle. But soon after Švejk climbed back into the cabin, the engine roared and the men began to applaud with great enthusiasm.

Švejk, his face glowing, waved from the cabin in acknowledgement of the acclaim, then he drove ahead, turning once to the left, once to the right, reversing and then driving in a circle. Like a flock of chickens, the fire-fighters moved now in one direction, now in another. Finally, Švejk parked the vehicle so that it faced the road, its rear end towards me, where I squatted in the bushes on the edge of the woods. Švejk turned the engine off and tumbled out of the cabin. Some of the fire-fighters went up to him and gave him a friendly pat on the shoulders. One offered him a beer, but Švejk politely demurred and signalled for his new friends to follow him.

They gathered at the back of the water tank, which even from a distance did not look in good condition. It was battered, deformed and rusty. Švejk explained something, and the others nodded. Then Švejk waved his hand, striking the battered rear end of the vehicle to add emphasis to his words. The metal was so corroded that it gave way beneath the blow, and Švejk's hand disappeared inside. This provoked general astonishment.

Most astonished of all was Švejk, who at first could not grasp what had happened. The others were waiting anxiously to see what he would say. First, he cautiously extracted his hand and examined it from all sides. When he saw it was still in one piece, a conspiratorial smile split his face. The fire-fighters began to laugh, at first only a few, the others doubting whether this was an appropriate reaction, but soon everyone joined in, particularly Švejk, for the unexpected mishap had endeared him even more to his new comrades.

Once again he began to speak and to explain something, while the others expressed their agreement by nodding. From his gestures it was clear that he was saying how he could fix the back of the water tank if they allowed him to. Some of the fire-fighters offered their views, and, in the end, general agreement was reached. Two of the men hurried inside and re-emerged with a flagon of wine. Once more they sat down, and this time even Švejk did not say no to a drop.

However, it was not difficult to tell that his thoughts were elsewhere. Several times when the others were speaking he gazed into the distance, and a few times he stared at the back of the fire engine as if he were trying to repair it by telepathy alone. Then he jumped up as though in a terrible hurry.

He offered his hand to those nearest to him, waved to the others, climbed into the cabin, started the engine and the aged fire engine lunged forward on to the main road, then the side road that led to our house.

I ran through the woods as fast as my legs would carry me.

15

I came panting through the orchard to see that the bright-red fire engine was already standing in the yard, the whole family gathered around it. Unobserved, I sneaked closer and pretended that I had been there from the beginning.

Švejk was explaining that he had just joined the village volunteer fire brigade, which had a century-long tradition. He had become the official driver of a fire engine should a fire break out in the local area. He had also been entrusted with the repair of an old vehicle, so that the fire-fighters would have two and thus be better equipped for extinguishing fires. Of course, the repairs would take some time, but he sincerely hoped that the repairing, banging and welding would not disturb anyone.

'Does anyone have any welding equipment?' he asked.

His words were met by silence. The sight of the red monster with the hole in its rear end, which in the relatively small space between the outbuildings looked incomparably bigger than it did in front of the fire station, had paralysed all those present – almost, I would say, in a similar fashion to the appearance of the mysterious object in the orchard.

More than anything, the fire engine in the yard evoked a feeling that it didn't really belong there. The way that Švejk had presented us with a *fait accompli* was experienced by all of us as an infringement of our right to decide – even, to judge from her grim expression, Aunt Mara, who was usually the greatest defender of Švejk's eccentricities.

We were all waiting to see what Dad would say. When he just stood and stared at the vehicle as if it wasn't at all clear how, on top of everything else, this could happen to us, Mum spoke up. As Švejk's sister she obviously felt obliged to take the initiative.

'Jaro,' she said, 'things have gone a bit too far.'

'But I thought –' Švejk began to say after a stunned silence.

But Mum interrupted him. 'I really don't care what you thought. Sometimes you need to consider what others think.'

'But –' Uncle Švejk began to say, but Mum interrupted him again.

'Take this horrible thing back to the fire station, or I'll take it myself.'

Dad cleared his throat, indicating that he intended to offer an opinion. We all listened but, most intently of all, Švejk, in the hope that he had an ally. When Dad had achieved the desired effect, he cleared his throat again, probably to underline the importance of what he was about to say.

'Švejk, if my memory doesn't deceive me, you indicated that your greatest and perhaps only pleasure was transporting people – delivering them to their destinations so that they arrive neither too early nor too late. How does that fit with the vehicle we see before us, in which you couldn't even transport rubbish let alone anything of value – not to mention people?'

Yes, the others nodded in agreement, carrying passengers was one thing, putting out fires was something else, especially with a vehicle that needed patching up first.

'How can I paint in peace', said Aunt Mara, 'if the yard becomes a body-repair shop?'

'To put it mildly,' said Elizabeta sarcastically, 'we are all somewhat taken aback.'

'Or not . . .' said my older brother Peter meaningfully and then immediately sank into enigmatic silence.

'I don't know what to say,' said Uncle Vinko with a sigh.

'To which I would add', said Vladimir, 'that then the wisest thing is to say nothing.'

Perhaps emulating Dad, Švejk now also cleared his throat. Embarrassed but stubbornly convinced that he was in the right, he observed that driving a bus and delivering people to their destination was quite a broad concept that allowed for at least some flexibility. One of man's noblest goals is that if the house in which he lives is struck by lightning it doesn't burn down. For that reason the fire-fighter was one of the noblest professions in the world. By chance – but also by divine providence – his desire to find a vocation to which to devote his life had been fulfilled. If, God forbid, our house should ever catch fire, the presence of an experienced fire-fighter would certainly be of assistance.

What was more, he had thought up a special way of repairing the fire engine. He wouldn't simply patch up the rear of the water tank but would make a hatch with a seal, which could be closed, locked, opened or even removed. In that way the vehicle could be used to carry water for putting out fires but also milk, wine, vinegar, oil, liquid manure and so on or, if the need should arise, bags of cement, leaves, wheat, flour, clothes, furniture, people. Here was an opportunity, with a small intervention and almost for free, at no cost to anyone in the family, to what you might call a universal vehicle. If they wished him well, if they wanted him to succeed and if they wanted to benefit themselves, then they should support his idea. If not, he could rent a room somewhere in the village or, if there was no other choice, with the gypsies.

Although we knew that in a nice way Švejk was coercing us, no one found the courage to call his bluff and say, 'OK, go.' We all waited, as was our custom, to see what Dad would say – for, in spite of his clearly growing uncertainty, it was still the case that he could not be wrong, at least not as wrong as one of us might be.

But Dad said not a word. We speculated in vain whether this was because he didn't want to offend Švejk or because he accepted his proposal in principle or because he was in shock at how much the idea of the vehicle that could be used for everything and at the same time nothing in particular resembled the mysterious object, the Great Unsolvable Mystery.

As if one of its effects was Švejk's arrival. As if the thing locked in the shed wanted once more to intrude in our lives but this time in a different form.

Švejk's eyes jumped from one person to another, waiting, checking, speculating, seeking allies. At the same time they challenged each of us in turn to go against him. When it appeared that no one would do this, he gave a friendly smile, rubbed his hands together and said, 'Right, so I just need a welding torch and I can get down to it.'

Then Mum spoke up. 'Sorry, Jaro, but I have to say again that this is not on. No welding, no panel-beating, no transport runs with a vehicle that belongs, repaired or not, at the fire station, not on the road. And definitely not in our yard. We moved to this village to find refuge from a world that most of us don't understand. With your arrival that world has followed us and now, through you, has presented us with a *fait accompli* in a way we cannot accept.

You can stay but this monstrosity cannot.' At which she turned and went into the house.

We looked down in embarrassment, even Dad, who was on the receiving end of Švejk's hurt expression most of all. Mum's judgement seemed too hasty and too harsh. We all had the feeling that Švejk wouldn't back down and that he would soon vanish from our lives. That filled us with sadness; in spite of everything, he had brought a great deal of fun to the family circle. So it was to be expected, especially seeing Švejk's growing despondence, that we would try to find a compromise.

The first to speak was Vinko, who knew Švejk best of all.

'Jaro,' he warned him, 'stubbornness won't help anyone. You know very well that you are absolutely welcome here, even if you weren't at first. You could say you've found a home. So I suggest you think the matter over and take the vehicle back to where it belongs. You can repair it there, and when you start to use it you can keep it there. I know the fire-fighters, and I'm sure that none of them will object. Quite the opposite – if you keep the vehicle here some may think that you have purloined it. Sooner or later they will come and ask for it back.'

Then Vinko looked at Dad, as if asking whether he agreed.

But before Dad could adopt a stance Vladimir spoke up.

'I know that I am also a mere guest in this house, but I'd still like to offer my opinion. Why not grant the new family member, if that is what he has become, the same rights as the rest of us? When we moved here I imagined that in our community each of us would be allowed to realize his dream and that the others would support him. We could build a big open-sided shed in the lower part of the orchard. Švejk could work there on his vehicle ten hours a day without disturbing anyone. He could get access straight from the road so that it would never come near the house. And when Švejk started to use it to transport things he could do it almost without us being aware of it – certainly discreetly enough for the rest of us to get on with our lives, as if Švejk were not even there.'

Švejk turned towards Vladimir, and they looked at each other in the sudden realization they had become friends. At the same time it was clear that Švejk was ready to accept the compromise if it received a positive response from Dad.

But Dad still couldn't decide whether to support Mum's decision or

Vladimir's proposal. If he did the latter, then he could get involved in a lengthy war of attrition with Mum, which it seemed he was not ready to do, since he knew her only too well.

He looked at Vinko to see what he thought of the matter.

But Vinko merely shrugged. In the light of Dad's indecision, he no longer knew whose side to take.

16

Aunt Mara decided it was time to intervene in the debate.

'This is what I think,' she said, somewhat offended that no one had already asked for her opinion. 'Vladimir's proposal is a reasonable one, and it could only be rejected by someone who doesn't like Švejk. But I'd like to modify it. The vehicle that now looks so hideous could, with a little imagination, become not only pleasing visually but a genuine work of art. If Švejk were to allow me, I would paint the fire engine with images from the Bible. It could be converted into a travelling gallery in which he could drive my pictures around the area and sell them at celebrations, festivals, fairs and other events. Art needs to be among the people. We have shut ourselves off too much, while the real world passes us by. With Švejk's help I could become a bridge to that world.'

'I have a different suggestion,' said Elizabeta. 'The vehicle must certainly stay close by – as far as I'm concerned it can stay right here. Švejk must remain with us. Can we live without him? I think not. We'd feel like a child that has had its pacifier taken away just as it got used to it. And, as far as the vehicle is concerned, it seems a shame to use it for fire-fighting. There aren't any fires – unless we start setting things alight so that fire-fighter Švejk isn't deprived of his fun. The vehicle is perfect for something else, and that is for addressing our inhibitions and our feeling that life is a torment that needs to be struggled with, through gritted teeth, right to the bitter end. I'm convinced that the majority of people would rather live freely. To quote the head of our family: a free society needs free people –'

'What are you rambling on about?' Aunt Mara started to interrupt her, but Dad indicated with a gesture that Elizabeta should continue. The malicious hussy didn't need much persuasion, and, emboldened, she began to outline her idea.

She said that we should paint on the vehicle the words 'Enter and enjoy a moment of freedom'. From what she could make out, having made her way through a number of learned books when she had nothing better to do, our feeling of entrapment stemmed from suppressed sexual urges. We were suppressing them because we were convinced, completely misguidedly, that they were necessarily connected with difficult and risky interpersonal relations. This, of course, was not the case, and it should be our mission to show people this. The interior of the water tank could be transformed into a softly furnished boudoir into which people would crawl in total darkness, without knowing what awaited them there, and satisfy their sexual desires without feelings of guilt or obligation. Troublesome factors like appearance, hair colour, social status, education, emotions, expectation, boring seduction games and establishing interpersonal communication would all become irrelevant. There would remain only the bare act without the presence of ego. Švejk, as the owner of the company for making people happy, and she, as his personal assistant, would ensure the anonymity of the users. No one should have the feeling that they were getting into a situation where their identities might be uncovered.

Elizabeta was unable to complete the description of her charitable vision, for Aunt Mara flew at her and began to kick her and beat her on the head with her fists. She knocked her to the ground and was just about to jump on her when Švejk and Vladimir took hold of her by the arms and restrained her.

'I'll kill you,' she yelled, saliva spraying on her daughter, who was rolling on the ground in pain.

This was the moment when Dad felt he could no longer stand there as if this barely believable scene unfolding in his yard had nothing to do with him. 'Mara,' he said and then, when it was clear she had not heard, much louder, 'Mara, calm down.'

But Mara was struggling to escape so that she could throw herself on Elizabeta, who had half risen from the ground.

'Take her away', Dad said to Vladimir, 'and lock her in the studio. Let her jump on her paintings for a while.'

'No,' said Mara, pushing away her two captors. 'No one's going to lock me up. I'm going on my own.'

Head held high and brush in hand, she stalked across the yard to her 'realm of art', as she liked to call it and slammed the door.

'You go to your room,' Dad said to Elizabeta, 'and make sure I don't see you for some time.'

Elizabeta put her tongue out, turned and ran into the woods.

'My God,' said Uncle Vinko, 'what's happening to us?'

'Nothing that we shouldn't have expected,' said Peter, going after Elizabeta, at first slowly then at a running pace to catch up with her.

'I think it's all my fault,' said Švejk, his head lowered. 'The only possibility is that I relieve you of my presence and leave you to the peace you enjoyed before fate brought me to your yard.'

'Švejk, listen . . .' said Dad, getting ready for a lengthy negotiation, but Švejk climbed into the fire engine and started the motor. Black smoke belched from the exhaust pipe straight into Dad's face, so that he had to take a leap back and cover his nose with his hand. Švejk skilfully reversed the fire engine. He turned the wheel and drove from the yard along the grassy drive to the road and then up the road towards the village. In less than three minutes the noise of the engine had faded and been replaced by silence.

'Everything will be all right,' said Uncle Vinko after a while. 'He'll reconsider.'

No one believed that. A strange fog descended on us. We all felt that something, God knows what, had pushed us over the threshold of the unknown. To judge by the look on her face Mum felt it, too; she had witnessed the whole scene through the window of her room on the first floor. When she saw how Dad, Vinko, Vladimir and I were standing there with heads bowed, she also hung her head.

Elizabeta and Peter returned two hours later with little to say for themselves and lost in their own thoughts. Aunt Mara could not be coaxed from her studio, where she had locked herself, even by the friendliest of words. Nor had Švejk returned. The next morning, when he was not at breakfast and Mum sent me to knock on his door, I discovered that his bed had not been slept in. He must have spent the night elsewhere.

This filled us with a concern that we each experienced in our own way.

'He's sure to turn up,' said Mum. 'He probably got drunk somewhere.'

But Švejk did not appear in the afternoon or the evening. And when, the following morning, Mum sent me to knock on his door, I found that his things had mysteriously disappeared during the night, right down to his toothbrush and socks, not to mention the clothes he'd bought using the money from the 'Švejk fund'.

'OK then,' concluded Mum.

17

We all knew that Mum's indifference was not genuine and that she felt at least partly responsible for Švejk's disappearance. Dad said nothing. Ever since Uncle's disappearance he had stared blankly into space, as if he had retreated to a parallel world. Whenever Mum asked for his opinion on something he did it more out of politeness than out of interest. He sank into a state of apathy in which we saw the reflection of our own gloom. We also felt the weight of events as a burden that showed no sign of diminishing in the near future.

Elizabeta volunteered to go into the village and find out whether anyone had seen Švejk and where he had taken the fire engine.

'No.' Mum was decisively against the idea. 'He was the one who decided to leave, so let him come back of his own accord if he wants to.'

'It would be good to know that nothing has happened to him,' observed Vinko, in the hope that Mum would reconsider.

'Yes,' said Vladimir with a nod.

'That at least,' agreed Aunt Mara.

'To make sure he didn't drive the fire engine into a ditch or crash into the corner of the inn,' said Elizabeta.

But Mum was firm. If they demonstrated in any way that they weren't indifferent to what happened to him he would sooner or later make use of the fact. We would wait for him to return, and that was that.

'But this is childish,' said Peter, suddenly plucking up courage. 'This is something left over from your childhood. I don't see why it should bind us as well. We are surely free to decide whether to be concerned about the fate of a person who has gone missing.'

'Absolutely,' Dad burst out. 'Personal freedom cannot become a subject of negotiation among family members. Everyone has the right to act in line with his conscience. But my freedom ends at the point where it begins to harm someone dear to me. If Mum doesn't want to look for the brother that was long concealed, she no doubt has her reasons, which she will share with us when the time is right. But that does not mean that she has an exclusive right to Švejk. All she wants is that we take her opinions into consideration – after all, she is the one who knows him best.'

'It's ridiculous', objected Peter, 'that a tyranny has suddenly become established in this family, which is far from the goals we had when we moved here. Mum's emotional trauma, or whatever the reason is for her infantile attitude to Švejk, cannot prevent me from building relationships with others based on my own judgement. So no one should hold it against me if I go into the village and start asking after Švejk. Nor if I ask him to return home.'

'I'll go,' said Mum. 'I'll go and find him and bring him home. If he is willing to return home without the fire engine. If not, you can have him, and I'll leave. I, too, am free to choose who I have in my house and under what conditions, am I not?'

'Absolutely,' we all nodded in agreement, I as usual with tongue in cheek – the others, too, as far as I could judge from their faces, with the exception of Dad, who had evidently decided that submitting to Mum's will would at least bring some peace – the thing he had yearned for over the last year.

I felt that he was torn. Part of him wished that Švejk had never appeared, but the oddball missing uncle had entertained him and stopped him thinking about the pointlessness of life and the cruelty of history. Of course, he would never admit this, but, as long as he dressed up his need for Švejk's presence in the house as concern for his well-being, he avoided the danger that any member of the family might suspect that the *capo di banda* also had human needs.

Except me, of course. And maybe Elizabeta. And Aunt Mara, who was far from as stupid as she liked to appear. And Vinko, of course. And Peter, who was not so lost in space as not to know what was happening right in front of his nose. Not to mention Vladimir, who as a long-time Party functionary, was particularly alert to pretence; thus the situation must have been crystal clear to him.

There was no one in the family who was unaware that Dad missed Švejk as much as everyone else did and that he was both amazed and delighted about this. Amazed because it was unclear to him how he could be won over by such an unorthodox individual and delighted over the realization that his feelings had not been totally subordinated to his reason. We all knew that Dad would be relieved if Švejk moved back into the guest room.

'At the end of the day,' he said, making sure that Mum could hear him, 'Vladimir's proposal is not such a bad one. We *could* build a shed down by the road, and Švejk could repair and park his vehicle there without it affecting us at all. Švejk would have his fun, and we would have the pleasant feeling that we will never burn in our beds. How many families can boast of their own fire engine as well as a fire-fighter?'

The same day Mum went to the fire station.

Although I knew that there would be no one there because the fire-fighters were volunteers and had their meetings and practice sessions on a Sunday, I didn't tell her this. I wanted to find Švejk on my own. I hurried through the woods to the house of the head of the local fire brigade. He was sure to know where Švejk had taken the vehicle they had entrusted to him for repair. But he wasn't there; he was at work in the hardboard factory in the next village, and his wife had never even heard of Švejk let alone of the loaned fire engine.

I took a short cut to the inn, which was not only the main talking shop and location for exchanging village gossip but doubled as the first repository for anything new or unusual that happened in the village.

I almost ran into Mum and Uncle Vladimir, who were arguing on the terrace in front of the entrance about who had the most right to look for Švejk. Vladimir was claiming that he had come only for a glass of wine and that he was not going to be stopped even by the new authorities, who would like to see every old Partisan dead and buried; he had about as much interest in Švejk as he did in last year's news.

'Don't pretend,' said Mum, wagging her finger at him. 'I heard you talking at the bar about the fire engine.'

'What if we were?' Vladimir snapped back. 'Doesn't the village community, in the middle of the summer when the risk of fires is at its greatest, have a right, not to mention a duty, to talk about the fact that one fire engine is not enough and that it is time to get at least one other? The days when there were only certain things we could talk about are past. What's the matter with you? Why are you acting like a tyrant with members of your own family?'

Mum turned bright red and almost hissed. 'If we were on our own now

I'd slap your face.' She spun around and, stubbornly offended, stomped off towards the road.

'God help us,' said Vladimir to himself. 'The woman's gone mad.'

I hurried after Mum to see where she would go next. She was marching in the direction of a poorly frequented bar that had been opened in the old school building and which served only in the evenings. Her gait had never displayed such relentless determination. If an elephant had blocked her path at that moment she would probably have blown it out of the way. Since I knew that at three in the afternoon she would be met by a locked door, I didn't follow her. I suddenly thought of the possibility that Švejk had driven the rusty old fire engine back to the fire station and had then disappeared or gone back to where he was before he came to us.

I ran back towards the fire station. In front of the inn I saw Peter and Vladimir. This time Vladimir was rebuking Peter in the way that Mum had rebuked him. Evidently Peter couldn't help himself and was also looking for Švejk. I rushed past so that they wouldn't notice me. I peered through the window at the back of the fire station. As far as I could see there was only one fire engine there. Slowly, my eyes grew accustomed to the dark interior, and there was no doubt. Švejk had not returned the vehicle.

But where could he have disappeared to with it? Certainly not into the town because he would have problems parking there. Was he driving from one place to another and sleeping in the water tank? If he got rid of the rusty rear end and put a cheap mattress inside he would have as much comfort as he had enjoyed in our spare room, so it didn't seem impossible that he had decided on a nomadic life. In that case, it would be difficult to track him down without the help of the police, but before the police would be willing to act we would have to report him missing.

Later, it was never clear to me why I thought about the most likely possibility last of all. Only when I was sitting on the grass beside the fire station and, looking at the slope of the hill opposite, did I see the wood where the gypsy settlement was and recalled Švejk's threat that he would seek refuge with the Roma. Although I could not imagine what a hero of the war for independence and volunteer fire-fighter would do there, my curiosity drove me along the narrow path into the valley, across the wooden footbridge over the stream and through the fields towards the wood that sat below the summit of the neighbouring hill.

18

The gypsies, now known as the Roma, lived in small settlements all around the area – not in the village where we had bought the house but near enough so it was not hard to come across them. It was said that they had lived a lot better in the past – more 'gypsy-like' lives, whatever that meant – but in recent years, mainly because they had been working over the border in Austria, they had become less 'gypsy-like', more like 'ordinary people', as my granny put it. This meant that they built new houses, bolted satellite dishes to them, bought second-hand cars, stopped begging in the villages and began acting like equal citizens of a free sovereign state.

Dad, who strove to adapt the mindset of the members of his family to the new spirit of the times, insisted in the name of political correctness that we should no longer speak of 'gypsies' but only of 'Roma communities' that had the same rights as other minorities, and so any kind of demeaning comments about them were unacceptable. But his words had not been received with the same level of understanding by everyone, especially Vladimir, who said that in their essence things did not change as quickly as that.

This was shown by Dad's choice of words: 'unacceptable' was reminiscent of the times when the most common socio-political phrase was 'that's unacceptable'. Behind the façade of a new name the gypsies could pretend that they were now different, and under the dictates of the new social norms we could also pretend that our attitude towards them had changed, but the fact was that the situation was still pretty much the same. For us, they were still different, dark-skinned, exotic, unintegrated and with a language, folklore and customs from elsewhere. And why not? After all, we could respect them in their difference, even if it did have negative connotations.

Aunt Mara added, 'Among the Roma there is roughly the same percentage of gypsies as among the non-Roma, so perhaps we should ask who the gypsies are among us.'

One way or another, for Peter, Elizabeta and I, who did not remember the 'leaden times', the gypsies or Roma, regardless of their name and alleged changes in their lifestyle, represented complete difference and an attractiveness that our older relatives could not understand. We were of a generation that regarded difference as a positive value – even something to boast of – so we respected more those gypsies who had not tried to submerge themselves in the evermore uniform world of consumerism and had clung to the old ways, the wandering life, idleness, fighting, music-making, fortune-telling and opportunist thieving; but, above all, even though we were perhaps only daydreaming about this, sexual freedom, which presented the possibility of a pleasant surprise in the near future for at least some of us.

There was a gypsy girl at school who, it was rumoured, was prepared to do 'it' for the price of a packet of chewing gum if you caught her at the right moment – although she couldn't have been described as pretty. Elizabeta had a gypsy classmate who earned enough offering sexual favours to older women to buy himself a motorbike and who was prepared, for a packet of cigarettes, to painlessly deflower any girl ready to enter the world of adulthood but who had no interest in forming emotional connections with clumsy 'romantic' peers.

For Elizabeta, who had decided to lose her virginity in a completely original way, such a routine deflowering was out of the question since she would be merely one in a long line, but she had often expressed the desire to be present when the gypsy lad with the motorbike deflowered one of her schoolmates. For such an opportunity she was ready to give him all of her savings. He was easy to convince, but she could not find a willing schoolgirl.

As far as Peter was concerned, I had long known that he was attracted to long walks in the woods not only because of the chance to reflect deeply on nature and the fate of the universe but also, or principally, because of the two gypsy girls who often sunbathed naked in the grassy glades, and that was also one of the reasons for my own peregrinations.

The settlement in the woods on the slope of the nearby hill was not on the way to school, so we didn't know much about it, except that of all the ones in the area it was the most genuinely gypsy, with only one satellite dish, no running water or gas, wood-burning stoves that caused spirals of smoke above the dense spruce trees in the winter and a pack of canine beasts that often set up such a loud collective barking that it could be heard all the way to our village. Because of the dogs I had never dared sneak into the woods to take a look at the settlement from up close, and even now I was unsure whether I would find the courage.

The closer I got to the settlement, the less likely it seemed that Švejk would seek refuge here, if only because it would be difficult to get the awkward fire engine down the steep unpaved track. And, if he had already manoeuvred it down the slope, it would be even harder to get it back up to the road at the top of the hill. But even before I got to the edge of the wood I could hear metal being worked. It sounded as if someone was beating something made of steel with a heavy hammer and, in between, drilling, filing and smoothing. There were no other sounds. It was as if everyone in the settlement as well as the dogs were gathered around this noise, listening.

I pushed through the low bushes and cautiously, moving quickly from tree to tree, approached the cluster of modest houses. I was met by a scene that at first did not seem credible, although the whole time I'd had a feeling that I would come across something unusual.

The fire engine squatted among the houses like a giant queen bee, around which swarmed a busy mass of workers. Actually, the scene was most reminiscent of an operation, with Švejk in the role of the surgeon trying to patch up the rear end of an enormous creature, while those around him, with a zeal that attested to the importance of the event, were passing him various tools. At the same time they were taking from his hands the tools he had finished with, almost fighting each other for them; all, especially the children, wanted to touch those items that Švejk had used to sand, file, remove, level and smooth the rebellious metal.

He kept demanding that they hand back what had just left his hands, so no tool could go so far away that he would have to wait for it and his assistants had to stay close by.

This meant that with the children, women, old men and even dogs, who were hypnotized by the metallic noise, there was such a crowd that at times Švejk didn't have enough room to gesticulate effectively; people had to shuffle back and make room. But only for a moment, for then they squeezed in again from all sides.

The role of chief assistant and controller of the curious crowd was played by a youngish-to-middle-aged dark-skinned gypsy with cropped black hair and a cruel face that was enhanced by a toothbrush moustache and disturbed, melancholy eyes. He was evidently some kind of village headman, and everyone obeyed him without question. He was also the only one who dared to give Švejk advice, while Švejk gave the impression that the advice did not bother him at all – quite the opposite. It seemed the 'Czech bastard' and the gypsy had become allies in the struggle with the disobedient metal.

The scene captivated me so much that it was only after five minutes that I noticed what else was going on. Two boys of my age, whom I didn't know because they must have attended a different school, were using large brushes to repaint the fire engine a new colour. From where I was, I couldn't see exactly what they were doing, so I cautiously moved in a large arc through the trees, hoping that the dogs wouldn't smell me, until I could see the full length of the vehicle.

I saw that the boys were not painting the whole surface but painting on the side in bright yellow letters the words 'Aranka, Gypsy Fortune-Teller'. They had already done the letters, and now they were highlighting them. I knew that Aranka was a gypsy woman's name, and I realized that Švejk, with the gypsies' help, was cutting out the back of the water tank so that a gypsy fortune-teller could be transported in it to fairs and other events – probably one of the women standing in mass of onlookers.

Something suddenly moved close by me. Afraid that it was one of the dogs, I froze and didn't dare look. Only when a soft hand touched me did I turn my head – and saw Elizabeta, who put a finger to her lips and barely audibly went 'Shhh.'

'What are you doing here?' I asked.

She replied, 'The same as you. And speak more quietly. If they catch us, we won't get out of here alive.'

'Don't exaggerate,' I said. 'They're gypsies not vampires. And Švejk is here. We could go over to him and tell him to come home.'

'Listen,' she said. 'Your mum doesn't want Aranka the Fortune-Teller on her land – that much is clear. And Švejk is no longer what he was. They have ensnared him here, stolen his soul, and now they will exploit him for their own purposes. And he, wimp that he is, will not be able to resist them.'

'You're exaggerating again,' I said. 'These gypsies are completely innocent. Švejk is here because we are wicked and heartless, us, his own family.'

'I found out', she said, 'that in this village there lives a murderer, who some years ago killed his mother's lover and has only recently got out of prison. If you ask me, I'd say that it must be no other than the one with the cruel face who is helping Švejk the most enthusiastically. And you know why? Because he wants to free his friends who stayed behind bars. One of them will start a fire, the prison will start to burn, fire engines will come hurtling up, among them Švejk's, five or ten prisoners will crowd into the water tank, the vehicle will drive off, saying they are going to get water, and the gypsy with the moustache will become the leader of a gang of robbers.'

'What kind of story is that?' I asked. 'It couldn't be more far-fetched if you tried. When I'm a writer –'

'You never will be because you have no imagination. Even Švejk has more than you. Look, now he'll drive around with some old woman and earn his living from fortune-telling. A nice end for a war hero.'

'No, he won't,' I said. 'I'll convince him to return home, and then he'll drive around a mobile exhibition of your mum's paintings.'

'Good luck with that,' said Elizabeta. 'I've had another idea, a lot less boring than yours. Actually, I'm not even going to tell you,' she pouted.

'Why not?'

'Because you'll tell the others and because you're too green to understand, let alone to value the decision I made a few minutes ago, the moment I saw the gypsy with the cruel face. He looks like a character in a film. I get goose bumps when I look at him. Killers have a particular power inside them.'

'But you've no evidence that he is a killer,' I said, 'and killers are usually feeble types. They have no internal power, only a desire to do evil.'

'You, child, you've no idea what makes the world go round. I'd bet my life's savings that you're still a virgin.'

'So what?' I said. 'Maybe I am, maybe I'm not, but I'm not going to discuss that with you.'

'The object,' she said, 'it has affected you as well. At the age of seventeen it has sucked out your interest in sex, and you're probably impotent. When did you last have an erection?'

'I get five a day,' I replied. 'And that thing in the shed has no power at all, at least not the kind you think it has.'

'Then show me you're capable of an erection.'

'Why should I?'

'You can't get it up,' she mocked.

I protested that I could in such a loud voice that one of the dogs in the gypsy pack pricked up its ears. Elizabeta covered my hand with her mouth.

'Get it out, and I'll jerk you off,' she whispered. 'Then I'll believe you. Has any girl ever given you a blow job?'

I shook my head.

'I will,' she said. 'If it goes hard I'll believe you, otherwise I'll tell everyone at school that you're impotent.'

'I don't care,' I replied, although I knew that from this point on her offer would give me no peace.

'OK, I will then,' she said, offended. 'Unless you do something for me.'

She beckoned me nearer. She leaned towards me, and I felt her sweet breath on my face. Her tongue quivered between her open lips.

'Listen,' she said. 'If you give a message to the gypsy with a cruel face that a beautiful fifteen-year-old girl would like to lose her virginity to him I'll keep the secret of your impotence to myself.'

'I can't believe that you'd want to do it with him.'

'Why not?'

'You said he was a murderer.'

'You know what?' She shook her head coldly. 'You'll never be a writer. You don't understand women. You don't realize that women are always wanting something that in reality they don't really want.'

'What do you know about women at your age? And what do you know about men or the world in general? You've no idea. You just provoke people and show off, and that's all. And you're not even that wickedly beautiful. You're just an ordinary pumpkin who, out of sheer stubbornness, refuses to look around and acknowledge that almost every other girl is ten times more beautiful. Look at the gypsy women standing around Švejk's fire engine.'

'They may be more beautiful,' said Elizabeta, suppressing a sob, 'but not one of them is sexier. Look,' she suddenly lifted her T-shirt and revealed her pert breasts. 'Did you ever see anything more seductive?'

'I didn't know you had such terrible problems with growing up. You fill your head with crazy ideas that will lead you to the lunatic asylum if you don't get them under control.'

She gave a sob and began to hit me on the head with her fists. This caused the gypsy dogs to snap out of their trance. They jumped up, pricked up their ears and begun to sniff the air excitedly.

19

Elizabeta and I were already halfway to the stream in the valley. Her outbreak had forced me to flee, but she was hot on my heels, as if she feared that I would get home before her and complain to Mara. Her fear of her mother was such that she found unusual reserves of inner strength and caught up with me just before the footbridge. She grabbed hold of my shirt from behind and pulled with such strength that I tripped and fell on to the grass. She ended up on top of me.

I expected her to keep pummelling me, so I instinctively covered my head with my hands, but instead she turned me over on to my back and fastened her bloodthirsty mouth on to mine. At first I thought she wanted to bite me, so I clamped my jaws together and only relaxed them when there was no longer any doubt she was kissing and licking me. Although a tiny voice inside me told me to resist, I slowly succumbed and finally unclenched my teeth, through which she kept pushing the end of her tongue.

When my resistance dropped, her burning tongue wrestled with mine, as if it wished to get past it and enter my throat. I began almost to choke, as did she. Several times her teeth banged noisily against mine. It struck me that she was not doing this for pleasure but to punish me. She wanted a weapon to use against me in case I tried to accuse her.

I was overcome by an unfamiliar feeling. At least twice I thought I was going to pass out. I began to respond to the sucking pressure of her mouth, I began to bite back and suck, and when she realized what I was doing she began both to challenge and invite me, to attack and withdraw, to succumb and to pull away. Whenever my passion began to wane and she felt I was beginning to go limp, she went on the attack once more to keep me in the game as an equal opponent.

Whenever I went on the attack, she began to retreat, as if afraid that blood would flow, or perhaps as if she enjoyed the feeling that I was trying to entice her back into the game that she had created. Thus we slid over the slippery ground of sensuality, together and separately seeking new thresholds of fear and bliss, until I, almost in passing, in a break between the struggle of mouths and tongues, realized that her right hand had found its way beneath the elastic waistband of my summer shorts and had begun to squeeze my swollen penis.

Suddenly she froze and I, too. We had both noticed at the same moment that we were surrounded by a pack of gypsy dogs. They sat there, their tongues lolling from their panting mouths. To judge from their postures they had been there for some time; they probably overtook us just after we fell on the grass, and our actions had confused them so much they just sat and watched.

Now that they scented our fear one of them began to growl. The others shifted on their haunches and bared their teeth. We looked towards the stream. The bridge was only three strides away. The distance was small, but the dogs would probably hurl themselves at us as soon as we rose. There were eight of them; some looked harmless enough, but the two large Alsatians looked as if they were craving blood.

'What shall we do?' whispered Elizabeta.

'Pretend they're not there,' I suggested.

'For how long?'

'Until they get fed up and leave.'

'And if they don't?' she asked on the verge of tears.

'Of course they will,' I replied. 'Sooner or later. If not today, tomorrow.'

'Are you mad?' she said. 'We're not waiting until tomorrow.'

She made a sudden movement with her hands, which again excited the dogs. The Alsatians growled and rose, ready to leap, while the three smaller hounds began to bark.

'Stay still,' I said. 'No sudden movements.'

'Why didn't they growl before?' she asked. 'We didn't even know they were here.'

'Dogs sense when we are afraid. Fear is connected with threat. What we were doing before didn't concern them.'

'So let's carry on,' she said, 'then they'll get bored and leave sooner than if we just lie here, afraid of them. Let's show them we don't care.'

'Right,' I said. 'Maybe they really will clear off.'

'Jesus,' she sighed. 'I never thought I'd be doing this just to avoid being bitten by a dog.'

She leaned over me and asked, 'Will it be enough if we just pretend to be kissing?'

'As far as the dogs are concerned, I'm sure it will.'

'Oh,' she sighed again, 'this will be hard work. A shame we have to pretend, but there's no other option.'

'No, we'll just have to grit our teeth and get on with it,' I said, trying to sound convincing.

'We can't kiss with gritted teeth,' she said decisively. 'First of all, it's harder, and, second, the dogs are not stupid. They'll know if we're cheating. If there's no other option but to pretend, then let's pretend convincingly. Otherwise one of the big ones might snap at you and bite off your prick. Do you want to be left without a future at seventeen?'

'No,' I replied, 'I wouldn't like that. So it would be better not to pretend at all.'

'I know that's what you want, but it's out of the question,' she said. 'I won't say that you disgust me, because it's not true, but my kisses, especially with my tongue down someone's throat, are reserved for the one who takes my virginity, not for you, you who remind me of a piglet rather than a man. So don't imagine that this is anything other than pretence.' She fastened her mouth to mine and attacked my tongue with hers, as if trying to remove a barrier.

Then she pulled back and asked, 'Do you think we're pretending OK?'

'Don't know,' I said with a shrug. 'Maybe less convincingly than before.'

'You know what,' she said, 'we can't do any better because, to be honest, it's pretty unpleasant, although probably less than being bitten by a dog, don't you think?'

'A bit less, I imagine.'

'So,' she said, 'it's better to continue.'

A wind blew across the valley, disturbing the grass and ruffling the dogs' coats. It got colder. Lightning split the darkening sky. There was no thunder. Elizabeta was so engrossed in what she was doing that she didn't notice the sudden changes. I knew that at any moment it would begin to pour down, but I didn't care. Elizabeta began to moan softly. She seemed to be struggling with herself, with some force that had awakened inside her and that she could not control.

All at once she succumbed, removed her mouth from mine, swung her legs across me, lifted her short skirt, put her fingers inside her panties and ripped them off, took hold of my penis, lifted herself slightly and sank on to it. I felt a soft barrier, which then gave way and I slipped inside her. The soft walls of her vagina gripped me like a mouth but one without a tongue to get in the way.

At the same moment a cry came from Elizabeta's throat, loud enough to be heard at the gypsy settlement if it hadn't been for the thunder. And then there was a torrential downpour. The dogs jumped up, their ears went down and they scurried ignominiously back home. Elizabeta's triumph did not last long because the downpour triggered another kind of outpouring, at which her body shuddered as if to prevent my sudden withdrawal from the game; and then, as she felt my penis go limp inside her, the almost ecstatic expression of her face distorted into one of despair, almost hatred.

'What have I done?' she began to cry like a madwoman, pulling at her wet hair. 'What have I done?' And she began to pummel me with her fists. 'Because I was scared of the dogs I've taken my own virginity, and, in return for nothing, given it to someone who is not worthy to lick my feet let alone bring me into the adult world. And I so wanted it to be the event of the century. What can I dream about now? It's all over.'

She put her head on my chest, shaking. When I tried to stroke her wet hair she knocked my hand away.

'Don't you touch me,' she hissed. 'Never again. I'll kill myself from sorrow. What will I say to the gypsy with the cruel face who was my destiny? I've betrayed him. And it's all your fault!'

She cried so movingly that I, too, began to be overcome with sadness. We lay helpless on the grass, surrendering to the power of the wind and rain in the hope that it would wash us clean and return us to the time when we merely dreamed about what was now behind us. But we knew there was no way back. The device had sealed our fate.

20

Now came a period of growing uncertainty within the family. Elizabeta shut herself in her room for three days.

'Leave me alone, or I'll hang myself,' she yelled whenever anyone knocked on her door and tried to persuade her to come out.

When everyone else had tried, Mum asked me to. She was sure to listen to me, as I was the only one she didn't resent.

'If I try, she's sure to hang herself,' I replied. 'And I'm going to close my door. You're all getting on my nerves. You're always sticking your noses in. There's no privacy in this house. I'm going to move out.'

'Will someone tell me what's going on in this family,' Mum pleaded tetchily, turning to Dad.

He merely shrugged and sank back into his newspaper.

'We all know what's going on,' said Peter with a resigned air, 'but no one wants to acknowledge it, let alone talk about it.'

'You know what,' said Mum, 'I'm sick of your mysterious hints, and I refuse to listen to them. Go and play with your telescope if you've no intention of studying and finishing your degree.'

'We miss Švejk,' said Peter. 'Why can't you accept that? Fate brought him into our family, and you did not grant him the right to do what would make him happiest. You're not the person you were.'

Mum's hand flew through the air of its own accord and slapped Peter's cheek. This was the first time she had ever hit anyone, and the strangeness of the change she had undergone filled us with the feeling that the last chance of peace and happiness in the house that Dad had bought so that we could become a loving family had vanished.

'Thanks, Mum,' said Peter calmly. 'A mother who dares to hit her son is definitely a successful one, a real pillar of the family. For at the age of twenty-three a son is too young to have a right to his own opinion, let alone to express it.'

'Oh God,' sobbed Mum, collapsing on to the sofa. 'What is happening to us?'

'If you'll allow me a small observation: too many secrets,' said Vladimir, coming forward. 'Secrets are like dry rot. If you allow them to spread unchecked the whole house can come tumbling down.'

'I agree,' said Aunt Mara. 'So it's time that you tell us what happened between you and your half-brother that makes you hate him so.'

'But I don't,' yelled Mum. 'I never have.'

'Let's not be so intrusive,' intervened Uncle Vinko, who evidently knew all too well what Mum was hiding. 'Everyone has the right to keep quiet about certain things. What's true for one is true for all. So let's not be unfair to someone who's in need but rather help them to extricate themselves.'

'And what does that mean?' asked Mara. 'It means we have to find Švejk and bring him home.'

'Find him,' sobbed Mum. 'Bring him back. And let him have his hideous vehicle. Let him hammer it whenever he feels like it. I can always plug my ears.'

At that moment I could have spoken and defused the crisis. I could have said I'd found Švejk and that I even knew what he was going to do with the fire engine. Why did I keep quiet?

Maybe I was waiting for Elizabeta to speak. I had a feeling that we shared a secret I could not divulge without her permission. On the other hand, I didn't want to be unfair to Švejk. Maybe he had found more trust and support with the gypsies than with us, who we had generally made fun of him, albeit good-naturedly. He was welcome at our house as long as he was prepared to play the family fool, but the gypsies had evidently taken him completely seriously, otherwise they wouldn't have decided on a joint business venture in such a short time.

Although I missed him as much as the others did, I didn't want to burden him with the attention of the family, who wanted him back because they felt guilty and because of his entertainment value.

At the same time I knew – or perhaps sensed rather than knew – that sooner or later I would go to see him and ask if I could be his assistant. In the middle of the summer it would be hard to find a more entertaining way to spend time than to visit fairs with a gypsy fortune-teller in a converted fire engine.

Except, of course, a duel of the emotions with Elizabeta, which I hoped would continue, regardless of how it affected others. I suddenly lost the feeling that I had to take them into consideration. Every man for himself, I thought – after all, they're all adults. And I didn't owe anybody anything. What had any of them ever done for me, other than frequently make my life difficult? The only exception was Dad, whom I didn't want to hurt. I thought he had been wounded enough by the way things had gone since we moved to the country. The move had been his idea.

But his motives had been noble ones. We had no right to blame him for things he couldn't have foreseen. Dad certainly wouldn't be angry if he found out that Elizabeta and I were playing secret games. Maybe he wouldn't exactly be delighted, as Elizabeta was not of an age when she should be getting involved in such activities. But Dad would understand and wouldn't cast us out. Vinko and Vladimir might simply shrug. What Mum and Aunt Mara would do didn't bear thinking about.

And Peter, who longed for the favours that Elizabeta had offered me? He'd probably kill me. Or himself. Maybe he'd go crazy and kill the whole family. The newspapers were full of grim tales of family massacres.

21

My hopes of spending an exciting summer evaporated as soon as Elizabeta emerged from her room. We were having breakfast, and she appeared so suddenly that we were left speechless. No one wanted to be responsible for her renewed disappearance through some poorly chosen words, including Aunt Mara, who could barely restrain herself from throwing herself at her daughter and stabbing her with a fork.

Elizabeta avoided our eyes and said not a word. She filled herself with three days' worth of cheese, salami and bread. Her eyes were red and swollen as if she had spent most of the time in her room crying. I felt sick at heart at the thought that the cause might be the incident by the stream.

After she had put away almost a whole loaf of bread, she spent about five minutes wiping her mouth with a paper serviette. She gulped from a glass of water, rinsing it around her mouth as if she wished to wash away the taste of the food she had eaten. She didn't swallow it but rather spat it into the sink. She then repeated the procedure.

Dad, Mum and Aunt Mara looked at each other. Something had obviously happened to Elizabeta. She had changed so much in three days as to be almost unrecognizable. She sat back down at the table and announced, 'I've decided to enter a convent.'

'Thank God,' said Aunt Mara in relief, 'I feared it was something much worse. I'm pleased you've finally entered a phase you should have got over long ago. It's usually thirteen-year-olds who decide to become nuns. When are you going and to which one?'

Elizabeta could not have missed Mara's sarcastic tone, but, surprisingly, she didn't react in her usual fashion but in a mild, dignified voice replied that she would leave as soon as she found one willing to accept such a great sinner.

'For your sins', observed Mara, 'even hell is too mild a punishment. The Devil will have to think up some new ones.'

'That's just it,' said Elizabeta. 'For sinners who cannot be adequately punished there is only forgiveness, which cannot be found in Hell. Only God can forgive – or sometimes a mother her own child. A convent is the only place I'll find penance and peace.'

'What should I forgive you for?' replied Aunt Mara angrily. 'Setting aside the fact that I've been forgiving you for fifteen years and sometimes several times a day, I'd like to know what I've not forgiven you for. Come on, don't leave me in the dark.'

'It's too late for discussion,' said Elizabeta. 'Evil has moved into this house. I feel it seeping through the walls, radiating from all of you. I have to withdraw, otherwise it will grow inside me as well – and then God help this family. One way or another you are all lost.'

She turned to Dad. 'Can I borrow the Bible from the library?'

Dad opened his mouth to speak, but when he noticed that everyone's eyes were upon him he merely cleared his throat, mumbled something, nodded and gestured as if to say yes, why not.

Elizabeta thanked him silently and left with lowered eyes. We also looked at the ground. Then Peter got up as if to follow her, but Dad's look fixed him to the table.

'Now this, on top of everything else,' sighed Mum.

Aunt Mara said nothing but merely made a vague gesture.

Dad suddenly realized his duty as head of the family. The look of certainty that we had long missed returned.

'The girl's growing up,' he said, as if stating something that would come as a great surprise. 'We have to take these things in our stride. It could be a lot worse. But it won't last long. After a few days she'll find something else to hold on to. So I suggest that we show as much tolerance as we can.'

'Well,' said Aunt Mara, noisily pushing back her chair, 'I'm glad someone is taking responsibility for my daughter's upbringing. I clearly didn't know how to raise her as a decent member of the family.'

'Mara,' Dad's voice suddenly grew louder and his tone sharper, 'childish behaviour does not become you. Calm yourself and sit down.'

Mara sank back into her chair without protest.

'Enough about Elizabeta,' Dad concluded. 'As far as Švejk is concerned, whoever wants to look for him, let them do so. I spoke to the chief fire officer on the phone, and he said Švejk hasn't brought the vehicle back. But they're not expecting him to, since they more or less gave it to him. Švejk's promise that he will make it suitable for fire-fighting once more didn't seem realistic to them. They actually wanted to get rid of it, so that it was no longer in their way, and Švejk must have been aware of that. And since he knows that the vehicle is his he could have gone anywhere. As enquiries in the village have led nowhere we need to cast our net wider. We could call the police and report Švejk missing.'

'There's no point,' said Uncle Vinko. 'The police won't search for someone who's not been proven to be of unsound mind or dangerous to others, who's not under age or in any way not entitled to move about freely. They'll say that Švejk has simply moved on and perhaps does not want to be found.'

'Then I don't know,' said Dad with a helpless gesture. 'Hire a private detective or put an ad in the paper. When you find him, tell me.' He got up and went to his room.

22

We entered a period that we would later remember as one of false normality. We all fell into a routine that was usual for that time of the year, but beneath the surface the forces that had invaded our life continued working and slowly undermining the foundations of our trust in the solidity of the family. These forces burgeoned in the terrible heat, an average of thirty-five degrees, which even Vladimir said he could not recall since his childhood. Every day there was at least one thunderstorm. Usually it began as a mass of black clouds beyond the western hills, where it hesitated for some time as if unsure which direction to take, then, with dramatic thunder and lightning, it lumbered towards our house and raged above it as if totally uninterested in the surrounding area. As soon as it retreated to the woods behind the house it calmed down, as if out of breath, and often simply disappeared.

It seemed something in the house or in us was attracting the destructive forces of nature.

Aunt Mara demanded that an effective lightning conductor be installed on the outbuilding where her studio was, since she thought it was only a matter of time before a lightning strike destroyed her work and burned her alive. Dad called a local tradesman, who installed lightning conductors on all the outbuildings and replaced the old one on the house.

'I'd still feel a lot safer', said Aunt Mara, 'if we had a fire engine parked in the yard and a fire-fighter in the guest room.'

This was the only comment made during this period in which any of us mentioned Švejk. And no one was actively looking for him.

Uncle Vinko decided he needed at least two weeks' holiday in his seaside caravan. For the first time he did not invite any of us to go with him, maybe because he knew that he would only hear the usual excuses. The caravan was extremely small with only one bed; moreover, it stood in a huddle of caravans three hundred metres from the sea, and it was without water or electricity.

Vladimir decided to bin his second attempt at his Partisan memoirs and to begin writing a book entitled *How to Survive the Years Leading Up to Death*. Peter observed that all years were years leading up to death, so why not just call the book *How to Survive*.

Mara said that most people spend the years leading up to death asking how to survive the years leading up to death, which was why almost no one was really living. That would no doubt happen to her, too, if she did not have her art.

After this she carried her paintings to the road and exhibited them on a long trestle table we found in one of the outbuildings. She then sat there every day on a wickerwork chair waiting for tourists to emerge from the woods and pass by our orchard on the footpath to the tourist farm at the top of the hill.

Some did stop, looked at the paintings, chatted with Aunt Mara, expressed their surprise that there was an exhibition of paintings beside a country path, almost in the woods, and then went on their way, convinced that the woman was not quite with it. Over the course of a week she did not sell a single painting.

But she refused to give up. Peter and I had to carry her easel to the road and place on it a garish sign saying 'Portraits painted'. The next day a middle-aged man really did ask to have his portrait painted but it turned out only because he wanted to take a rest in Aunt Mara's comfortable wickerwork chair. In the end he said he would not take the portrait because it did not look anything like him. But he did want to be fair, so he bought a painting of a calf that had just stood up for the first time.

'Skilfully drawn,' he praised Mara. 'Are you a member of the Farmers' Wives' Association?'

'I'll give you farmer wives!' said city girl Aunt Mara, blushing to the roots of her hair. She snatched the painting of the calf from his hands and smashed it over his head. 'Now take it,' she said. 'It's yours.'

The man was so stunned that he simply turned and went on his way. Only after several hundred metres did he remove the holed painting from around his neck and throw it into a wheatfield.

I watched all this from the window of my room, from where I could see much else besides; including Elizabeta, who was sunbathing among the wheat. Each day she left the house at ten, waded into the centre of the golden-yellow crop, as if it were ours and not the neighbour's, stretched out on a dark-blue towel and offered herself to the sun's rays while reading the Bible. She was wearing a small bikini. She always lay with her legs towards the house, and, although her eyes were concealed by dark sunglasses as well as the Holy Book, I knew from her posture and her movements that she knew all too well that two pairs of eyes were constantly trained on her, from the dark interiors of my room and Peter's.

Peter even watched her through binoculars. I discovered this by chance when I leaned out of the window to see who was wandering around restlessly outside the house; as always, it was Vladimir.

Uncle Vinko then decided that he needed some sea air straight away. He climbed into his battered Nissan and drove off. He forgot to take most of the things he normally took with him to the seaside, even his swimming trunks, as Mum discovered to her surprise when she examined his room. This was completely uncharacteristic of someone who was usually as precise as a bookkeeper.

'Oh,' said Dad with a careless gesture, 'sooner or later we all become prone to forgetfulness. He'll be back.'

But Vinko did not return, and when Mum discovered that he hadn't even taken the pack of cards that he played with every evening it became clear that he had not gone to the seaside but somewhere else.

'It's all very suspicious,' said Mum.

'He's a grown man, for God's sake,' responded Dad, barely containing his anger.

'I know where he's gone,' said Elizabeta mysteriously. Since deciding to enter a convent she had begun to speak with a soft, barely audible voice, in a tone that was a mixture of surrendering to one's fate and genuine friendliness.

'If you're lying I'll give you such a slap,' Aunt Mara threatened.

Dad felt obliged to protect Elizabeta. 'There'll be no slapping in this house,' he commanded like a high-court judge delivering sentence. 'In this house we are friendly and tolerant; threats are forbidden, and hands can be laid on others only in love.'

'If only,' muttered Peter in a low voice.

'OK, so where has Uncle Vinko gone?' Mum turned to Elizabeta with all the friendliness she could muster at that moment. I saw how she was gripping the edge of the table, trying to control herself.

'We agreed that he would go to look for a suitable convent for me,' said Elizabeta. 'One where I wouldn't have to work but could devote myself to reflecting on God's love.'

'Stop pulling our leg, you little hussy,' Aunt Mara hissed through clenched teeth. 'I've had it up to here with you.'

'No one will stop me realizing my plan,' said Elizabeta calmly. 'I'm a free person.'

'Oh no you're not,' replied Aunt Mara, raising her voice. 'You're an adolescent and can do only what I permit you to do.'

'Right,' said Elizabeta, 'then I must warn you that I will run away from home and work in a brothel.'

'A brothel's preferable to a convent,' said Aunt Mara. 'I'd be happy to leave you there but not in a convent. And you'd enjoy it more in a brothel. I know you only too well.'

'What can I say?' replied Elizabeta. 'Like mother, like daughter.'

Aunt Mara got up from the table as if she were about to throw herself at the girl. Dad, Vladimir and Peter had to use all their strength to restrain her.

'Let go of me, so I can kill her,' she spat across the table. 'Or let me go and kill myself. Oh God,' she sighed, 'take me to my room. I can no longer stay here and watch my daughter turn into a monster.'

When Dad and Vladimir took her, bent and broken, to the studio, which she had also made into a bedroom, Mum looked at Elizabeta and said, 'I've never known such a wicked girl.'

'I agree,' replied Elizabeta unfazed. 'The only safe place for me is a convent. Uncle Vinko realizes that and is trying to help me. To help you as well, for as soon as he gets back you'll be rid of me for ever.'

23

When after a few days Vinko returned, our questions about a convent took him by surprise. He said it was the first he had heard about it and he didn't want to get involved, since the girl had a mother who was legally responsible for her. Besides which, we had a head of the family, who always knew what to do for the best.

He said he'd had other fish to fry and had discovered things that would take our breath away. He placed a bunch of newspaper cuttings on the table.

'Read them,' he said, pushing them towards Peter. 'Read them out loud.'

'Why me?' said Peter defensively.

'Because you have the nicest voice,' said Mum.

'That's not true. Elizabeta has the nicest voice.'

'I'll do it,' said Mum, reaching for the cuttings, and she began to read the first one.

'"Top class fortune-teller answers all your questions, helps you find luck in love and marriage, removes curses and wards off black magic, opens the way to happiness in love. Call Aranka the Gypsy Fortune-Teller."'

She put down the cutting and picked up the next. '"If you have problems in love or with your health, if you think that black magic is affecting your life, if you think you are cursed or if you are interested in where your problems are coming from, you will get all the answers from Aranka the Gypsy Fortune-Teller."'

She picked up another one. '"Does your child find it hard to learn, or are there other problems? Call Aranka the biotherapist and success is guaranteed. Make an appointment, come and see us so that we can drive away your sadness, negativity and fears. Fortune-telling from cards, crystals, coffee grounds, talismans, disposal of curses."'

Mum threw the scrap of paper on to the pile and pushed the whole lot back towards Vinko. 'Why am I reading this?' she asked. 'Are you making fun of me?'

Vinko searched through the cuttings, pulled out one of the smallest ones and pushed it towards her. 'Read this one, too,' he said.

Mum sighed and raised it to her eyes. '"Do you wish to feel and embrace the pure positive energy of the universe but don't know how? Are many other things hidden from you? This and other secrets can be revealed to you by bioenergetic Švejk, great-grandson of the world-renowned Good Soldier Švejk, who materialized via astral paths and after several months touring Europe is with us once more. Call us."'

Mum put the cutting on the table and said, 'It's a good job I'm sitting down, otherwise I'd fall over.'

She looked at Dad, who turned away as if unsure how to react.

'As far as I'm concerned,' said Elizabeta, reaching for the newspaper cutting, 'I'd really like to feel and embrace the pure positive energy of the universe.'

'Not to mention me,' said Peter, also reaching out his hand and inadvertently taking hold of Elizabeta's.

'Don't touch me,' she said without even looking at him. 'I'm promised to Jesus.'

Peter withdrew his hand, and Mum snatched the cutting from between Elizabeta's fingers.

'That's not all,' said Uncle Vinko, taking some photographs from his bag. He threw them on the table, and they scattered so that several ended up in front of each of us.

The first one I picked up showed the back of Švejk's fire engine, which now boasted a hinged door, standing wide open. Inside, on soft cushions, sat an old gypsy woman dressed in colourful rags examining the outstretched hand of a young woman through a magnifying glass. Outside was a queue of people aged from fifteen to ninety, from simple folk to educated ones, from scruffy to elegant, all determined to hear the prognoses for their futures.

The next photograph showed a side view of the fire engine. In front of it stood Švejk and a gypsy woman, who must have been at least sixty-five, hand in hand and grinning broadly. On the water tank it no longer said 'Aranka the Gypsy Fortune-Teller' but 'Aranka Hudorovec and Jaroslav Švejk Ltd' and underneath in smaller letters 'Fortune-telling, crystals, tarot, black magic, biotherapy, psychotherapy, massage, astrological analysis, advice on love'.

'Oh my God,' gasped Mum, who was probably looking at something similar.

'Oh my God,' echoed Elizabeta, 'who is that gypsy with the moustache and the cruel face who looks like a killer?'

'The fortune-teller's son,' said Uncle Vinko. 'His name is Janek Hudorovec. And he really is a killer. When he was younger, still a student, he murdered a farmer in the next village, who, it was rumoured, was his mother's lover. He spent twenty years in jail, where he apparently got a degree in law and philosophy. When he was released he got a job as a legal adviser, but after a few years he grew tired of it and returned to his home village, where he became a kind of unofficial head man. Now he's involved in the fight for Roma rights.'

'He's dreamy,' breathed Elizabeta, unable to take her eyes from the photograph in front of her; she was gripping it so hard that the ends of her fingers turned blue. 'Perhaps I won't go to a convent; perhaps I'll become a gypsy.'

'Thank God,' said Aunt Mara. 'I'd rather entrust you to a killer than to nuns. I'll go today and ask him to take you away right now.'

'Thanks, Mum,' said Elizabeta with a strange laugh. 'You're such a great mother. Why don't you go straight away?'

Aunt Mara got up to sink her nails into her daughter's face, but once again Dad restrained her.

'Mara, please,' he said in a louder voice than he had used in the past two years, 'control yourself, or you'll end up among the gypsies before Elizabeta does.'

'Well,' said Mara, sinking limply back into her seat, 'how encouraging that the family is on my side when it comes to raising my twisted daughter.'

'Why am I twisted?' asked Elizabeta. 'Because I'm in love with a gypsy or because I'm in love with a murderer? Or just because I'm in love?'

'How can you be in love with someone you've never even met?' asked Mara, rising again. 'How can you fall in love the minute you look at a photograph, when a little earlier you said you were betrothed to God and on your way to a convent? When are you going to stop tormenting us? When are you going to stop saying stupid things just because you enjoy causing us to suffer? When are you going to start acting normally?'

'That's irrelevant,' said Mum, also getting up. 'No one takes her seriously – what do we care about the fantasies of a malicious hussy, which are constantly changing and have only one goal: to disturb us five times a day and divert our attention from events that really are important and tragic? No one gives a damn about my brother, who has been ensnared by the gypsies and is now being exploited by them for God knows what nefarious purpose. Because he is so naïvely good he does not know how to defend himself. It's our duty to rescue him from their clutches.'

'Is that so?' said Mara, literally frothing at the mouth. 'Says you, who kept quiet about him at first and then drove him away. Now we are once more responsible for your mistakes? You go and sort them. I've got enough on my plate dealing with my own. And it's becoming increasingly clear to me that I really don't belong in this family.'

She clumsily pushed the chair aside and left the dining-room.

'To me, too,' said Elizabeta and went to her room. I noticed that she took the photograph of the gypsy with the cruel face with her.

Peter and I both jumped to our feet. Dad, who knew where we were heading, pinned us to the table with a single look.

'Where did you take these photographs?' Mum asked Vinko.

'Different locations,' he replied. 'They drive from place to place. The gypsy's son is their manager.'

'Did you talk to Švejk? Did he see you?' Mum was becoming increasingly impatient.

'No,' Vinko shook his head. 'I didn't want to upset him. I stayed hidden. I used a zoom lens.'

'And why didn't you tell him to come home as soon as possible?' Mum asked.

'How was I to know I had the right to do that?' replied Vinko, raising his voice slightly.

'You not only had the right', said Mum with annoyance, 'it was your duty to do so when you saw him being exploited and ridiculed for some gypsy nonsense.'

'Calm down,' Dad placed his hand on her shoulder and gave it a barely noticeable squeeze. 'We shouldn't be having a go at anyone. Everyone has the right to live as they see fit. Švejk can hang out with whoever he wants; there's nothing on earth to stop him.'

'There's me,' said Mum, pushing Dad's hand away and getting up. 'I'll stop him.'

'You won't,' said Dad. 'Even I am ready to protect him from your violence.'

Mum looked to be on the verge of tears. 'I only want what's best for him, and you say I'm violent?' The next moment tears were running down her face.

'How do you know what's best for him?' Dad got up and straightened his back; he even raised his head a little. 'Did you ask him? Do you think what's best for him is only what you think he ought to do?'

'It's all so terrible.' Mum sobbed louder and sank into her chair. 'More and more terrible. I can't live with the thought that he's wandering around with the gypsies. One way or another we have to bring him back.'

'May I make a suggestion?' asked Vladimir, who had been sitting silently to one side.

We all turned to him. He got up and came nearer.

'We must put together a delegation,' he said. 'The interested members of the family must go to see him and convince him, not through emotional outbursts or threats but with sober arguments, to return home. Of course, we have to offer him concrete benefits,' he added.

'Let him tell us what he wants,' said Mum quickly, wiping away her tears. 'Let him state his conditions, and we will agree to them.'

24

The delegation set off the next day. After an hour on the phone, Vinko had established that there were no fairs or other events where 'bioenergetic' Švejk and his partner could solve the problems of unhappy people. It was very likely that he and his vehicle would be at the gypsy settlement on the slope of the neighbouring hill.

At first Mum tried to restrict participation to Dad, Vinko and herself, but the rest of us protested so vociferously that in the end Dad agreed to let the whole family go. Aunt Mara said she would take the opportunity to have her fortune read with cards. At the same time she would ask Gypsy Aranka to drive the devil from Elizabeta. And perhaps one of the gypsies would want their portrait painted – why not combine business with pleasure?

Elizabeta wore the shortest skirt she could find and a tight white T-shirt that covered only her breasts and left her tanned midriff exposed. She put on bright-red lipstick and painted her eyebrows and eyelashes with something she found in her mother's make-up bag. Her long black hair was in a ponytail, which she swished like a horse.

'A real nun,' said Aunt Mara mockingly.

Elizabeta smiled sweetly and chirruped, 'Thanks, Mummy.'

Aunt Mara took a deep breath, but Dad undermined her anger by saying, 'Anyone who fails to behave in a dignified fashion will have to come straight home.'

'That's right,' added Vladimir. 'This expedition is too important to be sabotaged by any one person.'

When we had crossed the narrow wooden footbridge over the stream, with Vinko in front, followed by Dad, Mum, Mara, Vladimir, Elizabeta, Peter and me, we soon came to the place where the gypsy dogs had caught up with me and Elizabeta two weeks earlier. The grass beside the path still looked slightly flattened to me. I overtook Peter and coughed behind Elizabeta's back to remind her of the madness that had overwhelmed us.

'Cough, cough to you, too,' she said in a loud voice, half turning. 'Do you want to add something more specific?'

This seemed to me very disrespectful of my feelings. The malicious hussy knew all too well that our parents would crucify us if they suspected what we had done. I merely wanted to remind her of the act that, at least in my eyes, bound us together for ever.

'What secret do you two have?' said Aunt Mara, turning.

'Don't ask,' said Elizabeta, 'because you'd probably kill me if you knew.'

'Don't you worry,' replied Aunt Mara, walking on, 'I'll find out one way or another, with or without your help. And then God help you.'

I felt Peter grab hold of my shirt and pull me back. We stayed a little behind the others.

'Do you really have a secret?' he asked.

I nodded.

'What?' he wanted to know.

'If you promise not to tell anyone.'

He raised two fingers and swore.

'We're screwing each other,' I said. 'Five times a day. Haven't you seen us through your binoculars? Next time we'll do it so you can see.'

I would have said more, but my older brother punched me on the jaw with such force that I almost flew through the air. Although I waved my arms to keep my balance, I fell to the ground and lay groggily almost on the spot where Elizabeta and I had lost our virginities. My head was spinning so much I had to close my eyes. When I opened them I saw a circle of seven faces above me.

'What happened?' I heard Mum's voice.

'He fainted,' I heard Peter say. 'I tried to catch him, but he fell.'

'You didn't hit him by any chance?' Dad enquired.

'Hit him?' Peter feigned offence. 'Why would I hit my little brother whom I admire so much?'

'They were fighting because of me,' said Elizabeta proudly, straightening her back.

'That's not true,' I said, sitting up. 'My head suddenly began to spin,' I added. 'Probably the sun.'

'They lagged behind and were whispering about something,' said Aunt Mara. 'I saw them.'

'It's clear they're hiding something from us,' said Vladimir. 'We should interrogate them both immediately and find out what before something worse happens.'

'Calm down, Vladimir,' said Dad. 'No one's going to interrogate my sons. They're not enemies of the failed social system but growing lads looking for support in a world of irresponsibility, which those in charge try to peddle to us as freedom. What's going on?' He looked first at Peter and then at me.

'Quickly because we've got to get on,' added Mum.

'They'll lie,' said Elizabeta.

'One more word and I'll slap you,' said Aunt Mara, raising her hand and then letting it drop.

'Nothing,' I said. 'We just have similar ambitions, which one of us realizes better than the other.'

'For now,' hissed Elizabeta. 'Tomorrow it could be the other way round.'

'You keep quiet,' said Mara, losing her temper and striking her on the head, but, in the face of Dad's disapproval, the blow was more like a caress, which even Elizabeta noticed.

'Thanks, Mum.' She half turned. 'Keep hitting me. It's nice. And keep calling me a little bastard. At least then we'll know what you were doing when you were forty.'

'For God's sake,' said Mum angrily, 'are we going to stand here in the middle of the meadow spouting nonsense, or are we going to carry on?'

'Just a moment,' insisted Vladimir, 'I have the feeling that something happened between the boys, and for the good of the family we need to sort it out.'

'Let him tell you.' Peter turned away.

'Nothing happened,' I said. 'I just mentioned the dogs.'

'Which dogs?' Mum wanted to know.

'The gypsy dogs,' I said. 'They'll smell us any minute. Then they'll go crazy, they'll run here and tear us limb from limb.'

'How do you know?' Dad asked.

'He's been looking for a girlfriend in the gypsy village and has been going there a lot,' said Elizabeta.

'Is that true?' said Mum, horrified.

'It's true there are dogs in the settlement,' said Uncle Vinko, 'but they're not dangerous.'

'Aren't they?' stammered Aunt Mara. She froze.

We all froze. While we were arguing who said what and what they meant by it, the gypsy dogs had silently run down the slope and surrounded us. There were eight of them and eight of us; among them were the Alsatians I remembered from last time, and this time they rose slightly and growled when they knew we had noticed them.

'Sweet Jesus,' whispered Mum. 'There are eight of them.'

'Some of them must be bitches,' commented Elizabeta, 'just like in our family circle. But what will the poor boy do who is caught in both circles, family and doggy? Will he finally tell the truth?' She gave me a gentle kick.

'The moment will come when I will,' I hissed. 'Especially if someone goes too far.'

'Unless, of course, he's counting on a repeat, which there won't be,' she said with a wink.

She took hold of the hem of her skirt and quickly lifted it. Thankfully, the others were occupied with the dogs, but Peter noticed, and it became clear to him that I hadn't been lying. His head sank on to his chest and he looked as if he was about to start crying.

'There's no need to be afraid of the dogs,' said Vladimir confidently. 'They are primitive beings that always act instinctively and never cunningly. All we have to do is pretend they're not there.'

He took a step towards the wood below the hilltop. Some other members of the family were about to follow him when the smallest of the dogs, a ratty little mutt, growled and sank its teeth into Vladimir's trouser leg.

Vladimir froze mid-step in quite an amusing pose and waited for the dog to grow tired and let go of him. But the dog evidently had no intention of doing so; it gripped the soft material even harder, snarling like a police dog that has just got hold of an infamous criminal.

'Are you all right, Vladimir?' asked Dad, who was also frozen in an unusual posture.

'For now,' replied Vladimir, 'although a different position would be easier on my back.'

'Evidently we're not pretending convincingly enough that we can't see them,' commented Aunt Mara.

'I agree,' said Elizabeta, 'but there are those among us', she winked at me, 'who would get something much more enjoyable out of pretending in front of dogs than a pain in the lower back.'

'What are we going to do?' Mum asked again, still expecting simple answers to complicated questions.

'I think someone's coming,' said Vinko.

25

We turned as one towards the woods above us, where a middle-aged man was approaching along the grassy path.

'Oh,' sighed Elizabeta, immediately recognizing him as the gypsy prince of her dreams.

'Who on earth is that?' asked Mum in alarm.

'The son of the gypsy fortune-teller,' said Vinko. 'The one who is said to have killed someone when he was younger.'

'I hope he isn't going to kill us,' said Aunt Mara, only half joking.

'He will me,' said Elizabeta. 'But I hope with the right weapon. Come, sweet death,' she sighed.

'This is all so pathetic,' observed Peter. 'Disgusting and pathetic. I'm off.'

He turned and went towards home, but at that moment a black dog, the second smallest, snapped at him and grabbed hold of his trouser leg so that he, too, froze in a rather unusual posture. Evidently the dogs had been trained to do precisely that. All that remained was to guess which of them would snap at which of us if we all moved at once and what they would grab hold of in the case of those of us who were not wearing long trousers.

'I see you're having problems,' said the gypsy with the moustache when he reached us.

From close up he really did look like a killer, with hard, rough features and wild, deep eyes with a slight squint, quite dark skin – he could have played a gangster in a Bollywood film – a threatening posture but with gentle, soft movements that negated the general impression that he would attack you merely for giving him a black look.

He was wearing black trousers, a white shirt and a grey waistcoat; a gold chain hung from his breast pocket. It was clear he took some pride in his appearance, although there was nothing to indicate that he was at all vain – except perhaps for the dangling earring in his left ear and the slightly smug satisfaction with which he observed our embarrassment.

I noticed that his eyes lingered longest on Elizabeta and that he even looked towards her a second time, probably because she was staring at him as if bewitched.

'Not serious problems,' said Dad, 'but, to be honest, we're momentarily a bit more restricted with regard to free movement than we are accustomed to.'

'How dare you,' Aunt Mara went on the offensive. 'Setting dogs on innocent people coming to you as customers. If you don't get them off us this minute we're going to turn around and go home.'

'Easier said than done,' observed Vladimir, whose trouser leg was still being gripped by the ratty dog. 'I suggest we stop insulting this man, who perhaps has no connection with the dogs, and ask him instead what he thinks we can do. I've got to change position soon, otherwise I'll collapse.'

The cruel-looking gypsy clicked his tongue, and all the dogs jumped up and ran back towards the settlement in the woods with their tails between their legs. As they fled some of the smaller ones yapped once or twice.

'Would you believe it?' said Mum, relieved. 'Can we go on now?'

'Follow me,' said the gypsy, heading uphill.

'Slow down,' gasped Vladimir, holding his lower back. Vinko hung back to help him, while the rest of us followed the gypsy, fastest of all Elizabeta, who soon caught up and walked alongside him. I also speeded up so as not to miss what they were saying. The next moment Peter was right beside me. The others were panting up the gentle slope, each at their own pace.

'Did you really kill someone?' said Elizabeta to the gypsy.

'Of course,' he replied without surprise or excitement. 'Not just one but at least ten. But I can't say how many more I might kill.'

'I'm serious,' said Elizabeta. 'They say that you killed your mother's lover and spent twenty years in jail. Is it true?'

'Ask my mother.'

'Then you're Janek Hudorovec?'

'That I am,' he said and looked at her. Actually, he examined her from head to toe. 'How old are you?'

'Eighteen,' lied the malicious hussy without batting an eyelid.

'And,' he asked, 'have you killed anyone yet?'

'No, I'd rather be killed. I dream of someone savagely raping me then strangling me. Do you know anyone who would be prepared to do that?'

'For a reward or for free?'

'The reward would be me,' said Elizabeta. 'And there's no need to kill me straight away. In fact, I wouldn't want that. He could keep raping me for a month or two, even years, and kill me only when I said it was time. His eventual reward would be the feeling that he'd done something good. Before that we would feel and embrace the pure, positive energy of the universe. Like it says in the ad.'

The gypsy cleared his throat and for a while seemed to have no idea how to respond. We were approaching the edge of the wood where the settlement was hidden. Just before he turned into the trees he looked at Elizabeta and said, 'Come on your own some time and we'll discuss it.'

'What about tomorrow?' Elizabeta asked.

'That's too soon,' he replied. 'Come in two years, when you really are eighteen.'

'You'll be sorry,' said Elizabeta, and she stuck out her tongue.

26

In the woods we were met by an unusual scene. On the road among the houses stood Švejk's fire engine. The rear door was open and inside, instead of Aranka the Fortune-Teller, who we had seen in the photographs, was a television set showing a video recording of her telling fortunes in the middle of a crowd at a fair. Evidently the fortune-telling company was always accompanied by someone with a camera.

In the semi-circle in front of the television were gathered all the residents of the gypsy settlement, from babes in arms to crooked old grandfathers. Some were squatting or sitting on the ground, others had brought chairs, some were standing and some boys had climbed into a nearby beech tree. The scene was reminiscent of a religious ceremony. In the first row, on beautiful carved chairs, sat the special guests Aranka and Uncle Švejk, who were watching with a mixture of pride, embarrassment and the critical air of someone who has realized that something could be better.

Only a few heads turned when we arrived, for the rest, the scenes unfolding on the screen were mesmerizing. The camera showed Aranka the Fortune-Teller in big close-up, and we could hear her words clearly. 'Listen to the reply,' she was saying to a young woman wearing a headscarf. 'Don't forget that adults also play games, like children. Everyone does something and then watches how it is received. From this they learn and do not condemn others but alter their role so that they enjoy it and, if possible, their fellow actors are also satisfied. Don't tell others that they are responsible for you. Look for a role that will attract them. You understand?' she said, looking in the young woman's face.

The woman shook her head and asked, 'Can I have my money back?'

A wave of laughter rippled through the crowd.

'She's not stupid, that Aranka,' said Aunt Mara. 'I've got some questions for her, too.'

'We haven't come here to have our fortunes told,' said Mum. 'We've come for Švejk. Do something.' She turned to Dad.

But he just shrugged. Because we had come from the back and stopped behind the crowd, and because the gypsy with the moustache had not moved forward but stayed with us, we had no choice but to wait.

'Shocking,' said Mum. 'There are eight of us, and we don't have enough intelligence between us to attract Švejk's attention.'

Suddenly Elizabeta put her hands in front of her mouth and shouted so loud that we could hear the echo, 'Švejk, turn around!'

Every head turned, babies yelled, dogs began to bark and some of those watching jumped up, Švejk included, who at the sight of the family turned a dark red.

'I didn't know you knew him', said the gypsy with the cruel face looking even crueller.

'Not only do we know him,' said Mum with determination, 'we're going to take him away.'

'I don't think so,' replied Elizabeta's Prince Charming, adopting a threatening pose.

'Oh, really?' said Mum, pushing him roughly aside and going to the front of the crowd. Dad followed her, as did the rest of us, for we all felt our place was by her side – even Elizabeta, who probably went with us to stay near the gypsy, who had decided to follow us.

After a few steps we found ourselves face to face with Švejk. We were completely blocking the television screen, but the audience did not seem to mind too much, as they sensed that a more entertaining performance might be in the offing.

'Do you know these people?' Švejk's business partner turned to the fire-fighter manqué.

'How could I not?' replied Švejk hesitantly. 'I lived with them before I found a home here.'

'Jaro,' said Mum, 'we've come for you. Look,' she gestured, 'everyone is here. We all miss you. We all want you back.'

'Except for me,' added Elizabeta. 'I want you to do what you are sure is best for you.'

'Stop sabotaging our efforts,' Mara hissed in her ear, 'or you'll get a kick up your half-naked behind.'

'Did you hear that?' Elizabeta turned to the gypsy with the cruel face. 'Protect me.'

'I can't go anywhere right now,' said Švejk, indicating the crowd with a jerk of his head, 'but I'll think about it.'

'There's nothing to think about,' said Aranka the Fortune-Teller. 'You, me and my son have registered the company. You promised not to break the contract. Can't you see the hungry children in their mothers' arms? We said we'd do everything to improve life in this village. And you're thinking of abandoning us just because someone clicks their fingers?'

'Of course I'm not thinking of that, Aranka,' said Švejk, shuffling in embarrassment.

'For your information,' said Mum, suddenly full of self-confidence, 'I'm not just someone; I'm Švejk's sister. This gentleman beside me is his brother and the others are all members of his family, who have more right to Švejk than do you, who hardly knows him.'

'Švejk,' said Vladimir, stepping forward, his hands still on his lower back, 'we'll build you that shed down by the road, just as you wanted. You can keep your vehicle there and make as much noise as you like. I haven't told the others this yet, but I had a word with the head of the fire brigade. He promised that if you managed to make the vehicle suitable for fire-fighting you can become one of them. If not, you can drive their other fire engine. In any case, you can become a fire-fighter. That was your dream, Švejk. What you are doing now – and I don't want to offend anyone here – is just superstition, unworthy of a hero of the war for independence.'

'You tell him,' Mum turned to Dad.

'What can I say?' he shrugged. 'We have no rights regarding Švejk. I hope that's completely clear to you. It does pain me when I see how he's making a fool of himself, but he's free to do that if he wishes.'

'You and your precious freedom,' snapped Mum. 'It has blinded you. For you, every kind of opposition to something that is wrong is violence.'

'Oh,' said Dad, 'that's emotion talking. That's not an argument.'

'She's right,' Mum suddenly received support from an unexpected source. Peter moved closer to Dad and said, 'This extreme liberalism of yours, and which you unsuccessfully try to combine with an outmoded form of family paternalism, is built on very shaky foundations. In the world of freedom that you propose, we are most restricted by rigid adherence to abstract principles.'

'What are these people on about?' interrupted Aranka. 'Are they in their right minds? Are they really your family, Švejk?'

'Yes and no,' replied Švejk, once more trying to wriggle his way out of a difficult situation. 'I certainly don't want them to suffer because of me.'

'Because of you?' said Aranka, getting up and moving towards us. 'They're not suffering because of you but because of their own messed-up ideas. There isn't one of them whose face radiates health and inner peace. They're all sick.'

'Mum,' the gypsy with the cruel face tried to intervene, 'go easy on them.'

'Why should I?' said the old gypsy woman excitedly. She seemed to have considerable inner strength and must have been beautiful and spirited when she was younger. 'You could have thought of me and not brought them here.'

'I thought they were customers. I'd no idea they wanted to take Švejk away.'

'Well,' said Aranka, 'if they are customers and want to know what is wrong with them, I'll tell them for free. That one there', she pointed towards Mum, 'made a mistake in her younger years for which she is now punishing those closest to her. With each move she makes, she is pushing her family nearer to the abyss.'

When Mum burst noisily into tears, Aranka turned her attention to Dad, who instinctively took a step back.

'A weakling,' said the fortune-teller, getting the wind in her sails. 'An educated ditherer, who has five answers and ten fine expressions for everything but who in reality is a secret drinker who sits up at night because he can't fit the world into a box where he can control it.'

Dad blanched and took another step back.

'That one', Aranka considered Mara, 'is a spoilt ninny who has learned to live at others' expense, using as an excuse her special talents at which people laugh behind her back.'

I didn't get a chance to see Mara's reaction, because Aranka the Fortune-Teller then turned her attention to me.

'A liar of the first order,' she said. 'The world isn't enough for him, so he makes his own up, scattering the germs of his imagination around like a virus with which he would like to infect as many gullible people as possible. If you accuse me of superstition, then you should call what he has rolling around his head madness. He'll end up in prison or as a writer, which is just as bad – a prisoner of his own stories.'

'As for that one,' she looked at Peter, 'I'd bet my life that he's a dreamer and is incapable of finishing anything. He prefers dealing with things that are remote and that others don't know much about. He has a problem there because he can't touch anything real, not even the thing he wants most. I bet he's still a virgin.'

Peter hung his head in shame.

'As for him,' she pointed at Vladimir, 'even from a distance he looks like an old Partisan, probably someone in the pay of the secret police who put quite a number of innocent people behind bars and in doing so used the most brutal interrogation methods. Now he's tormented by guilt, but his repentance is only skin-deep, and he's still obsessed with the desire to lure people into a trap.'

She stopped in front of Vinko and looked at him for some time. 'Colourless,' she said. 'He's not stupid but not all that bright either. He's not a bad man, but he dare not be a good one. A little opportunist who follows the prevailing wind and prefers to be alone. He likes tidying up, he likes order, he can't stand uncounted numbers or unsolved problems. Boring but probably the most normal of the lot.'

'Which can't be said for the young lass,' she came to Elizabeta.

Elizabeta bent her knees slightly, put her hands on her hips and struck a provocative pose. 'So what, then?' she said, the only one who dared open her mouth during the gypsy's character assassination of the family.

'I'll tell you,' said Aranka and looked her over for some time. 'Or maybe not,' she reconsidered. 'You remind me too much of myself at your age. I made a lot of mistakes, and so will you, perhaps even more, and all your mistakes will harm others. And you'll like that, as I once did. You've got a devil inside you – a small one for now, but it might grow into an insatiable monster. You're the only one in the family that others should fear. Whatever curse has been placed on all of you – and one has, there's no doubt about that – it has affected this little show-off most, so I warn you all seriously to watch your every step. If anyone takes you over the edge, it will be her. Send her away as soon as possible. Or leave her to my son. He's very good at taming beasts that no one else can cope with.'

'So I can just stay here?' said Elizabeta. 'The sooner your son tames me, the sooner my family will be safe. But I must warn him that he needs to be really strong to take me on. Whoever wishes to ride the Devil needs more than sharp spurs.'

'Damn it all,' sighed Aunt Mara, 'what's happened to us?'

'Let's go,' said Mum decisively. 'What are we waiting for?'

'You're right,' said Dad, as if he was speaking down a telephone from a great distance.

'Mother, that was wrong of you,' said the gypsy, his cruel face suddenly melting into an apologetic smile.

'You be quiet', said Aranka, 'and convince the girl to stay here. I'll teach her to dance, and she can earn us some money.'

'Can I stay, Mum?' Elizabeta asked Mara.

This time it wasn't Mara who lost her temper; it was, surprisingly, Dad, who went over to Elizabeta and gave her such a clip around the ear that she almost fell over.

'We're going home,' he said. 'All of us.' He turned to leave.

Then we heard Švejk's voice. 'Wait,' he said, almost pleading.

We turned. Švejk hesitated. Then he spread his arms and looked at Aranka. 'They're family,' he said. He twisted awkwardly, as if he had stomach cramps, opening and closing his arms. 'They're family, and I'd like to take them on a small trip in the renovated fire engine. I promised them that when I was staying with them.'

'Now?' Aranka couldn't believe her ears. 'Now, when we're watching the first days of our business venture together?'

'We can carry on with that when I return,' said Švejk, sounding increasingly determined. 'I'll just drive them around a bit and drop them where they live.'

'Go on then,' said Aranka with a wave of her hand, moving towards the nearest house. 'Go on, if they mean more to you than I do.'

'Aranka.' Švejk made as if to go after her, but the gypsy with the cruel face held him back and said, 'You take them. Don't worry about her. She's like that. She'll calm down.'

He picked up the television set and placed it beneath a tree. One of the gypsy boys took the video player and cables away.

'Get in,' said Švejk to us.

'In the water tank?' Aunt Mara protested. 'Never.'

'It's lined with soft mattresses,' said Švejk, pointing inside.

'Even if it is,' Mum objected, 'I'm not rolling around inside a fire engine.'

In the end Mum, Aunt Mara and Dad climbed into the cabin with Švejk, while the rest of us made ourselves comfortable on the mattresses in the water tank, with Uncle Vladimir, who was still holding his back, complaining the most. Švejk closed the newly installed door, and we found ourselves in the dark.

'We'll suffocate,' said Uncle Vinko.

'Isn't this great?' said Elizabeta with a laugh. 'I've never ridden inside a fire engine with four men. How will I know who is who? I'll have to feel you.'

'Keep still,' Vinko ordered her, 'and stop wittering.'

'That will be difficult,' said Elizabeta. 'I'll have to fill my mouth with something.'

The vehicle shuddered and moved. In the darkness we lost sense of time and distance. It threw us around so that we rolled about on the mattresses, bumping into each other; it moved us apart again, banging our heads and hips together, and we held on to whatever we could. On Elizabeta's thigh I felt a hand that did not want to withdraw, and I was sure it was Peter's. But when I moved my hand across her stomach to her exposed breasts beneath her raised T-shirt I encountered another hand. When I felt it I realized it was someone's right hand, like the one on her hip. Strange, Peter didn't have two right hands. Then, on her knee, I discovered a third hand, I don't know whose, while a fourth one was rummaging between her legs. Wherever I touched, someone was there before me.

I was left with the feeling that I had been excluded from the game. When the vehicle finally stopped the door opened and we climbed groggily into the blinding light, the whole thing seemed like a dream to me. Elizabeta, her hair tousled and her lipstick smeared across her face leaned towards me and whispered, 'Now speculate, my dear. Speculate until you go mad.'

My pain was indescribable. I felt as if my world was falling apart. I was not roused from my depression even by Švejk's confession that he had stuffed us into the water tank only so that he could flee the gypsies and that he had no intention of returning to them. The others hugged him. I hurried to my room and gave in to the tears that had been welling up inside me.

27

There followed days of crystal-clear skies and a gentle breeze, which made the hot afternoons bearable. We effortlessly slipped into the routine we had known before, and there was a feeling that things had sorted themselves out and that everything would be as it was. Early every morning, usually before we were awake, when it was pleasantly cool, Mum ran her mini-marathon. Upon her return she would stand in front of the house for some time looking at the surrounding hills and the wide valley. It was already lively in the fields: haymaking had started, and crops were being harvested, while playful children and dogs frolicked.

At such moments we did feel that our move to the country really was the fruit of Dad's higher wisdom, for the sense of freshness and health, attainable if not attained, was as close as in the initial months when it seemed that life in the village would not only bring us peace and happiness but would transform us into demigods.

We were no longer able to cultivate such hopes, which were unrealistic considering the things that had happened, but there was a promise in the air of a truce or at least a shared desire to return to less choppy waters.

This was most evident when we had breakfast after Mum's morning run in the spacious open kitchen, where the early-morning breeze brought the pleasant scent of the orchard. The table was once again richly spread with eggs, salami, ham, fish, preserves and tasty French cheeses that Vinko brought every day from the supermarket in town on his way home from work.

Life was far from poor. It was not luxurious, but Vinko's salary, Mum's and Dad's pensions, Vladimir's special payments and the mysterious contributions to the common purse made by Aunt Mara meant that we could live in real comfort.

We weren't as talkative as we had once been at shared meals, but the conversation flowed and the tension of the previous weeks evaporated. A great contribution to this was made by Elizabeta, who stopped trying to provoke and was largely silent; she usually read at the table, no longer the Bible but de Sade once more, in whom she became so absorbed that she sometimes forgot to eat and absently chewed the same piece of sausage for five minutes.

But the main reason for the change in family relations was undoubtedly Švejk, who had already built his shed next to the road and begun to reconvert his vehicle back into a fire engine, since the local fire-fighters had been as good as their word and accepted him as an honorary member with the promise of full membership when he had completed the necessary training and passed the examination for volunteer fire-fighters. Those were the rules of the National Fire-Fighters' Association.

The metallic clanging and piercing sound of drilling that reached the house disturbed some of us, but no one said a word, not even Mum, who preferred to wear ear plugs. Since we had reclaimed Švejk she had been unusually friendly towards him, and the rest of us had stopped teasing him about his clumsiness.

There was less and less of this, although on the first day after his return he had taken a step backwards in the dining-room and knocked into the dresser with such force that Mum's beloved collection of porcelain had fallen from the shelves and ended up on the floor in fragments

'Never mind,' she said through gritted teeth, going to fetch the brush. 'It could have happened to anyone.'

Dad was astonished at the change in Mum and did not try to hide the fact, while the rest of us couldn't help being curious as to what had brought it about.

Perhaps the incident in the gypsy village had helped ease family tensions. With her cruel analysis of our characters, Aranka the Fortune-Teller had so completely laid us bare that we had no choice but common denial. We all wanted to create the impression that we were anything but how she had described us, although we each knew all too well that she had not been mistaken or, rather, that she had erred only to the extent that she had deliberately failed to mention that each of us also had a positive side or at least a wish to overcome our faults. Through our behaviour, we tried to establish precisely what she had not wanted to acknowledge.

And thus her brutal attack had a benign effect on us, even though that certainly had not been her intention. We felt she had wanted to lay a kind of curse upon us, and so we did not have the courage even to mention the gypsies, although we knew that Švejk had left all his things with them except the tools he kept in the fire engine.

We knew that things were not settled and that sooner or later the gypsies would try to get Švejk back, by fair means or foul. But it seemed impossible that they would try to carry him off by force, so we were not worried. Švejk had evidently not overlooked the fact that he had more freedom with us, as well as more comfort, and so we were convinced that nothing on earth could lure him back there other than black magic

In the succession of wonderful summer days there was nothing to suggest that soon things would get dangerously complicated; like a clear blue sky, across which fluffy white clouds occasionally drifted, it was hard to imagine that it would ever rain, let alone that there might be thunder and lightning. Mum and Dad became close once more and every evening went for a long walk in the neighbouring hills. During the day Dad listened to classical music in his room – Tchaikovsky, Beethoven, Berlioz and other Romantic masters that we had not heard for some time – and from Mara's studio baroque arias rang out.

Vladimir had abandoned the idea of writing a book about the years before death and had decided to have another go at his Partisan memoirs, this time from a different angle: not as an attempt at justification before those who now belittled the 'brave efforts of men and women in the fight against the occupier' but as an objective chronicle of events allowing readers to make up their own minds.

Vinko was newly obsessed with the idea of growing a record-breaking cabbage and immortalizing his name in the *Guinness World Records*. He said that, as an ordinary bookkeeper, this was the only way of making his mark on history. Every day, when he came back from work, he wolfed down his supper, got changed and set off with his small spade for the orchard, where he dug up soil samples at different locations and took them to his 'laboratory' in the cellar of one of the outbuildings. There, through biochemical analysis, he tried to determine where a cabbage would have the best chance of achieving better than average growth.

Aunt Mara was also in the grip of a creative fever. Peter and I had to carry her easel to Švejk's open shed, where every day she painted the hero of the independence struggle working on the reserve fire engine. In between, she did a number of portraits of him as well as of tourists who stopped by before continuing on their way to the tourist farm at the top of the hill. It was summer, and the number of walkers greatly increased. Švejk's hammering and welding evidently fascinated them so much that they often stood around in groups watching.

Many of them thought that it would be appropriate to take home their portrait as a reminder of this unusual scene, and so the commissions flooded in. What was more, passers-by also bought paintings of the fire engine and Švejk at work and even portraits of Švejk himself. Completely unexpectedly, a profitable business developed, which, according to the rules, Švejk and Aunt Mara should have registered for taxation purposes.

But, of course, they didn't give this a moment's thought. Whenever there were no visitors they liked to sit in the wickerwork chairs and chat. As soon as they heard the voices of approaching walkers, Švejk jumped up and started drilling, welding and hammering like one possessed; Peter was convinced he did the same bit of work at least ten times over. And thus Švejk's preparations for a career as a village fire-fighter became the driving force behind Mara's success as an artist. Sooner or later it became clear to both of them that the work on the fire engine was finished; however, Švejk had no choice but to continue, otherwise Mara would not sell any paintings. That this was really the case was proved when he took a day off.

Peter gave up wandering through the woods and the neighbouring villages (watching young gypsy girls sunbathing naked in clearings no longer appealed to him, nor to me), and he devoted most of his attention to his computer, which he wanted to protect against a virus that would supposedly bring about the collapse of the entire virtual world and perhaps lead to economic catastrophe, war and the end of civilization. It was 1999, and the historic date of the transition to numerical *terra incognita* was fast approaching. The newspapers began to be full of warnings of the catastrophe that could be caused by the millennium bug as well as advice on how to avoid it.

Peter decided to set up his own defences. Everyone else was just interested in making money and because of this were making prophecies of dire consequences. The older members of the family did not believe it possible that something which existed only on a screen and was by definition not real could cause the end of the world, but Peter eventually convinced them that, setting aside a possible collision with an meteorite, the end of the world could be triggered by an idea alone (Dad was the first to agree with him), and for an idea it was not important whether it was on a screen or in print or spread around the world in the form of a virus.

'The only defence against a destructive idea is a constructive idea,' he stated emphatically.

I don't know how many members of the family knew or at least sensed how much we were striving to realize this maxim in all the different areas of our lives. That heaven and hell were primarily or only in our minds, and that one could be defeated by opposing it with the other, was felt instinctively at least by Elizabeta, and perhaps most strongly by her, for after de Sade she had turned again to the Bible. Once I even came across her under the trees in the orchard with the Holy Book in one hand and *Juliette* and *La Nouvelle Justine* in the other, reading first from one and then the other two, as if playing table-tennis with the forces in her psyche.

I think it was Elizabeta who most strongly felt that life was a tightrope walk, where only skill or God's grace prevented you from tumbling into the depths. Whenever skill becomes clumsiness we instinctively cling to God's grace; whenever we feel we have enough of God's grace we are tempted by risk.

Two days later she began frantically ringing around her friends to ask whether anyone would like to go to the seaside with her. But some had already left, some had just come back and others were going with their parents or simply didn't fancy it. Elizabeta was well known at school as a 'difficult' girl and didn't have many friends, although there were always plenty of boys buzzing around her. When the idea of a trip had proved impossible she shut herself in her room, and I could hear her muffled sobs. I knocked on the door and offered to go with her to the seaside, the mountains, wherever she wanted.

'Get lost,' she yelled. 'I don't like guys who suck up to me. Be grateful for what you got and leave me in peace, otherwise I'll spill the beans and make your summer one that you'll never forget.'

After this vitriolic outburst I, too, didn't want to leave my room. I decided to forget about this cruel life and devote myself to my imagination.

I began to write a story entitled 'The Thing'. I wanted to pour into it the sense of hurt that had built up inside me.

28

Three days later we received a visit. We were having lunch, and Švejk's fire engine had been left unattended beside the road along with Mara's easel and stack of paintings, waiting for passers-by. Thus there was no one to warn us who might be approaching. We saw them only when they were already standing in the orchard near the open dining-room door.

'Jesus,' exclaimed Aunt Mara.

Švejk seemed to be having difficulty swallowing. Mum and Dad looked at each other, while Vladimir quietly cursed.

Vinko said, 'I knew this would happen.'

Elizabeta held her breath and stopped eating.

The delegation was led by Janek Hudorovec, whose face looked particularly cruel now. From the breast pocket on his waistcoat protruded something reminiscent of the sharp blade of a knife. He was accompanied by his mother, Aranka the Fortune-Teller, who was frowning as she regarded us with a mixture of scorn and, so it seemed, envy. The image of a happy family, lacking neither food nor comfort, evidently did not fill her with affection for those who had stolen her business partner.

The other members of the delegation also created the impression that they would not leave without what they had come for. Three stocky youths with cropped hair and dark glasses – dressed, despite the heat, in leather biker jackets and boots with metal trimmings – had their thumbs confidently tucked into their jeans. They were chewing gum in an almost synchronized way. Behind them stood an older clown-like gypsy with a hat, grinning idiotically.

There were also two young gypsy women, rather scantily dressed; one of them had cropped hair, the other a lush mane of black hair that fell across her ample bosom to her waist. They had probably been brought along as bait, for one of them had her eyes fixed provocatively on me and the other on Peter. In front of the adults stood four ragged barefoot children, two sucking their thumbs, who were probably supposed to arouse the pity of the more socially conscious among us.

And in front of them sat all eight gypsy dogs, their tongues lolling in the afternoon heat. The two Alsatians sat bolt upright, their posture giving the impression that they were willing to intervene in events as soon as they received the order.

Faced with an uncertain outcome, we eyed each other hesitantly.

The gypsies were waiting for us to say something, and we were waiting for them to say why they had come. Švejk was clearly nervous and began to hiccup.

'They're a real work of art,' commented Aunt Mara quietly. 'Shame I left my brushes and paints down by the road. If I portrayed them as they look now I could send the painting straight to the National Gallery.'

'Band of gypsies,' muttered Vladimir. 'Ten years ago we'd just have stuffed them in the car and taken them to prison. The world hasn't changed for the better.'

'I don't think it's the right moment for nostalgia,' murmured Dad. 'We need to use our common sense.'

'I'm afraid common sense will fall on deaf ears,' observed Vinko.

'I'll sacrifice myself,' said Elizabeta. 'Let them take me instead of Švejk.'

'Be quiet,' hissed Mara.

'Švejk is dearer to you than a malicious hussy anyway,' Elizabeta persisted. 'I'll become a gypsy princess and marry a murderer. You'll get to live in peace, and I'll get what I deserve: an ecstatic death.'

'Not now, please,' said Mum almost hysterically. 'Can't you see we're faced with a very delicate situation?'

Suddenly, the four barefoot gypsy children unrolled a narrow strip of canvas on which were written the words 'Švejk, come back. We love you'.

'Pathetic,' muttered Peter.

'In bad taste,' agreed Mara.

'A low blow,' muttered Vladimir, 'but in line with expectations.'

'It'll get worse,' said Vinko.

The ragged children rolled up the banner and unfurled a new one, which said 'Švejk, this is not your home. Your home is with us.'

Švejk was so embarrassed that he didn't know where to look. Aware that the eyes of the family were upon him, he emitted a muffled sigh and turned his attention once more to his steak. He was trying desperately to create the impression that he was in the middle of his lunch and had not the slightest interest in what was happening around him.

The little gypsies unfurled another banner, which said 'See these two young girls – they are yours.'

'Scandalous,' said Mum with quiet anger. 'How thoughtlessly they exploit their poor children. Isn't that against the law?'

'We live in times,' complained Vladimir, 'when the only illegal thing is tax evasion.'

Švejk couldn't help himself and glanced at the banner. I saw how he started slightly, especially when he saw the gypsy girls. Now he was so embarrassed that he no longer knew what to do. He tried to cut a piece off the steak that he had already finished.

'Well,' said Vinko, 'that was their trump card – I wonder what else they have up their sleeves.'

'We must be prepared for the worst,' said Vladimir. 'It's time I went for my pistol.'

He got up, but Dad pushed him back down on to his chair. 'Have you gone mad?' he said. 'Since when do you have a pistol?'

'Since I realized that I was the only one capable of defending this wretched family,' replied Vladimir.

These words had a visible impact on Dad. 'We're not a wretched family,' he said to Vladimir, 'and we don't need defending by Partisans. Certainly not in a style that has long been out of fashion.'

'Really?' said Vladimir with a frown. 'What is in fashion now?'

'Dialogue,' said Dad, getting up. 'Diplomacy, negotiation, seeking agreement.'

'But not with your opponents,' Vladimir objected. 'Dialogue is only possible with those who are on the same wavelength. The others need to be suppressed.'

'You should be ashamed of yourself,' said Dad. 'Protecting the family is my responsibility, so allow me to protect them in line with the spirit of the times. After all, we are on the threshold of a new millennium. Have we learned nothing from two thousand years of civilization? In a few months we shall be living in the twenty-first century.'

'I agree,' said Vladimir, 'but it doesn't apply to those standing outside. They are gypsies and will always be gypsies.'

'What rubbish I have to listen to . . .' said Peter. 'This house has become a hotbed of prejudice, racism and extreme selfishness.'

'So go and live with the gypsies,' snapped Mum, never imagining how she would soon come to regret her words.

'Please,' said Dad, turning, 'if you can't support me, can you at least keep quiet?'

'It's all my fault,' said Švejk, awkwardly pushing his plate aside. He took out his pocket handkerchief and spent some time wiping his mouth. Then he sneezed and wiped his nose. 'Whatever I do, it always ends up like this, with others suffering. That's my fate. It'll be best for you if I go and earn money to help the Roma community.'

'Švejk,' said Dad, looking at him, 'it'd be a great help if you stopped playing the hurt child.'

Švejk hung his head in shame.

'I won't let gypsies exploit my brother,' Mum broke in.

'We are the gypsies,' said Peter, 'at least, that's how we're acting.'

'Now I've had enough,' Dad raised his voice. 'If I hear another statement like that I'll go mad, literally. Do you understand?' He looked at each of us in turn. His face was red in a way I had never seen it before.

'Let's be quiet,' whispered Elizabeta. 'He's going to have a stroke.'

'What did you say?' Dad lowered his voice threateningly.

'Nothing,' said Elizabeta, scared. 'I was just praying that it will all end well.'

'You go ahead and pray,' snapped Dad, 'but silently.'

He waited a while to see if he had succeeded in frightening the family; then he straightened up to make himself look taller and faced the gypsies.

'It's nice of you to come,' he began in a conciliatory fashion, but Aranka the Fortune-Teller interrupted him.

'We're talking to Švejk. The rest of you don't interest us.'

'You're speaking to his legal representative,' Dad persisted. 'Whatever you have to say, you can say to me.'

'I didn't know you were a lawyer,' said Aranka.

'I'm not,' Dad admitted, 'but I'm the head of the family, and Švejk is one of those I'm responsible for.'

'You're not a lawyer?' said Aranka scornfully. 'Then it's good that we do have a lawyer – a real one, with a degree,' she patted her son, who stood beside her. 'Tell them,' she elbowed him. 'Don't wait for me, because I won't try to win them over. I'll curse them and be on my way.'

The gypsy with a cruel face calmly explained. 'It's like this: unilateral withdrawal from a business agreement that causes financial harm to the other partner carries certain consequences. The damage caused can be assessed by a court, and the aggrieved party can demand reparations. If the person is unable to pay, then the matter can end with seizure – including, in extreme cases, the property of his relatives.'

We all waited to see what Dad would say. Probably he was as shocked as we were. We had expected many things but not the threat of legal action. We had expected them to set the dogs on us or that the three leather jackets would attack us and grab Švejk. The last thing we had expected was a polite warning that Švejk had broken the law. This confused us, particularly Dad, who was a great advocate of respect for the law.

He turned and looked at Švejk. 'Švejk, did you sign anything?'

Švejk hesitated for some time then said, 'I won't pretend I didn't. But nothing important. Or I didn't know I was signing anything important. The agreement was that I would supply the transport and Aranka would do all the rest. But I made it clear that the vehicle belonged to the fire station, that I was making it suitable for fire-fighting again, and I could use it for other purposes only until it once more became a working fire engine.'

'Well done, Švejk,' said Dad. 'You acted sensibly.'

He turned back to the gypsies and said, 'I am informing you that Švejk is a registered fire-fighter, that the vehicle is not his property and that he was possibly in the wrong when he used it for other purposes. So, I'm advising you to address your damages claim to the actual owner of the vehicle, the local fire brigade. I wish you good day.'

With these words he triumphantly turned and sat back down at the table. Mum and Aunt Mara applauded.

'Švejk,' said Aranka the Fortune-Teller, 'come here. I'd like to talk to you.'

Švejk looked at Dad. Dad shook his head.

'Švejk,' Aranka pushed aside one of the barefoot little gypsies and took a half-step forward, 'don't forget I have unusual skills that I can use for good or ill. Don't imagine that you'll get out of this just like that.'

'As a lawyer,' said Dad to the gypsy with the cruel face, 'you should warn the lady that issuing threats in front of witnesses is a criminal offence.'

'You'll all be punished.' The fortune-teller lost her cool. 'Every last one of you. A curse on this house. A curse on all of you – and that goes for you, too, Švejk.'

'I'm already cursed,' murmured Švejk.

'Me, too?' said Vladimir, jumping up and taking a step towards the gypsies. We saw he was holding a pistol. The dogs immediately sprang up and started growling. The barefoot children leaped back and grabbed the nearest leg.

'Vladimir, for God's sake,' said Dad.

But Vladimir was not listening. With his weapon raised, he went out from the dining-room into the orchard and said, 'I'll count to five. Slowly, so no one gets hurt. One . . .'

The gypsy delegation hastily withdrew. The hastiest were the three thugs in leather jackets. The girls looked over their shoulders. The gypsy with the cruel face walked with head held high and did not look back. His mother had her fists clenched and was protesting angrily, but she was already too far away for us to hear what she was saying. The dogs followed, their tails between their legs.

When they had disappeared from sight, Dad got up and said, 'Vladimir, come here.'

When Vladimir came back inside, Dad said to him, 'It's quite possible that you've earned us a visit from the police.'

'Let them come,' said Vladimir, putting his pistol into his trouser pocket. 'I have a licence. I was defending private property, which has replaced the communist ideal as the highest value. What can they do to me?'

'Perhaps nothing,' said Dad, 'but if you're thinking of doing anything like that again, warn us in advance.'

Vladimir promised he would. Then he said, 'It would also be nice if Švejk kept us informed about his plans.'

Švejk hung his head.

'Please, no recriminations,' said Mum. 'We have survived the ordeal, and everything will be all right. The gypsies won't return, and they didn't do us any harm. Let's carry on with our lunch.'

We took her advice. But the gypsies' visit had not improved our appetites, so we quickly finished and dispersed. As for the gypsies not having done any harm, Mum was wrong, for half an hour later we heard Aunt Mara down by the road cursing them in every way she knew how.

It turned out that the gypsy delegation had disappeared, taking with them her stack of paintings as well as Švejk's tools, right down to the smallest screwdriver. And on the left-hand side of the water tank was a gaping hole caused by several blows of a heavy hammer.

29

At the beginning of August the village fire brigade celebrated its seventieth anniversary. The event exceeded all expectations. A wooden stage was erected in front of the fire station, and a number of simple metal chairs were placed on it for the guests of honour: the head of the fire brigade, the mayor, the president of the National Fire-Fighters' Association and a well-known writer who was to be the guest speaker. It was a nice sunny Sunday morning, and by eleven the guests of honour were already sweating profusely. Nobody had thought of providing any shade for the dignitaries. Anyone actually taking any notice would have seen that things were unravelling; if they extinguished fires with the same level of coordination they might as well give up altogether.

But the festive atmosphere filled most of those present with more than the usual measure of patience; and in the shade behind the fire station there was an aroma of sausages and goulash. We were all quietly hoping that the formal part would quickly give way to celebrating, which promised to last through the afternoon and well into the night. As a sign of good neighbourly relations, the fire-fighters from a village across the Austrian border, less than two kilometres away, had also been invited.

The Austrians came in funny little hats and lederhosen with a mass of multi-coloured flags. By comparison, our local boys in their dark-blue uniforms looked rather shabby, but they tried to make a better impression with their proud posture and firm step. The Austrians had brought a brass band with them, which played out of tune but loud enough to smother all conversation by striking up a march to which both brigades paraded from the church to the fire station where they all lined up.

Švejk was among the fire-fighters. His hastily made uniform did not exactly enhance the positive aspects of his figure, quite the opposite, and he marched out of step with the others. But his face was glowing with pride, for on the forecourt stood two fire engines waiting to be blessed by the local priest. One of them was his. Two days before the celebration he had managed to patch up the hole made by the revengeful gypsies and to weld a new back on to the water tank – he had even mended the pump.

He hadn't had time to check whether the vehicle was working as it should, but the fire-fighters (I think, following some persuasion by Dad) were sure that at least it would not explode in front of the visitors. They were proud to be able to appear before the Austrians with two fire engines – a single vehicle would have made much less of an impression. Through the red paint with which Švejk had quickly painted the water tank the discerning eye could still easily make out the words 'Aranka Hudorovec and Jaroslav Švejk Ltd', but few in the crowd were paying much attention to such details.

There were around five hundred people there. They were on the road, behind both lined-up brigades and in the lower part of the forecourt; some were already sitting on the benches at the tables beneath the canvas roof where the celebration was to take place. We were looking forward to the merrymaking, although Mum was threatening to go home as soon as the speeches were over. She was embarrassed because Aunt Mara had brought her easel and was, to general amusement, churning out one watercolour after the other.

'Wouldn't it be easier to buy a camera?' Mum muttered.

'Have you never heard of art?' replied Mara.

'I certainly have,' snapped Mum, 'but I'm asking myself whether you have.'

But Mum got the worst of the argument, for some of those standing near by had already asked whether the watercolours were for sale, and Aunt Mara had begun to make money even before the event had properly got going.

In line with expectations, the speeches were boring and some of them simply funny. Fortunately, every minute or so the microphone crackled or howled, which provided momentary relief. Of course, we were not expecting verbal fireworks from the head of the local fire brigade, who was employed in the local hardboard factory. We learned that the brigade had acquired the modern Iveco fire engine three years earlier and the older 800-litre fire engine in 1974. Three years ago the brigade had also organized the fourth cross-border fire-fighting competition and that seventy-two brigades had taken part. And so on.

Then it was the turn of the mayor. He could at least have tried to say something worth hearing, but evidently the sun had already got to him, and he merely mumbled pointless phrases about 'an important celebration' and 'lucky villagers' who could sleep peacefully thanks to their 'alert fire-fighters'.

'How can I sleep peacefully', came a drunken voice from the crowd, 'if next door's dog barks all night?'

This observation eased the painful atmosphere somewhat and received some applause.

The president of the National Fire-Fighters' Association read his speech out. Anxious to be heard, he strained so much that his neck muscles twitched and shook, and his mouth was almost glued to the microphone, so his every other word was swallowed up by feedback, and the more he tried the less we understood him. The Austrian fire-fighters smirked. The audience exchanged impolite comments.

But the gathered multitude was most disappointed by the guest speaker, the Important Writer who was supposedly invited because he had been born in the village and perhaps, in the hope that as a world traveller of some renown, his presence would help raise the tone of the event.

'Oh, he's worth listening to,' enthused Elizabeta, who had to read one of his books in school. 'He can be quite witty. I don't know whose photograph is on the back of his book, though, because there he looks young and fairly tasty, even though as a rule I don't like men with beards. But this guy doesn't look like him at all. Maybe he couldn't come and has sent a stand-in.'

'You're right,' said Aunt Mara. 'He looks rather funny in his trainers and jeans and light-coloured jacket. Who's seen a combination like that before? The jacket doesn't go with that shirt at all. It's way too dark.'

'He could do with a haircut, too,' observed Vladimir.

'What can he cut?' said Elizabeta, 'He's already bald on top. He needs some hair somewhere.'

Mum and Dad also knew his work. Mum said she had read one of his books three times and that she had a copy at home in the library, although it wasn't suitable for youngsters.

'Then I'll start it today' said Elizabeta. 'I didn't know he wrote that kind of book as well'

'He could with losing a bit of weight,' commented Aunt Mara.

'Yes, I'd imagined him thinner', said Mum, 'and taller. But I think he has nice eyes, as far as I can tell from this distance anyway. Big and sad.'

'I saw him in some magazine wearing tails,' said Aunt Mara. 'He looked a lot more elegant. Shame he's let himself go. Anyway, I'll paint him as he is.' She grabbed her brush.

'He doesn't look like he's let himself go at all,' said Elizabeta. 'He's dressed appropriately for the occasion.'

'It really doesn't matter,' said Dad in irritation. 'He's a writer not a model. What matters is what he says.'

'Exactly,' agreed Peter. 'But he won't say anything of any note. He'll just dispense some cheap wisdom.'

'If he ever starts his speech . . .' grumbled Vinko.

30

The Important Writer really did seem to be buying time. First he spent a good minute altering the height of the microphone so that it was directly in front of his mouth – evidently, the crackling and howling of the loudspeakers had made him concerned that he wouldn't be heard. Then he started rummaging through his pockets, as if trying to find something extremely important, looking all the more worried as he did so.

'What the hell is he doing?' grumbled Vladimir.

'He's just noticed that someone has stolen his wallet,' said Elizabeta.

When the Important Writer had thoroughly searched himself for the second time, he approached the microphone, cleared his throat – ahem, ahem – as people do when they are about to say something and once more in panic went through his pockets. Then he humbly confessed that he had left his prepared speech at home. Regrettably, he had no choice but to improvise, which, of course, would be far from what he had intended, for which he apologized.

'I can't believe it,' said Peter. 'What's he like? And a writer . . . Does he really think we're stupid enough to fall for an old trick like that? Like Demosthenes, who began each speech with the words "Sadly, I'm not much of a speaker" and then proved the opposite.'

'What are you talking about?' asked Mum.

'That your beloved author has learned his speech by heart,' said Peter. 'Now he'll pretend to be making it up as he goes along and people will say that he really knows how to speak in public.'

'How do you know he didn't leave it at home?' said Mum, sticking up for her author. 'And perhaps he really does know how to speak in public. Wouldn't it be better to wait and see?'

But in the end Mum, too, was not satisfied with what she heard, and the question as to whether he had memorized or was improvising became academic. Peter found the writer's words turgid, sentimental and tailored to the needs of an audience of which the writer clearly did not have a high opinion, since he tried so hard to be understood by everyone that he came across as patronizing and at the same time rather pathetic.

'Time passes, and whenever I return to my birthplace I cannot but help feel this sense of time passing with a certain amount of pain. When I'm here I have the feeling that the life I have lived elsewhere never really existed. Absence ceases to be real, it becomes dream-like, as if I had never left here and I only dreamed my life.'

And so on. He spoke slowly, with pauses during which he searched – or, at least pretended to – for the right words in a soft, dreamy voice that immediately put Aunt Mara off; she said it sounded like moaning and almost effeminate and that men should speak decisively and give the impression that things were clear to them.

'But things are not clear to men,' said Mum, still defending her beloved author. 'And it's nice that one of them dares to acknowledge this. He's got a nice voice, sensitive, caressing, although weary from all the experience that life has thrown at him.'

'What do I care about his life experience?' said Vladimir. 'This is not a confessional; it's a public event. He should speak of things that interest everyone: politics, history, the future, the nation.'

'Because I'm practically a local, it's appropriate that I speak somewhat more personally,' the guest speaker continued.

'Well,' said Mum to Vladimir, 'there's your answer.'

'Personally? Ridiculous . . .' Vladimir continued to be annoyed. 'No one has the right to speak personally in front of two fire brigades, who are soon going to succumb to the heat – especially if one of the brigades is from Austria.'

'Vladimir,' said Dad, 'be quiet and listen.'

'Time changes us, and we change with time,' the speaker continued. 'And with us the world around us changes.'

'Such profundity . . .' muttered Peter. 'Words that will change my life. I'm going to fall over.'

'I can no longer find the stream where I bathed with my cousin. It has dried up, like our hopes, our dreams. Where are those beautiful girls who swam with us and who I dreamed about? Now they are mothers, perhaps grandmothers. Time is unfair to us all.'

'There's one beautiful girl here,' said Elizabeta in a half-whisper. 'She's not yet a mother let alone a grandmother. Time is unfair to her because it moves too slowly and does not let her grow up. Have you forgotten your youth, Mr Writer? Would you like me to remind you of it?'

'What are you planning?' I hissed in her ear. 'Surely you're not going to offer yourself to *this* guy?'

'I'm not sure,' she said absently. 'Maybe then I'd end up in one of his books. For that privilege I'm sure plenty of girls have already spread their legs.'

'You know what?' I said. 'You're perverse.'

'Do you think he is as well?' she replied, full of hope.

I trod on her foot as hard as I could. Because she was wearing sandals and I shoes, it hurt so much she yelled out loud. People's heads turned. The cry was heard by the guest speaker, who turned in our direction. At that moment Elizabeta raised her hand and waved to him. This confused him.

'Have you gone mad?' said Aunt Mara.

Before Dad could restrain her she had hit Elizabeta on the head twice with her box of paints. Now quite a lot of people were looking at us. Elizabeta pushed her way through the crowd and disappeared. Mara wanted to go after her, but Dad grabbed hold of her collar and pulled her back.

'Mara,' he said, 'you've shamed us enough already.'

'I am delighted', continued the Important Writer, 'to be able to address you at this important celebration.' A number of fire-fighters from both brigades had started to yawn. 'But don't expect to hear a political speech today.'

'So,' said Peter, 'he began at the end and is ending at the beginning. At least that's original.'

But the Important Writer could not finish his speech one way or the other, because the next moment the sound system packed up. A collective sigh of relief could be heard from most of those present. The speaker also looked relieved; he pulled a face and gesticulated as if to say, 'Act of God. What can you do?'

The Austrian brass band seized the opportunity and blasted out a fire-fighters' march. A group of schoolgirls in national dress hurried on to the stage and handed bouquets to the guests of honour. The president of the

National Fire-Fighters' Association went over to the Important Writer and congratulated him on his speech, as did the mayor and the head of the local fire brigade.

The writer was not happy with himself, and I got the impression that he would rather be anywhere else but here. He also gave the impression that he had not attended the event with any particular enthusiasm; nor that he was particularly enthusiastic about life. I looked at Mum and saw that she was also thinking this. She seemed to feel sorry for the Important Writer and not just because his speech had been a disaster.

I saw that he was trying to leave the stage as quickly as possible and hide in the nearest corner. But the head of the fire brigade wouldn't let him go. The official part was not yet over. As soon as the last Austrian trombone fell quiet he indicated that a demonstration of fire-fighting skills would follow. The fine upstanding men would show how quickly they could put out a fire. In recent years there hadn't been so many fires in the area, not like in 1953, when on Good Friday three houses had burned down, but being prepared was a fundamental fire-fighters' rule.

Above all, local citizens should be free from worry; the demonstration would show that their brigade was modern, mobile and reliable.

'Especially now,' said the fire brigade head, 'when we once more have two vehicles. The credit for that goes to our new honorary member, Jaroslav Švejk, the well-known hero of the war for independence, who tried to stop a column of tanks with a city bus and to change the course of history. He recently moved to our village and managed to repair the 800-litre fire engine, which had been written off long ago. He deserves a round of applause.'

Švejk stepped out of line and gave an awkward bow. People clapped. Some shouted bravo. He blushed. The family were proud – although maybe proud is the wrong word; it was more relief that there was no longer any reason to feel ashamed of our lost uncle.

Mum was also comforted. She had tears in her eyes. Vladimir clapped louder than the others. The hero of the Second World War applauded the hero of the war for independence. For the family this was an important moment. Aunt Mara tried to immortalize it with some rapid strokes of her brush. Dad swallowed, and his Adam's apple jumped. He was moved.

31

Then a blaze appeared in the field in front of the woods. Only then did we notice that someone had built a large bonfire of dry branches there. In the hot sun, the flames had an easy job and grew quickly.

'The fire will die before they get their hoses out,' said Vladimir.

But the fire-fighters sprang into action as if it was their own homes burning down. The Austrian guests, who evidently hadn't been warned, withdrew like a flock of startled sheep, not knowing whether to join in or to make room for a rapid manoeuvre by the locals. The newer fire engine started to spray water on the fire in less than thirty seconds; people gasped in surprise and then applauded.

But the general attention soon turned to the older vehicle. To judge by the noisy whirring, there was nothing wrong with the pump, but Švejk and two other fire-fighters were trying in vain to unroll the hosepipe. It was awkwardly twisted and caught somewhere. Švejk pushed aside his two assistants and tried to deal with it on his own. He pushed and pulled and in the end kicked the disobedient hosepipe. And suddenly it found itself in his hands. People applauded.

But that was a mistake, because Švejk couldn't stop himself from acknowledging the public's attentions, and, as he did so, one of his assistants turned the water on a second before Švejk had managed to aim it at the flames.

The jet came out with such force that it threw Švejk back into the water tank. It was not directed at the fire but towards the stage with the guests of honour. It battered the president of the National Fire-Fighters' Association, knocked the mayor off the stage and lifted the Important Writer into the air, pinning him to the wall of the fire station, his arms and legs splayed like a squashed frog. He first squeezed his mouth shut and then opened it to expel the water that was choking him; the next moment he closed it again so as not to swallow more as it continued to pound him.

When Švejk finally managed to redirect the hosepipe the soaked guest speaker slid down into the space between the stage and the wall of the fire station and ended up lying on the grass under the platform. Meanwhile the jet of water from Švejk's water tank described an arc through the air, first destroying the amplifier and then flooding the tables and benches beneath the canvas roof of the covered bar area, soaking those present, some of whom were already drinking wine and eating sausages, breaking innumerable plates and glasses and literally tearing the food from people's mouths.

It reached as far as the cauldron with hot oil, which on contact with the water spat viciously, but luckily it did not overturn. Švejk's assistants, whom he had pushed away, now rushed to help him control the angry hosepipe. But Švejk stubbornly wanted to do it on his own, and it looked as if they were engaging in a tug of war. In so doing they turned it in the wrong direction, and the jet of water attacked the Austrians – some were knocked to the ground, others lost their hats, some had trumpets and trombones knocked from their hands, while those who had taken to their heels were soaked from behind – and finally the village policeman, who was there to ensure law and order was maintained, had his cap knocked off.

Then the flow of water suddenly ceased, not because the water had run out but because one of the fire-fighters had realized he simply needed to turn off the tap on the side of the water tank. Švejk looked stunned when the pressure suddenly dropped. Instinctively, he bent over and looked into the pipe to see if anything was wrong. In so doing, he got the last powerful spurt full in the face.

He threw down the hosepipe, which for some time writhed on the ground like a dying snake, and banged his chest so as to cough up the water entering his bronchial tubes.

The spectators laughed and clapped, showing that they had forgiven him – although those applauding were largely those who had escaped the great wash.

'That finished too quickly,' complained Aunt Mara. 'Shame, because if I'd captured that in paint I could live off selling copies for a hundred years.'

'Come on,' said Peter, 'at least a hundred people will have taken a photo or videoed the scene. No one will miss your paintings.'

'You have no idea what art is,' snapped Aunt Mara.

'Let's go and look after Švejk,' suggested Vladimir.

'I feel like sinking into the ground,' said Mum.

'Oh, come on,' replied Dad angrily, 'we have to stand by relatives when they need us, not when we need them.'

But Švejk was no longer beside the fire engine. He had rushed towards the remains of the smouldering bonfire that the other fire engine already had under control. However, the branches were still smouldering, and when Švejk opened his arms and hurled himself stomach first on top of them, the head of the fire brigade yelled an order, the pump shuddered and the fire-fighters directed a jet of water straight at Švejk and the hot charcoal sizzling around him. Although no one actually timed it, it seemed that the water fell on him for a good five minutes – long enough to drown him had he not already been carbonized.

But when we rushed to help Švejk and pushed aside the fire-fighters who were bending over him, the lost uncle rose like a phoenix from the ashes and calmly said, 'Never in my life have I drunk so much water. I hope there's enough room left at least for a glass of wine.'

'Why, for God's sake, did you jump on the embers?' Mum wanted to know.

Švejk confessed, 'I was so disappointed with myself I wanted to burn. My thanks to all those who were wiser than me and saved me.'

These words greatly endeared him to those who were gathered around. Above all, they disarmed the head of the local fire brigade, who was about to give Švejk a piece of his mind. After his face had run through various shades of red, in the end it was he who offered Švejk his hand and helped him to his feet.

'Let's put it all behind us, Švejk,' he said. 'Thanks for repairing the fire engine. The official part of the event is over. Now it's time for wine. You make a start. I have to check whether the Austrians have fled back across the border.'

Švejk had won so many new friends that he soon disappeared into their midst, and we could not reach him. People pressed in from all sides. They were all trying to get to the goulash, sausages and wine. Children were demanding ice-cream. When they found out there wasn't any some started to scream. Quite a few of them received a slap in response.

I wondered what had happened to the Important Writer. There was no sign of him anywhere. On the cut field in front of the fire station was a group of people who had been soaked to the skin by Švejk's demonstration of fire-fighting engagement. They had stripped off, spread their wet clothes out in the sun and were sitting or lying beside them as if they were on a beach. It was an unusual scene. Some were eating hot dogs with mustard and country bread; others were slowly sipping wine and toasting each other. The shared mishap had made friends of complete strangers. There was a lot of good cheer and laughter. The visitors from the town were less reserved than the villagers: some had stripped to their underwear. The local priest was walking past them, his hands behind his back, shaking his head. Because of the unexpected bathing, which was not part of the programme, the blessing of the fire engines had been called off.

Among the boldest was Elizabeta. I didn't know that Švejk's jet of water had also hit her. She was lying at the end of the row, wearing only a tiny pair of transparent black panties. She was leaning on her elbow, staring at the gypsy with the cruel face who was lying beside her dry and fully dressed. He had a stalk of grass between his teeth and was chewing it ruminatively. He took it from his mouth and slowly drew it across Elizabeta's breasts. She took hold of his hand and began to suck his thumb.

I ran into the woods, leaned against a tree and began to sob loudly. The pain within me became unbearable. It was now clear to me that I would have to kill the gypsy.

A sequence of unbearable images of their lovemaking flashed through my mind. The desire to kill the gypsy arose in me, not to prevent the terrible scene I couldn't banish from my thoughts but to punish him after the event. For the act itself I wanted to be present. I wanted to see every last detail, hear every word, every rustle, every intake of breath. I wanted to see every expression on Elizabeta's face, every gesture. I wanted to hold her hand. I wanted to be there, part of the game, even if only as an observer.

At the thought of this I became dizzy with lust and a sense of utter, untarnished despair, as if at the end of the suffering lay a heaven which it was possible to reach only via hell. And only then would I kill the gypsy. After their shared orgasm I would stab him with a knife. Perhaps not after the first time but maybe the second or the third, so that the intolerable suffering and passion could be repeated.

And maybe I wouldn't kill him, maybe I would force him at knifepoint to repeat the performance for my pleasure. I felt as if I would prefer to transform Elizabeta and the gypsy into willing actors who would enact sexual scenes whenever and wherever I wanted. And that I would be able to take part as I wished without either of them objecting. Without either of them even being aware that I was taking part, that I was touching them. I wanted to be both present and absent at the same time.

I stopped crying. I felt that in a special way I was pleased about the inevitability of what would happen, even though less than a minute ago the very thought of it had filled me with horror. At the same time I was stung by the realization that this sense of pleasure could not be normal – I couldn't imagine any other boy of my age would wish for this. It was clear that madness was sprouting within me.

The device, I thought.

No one had escaped its power. Why should I be the exception?

32

I thought that I could talk about these things to the Important Writer. After I crept out of the woods I saw that most people's clothes had dried and they had put them back on. There was no sign of Elizabeta and the gypsy. I wondered if they had sneaked into the woods and that at any moment, concealed in the bushes, they would do the deed in my absence. My first impulse was to go back among the trees and look for them. But where to start? There were hundreds of spots where they could hide in the undergrowth, and even if I did find them it would be too late.

I decided it would be smarter to look for the Important Writer first. More than anything, I needed advice.

With relief I saw that he was sitting beneath one of the canvas roofs. There was quite a crowd around him. Some were squeezed together on the benches; others were forced to stand. They were all listening to what he was saying, some out of politeness; others genuinely interested. Among those sitting I saw the gypsy with the cruel face. There was no sign of Elizabeta. But the mere fact that the gypsy was there lifted a terrible weight off my shoulders. I rushed over and pushed among the people standing around the table.

It was hard to hear what the writer was saying because the village band was playing a dance tune close by. People had already had quite a bit to drink; they wanted more goulash and sausages. There was a lot of pushing, shouting and laughter. I fought my way to the centre and squatted by the writer's elbow. He was still soaking wet; evidently he had no inclination to go into the sun to dry out, preferring to have some wine. On the table was a chaos of bottles and glasses, and his tongue was getting slightly tangled. Sitting at the table, he had assumed some of the authority that had been missing while he was making his speech.

He was saying how he had learned most about writing and about life from his father, who was a tailor, and his grandfather, who was a carpenter. He said that for him writing was manual work, like cutting out, putting together, sewing. Or like cutting, planing and joining pieces of wood together to make a piece of furniture that must be beautiful but at the same time functional – it must have drawers that things could be kept in, but it must also have hidden drawers that only some knew how to open, those who found the key. That key should not be too obvious so that it could be seen from afar, for then the hidden drawers would cease to be hidden and the piece of furniture would lose its value and become an object of mass production available to anyone. The hidden drawers were for keeping precious items in, so each piece of furniture, although interesting and beautiful, should be a kind of puzzle.

'Can I ask you something?' said Mum, whom I suddenly saw on the other side of the table sitting next to Dad.

'Go ahead,' said the Important Writer, pouring himself some more wine.

'When and how can the readers of your books know that they have found the right key and all the hidden drawers? Is it possible that they deceive themselves? That they are opening drawers that are available to everyone else and, like them, they fail to see what is really precious?'

The Important Writer drank some wine and cleared his throat twice. He did so almost inaudibly; he did not wish to create the impression that he did not know how to reply. In spite of that, he was clearly giving the matter some thought.

'Of course,' he said eventually. 'That isn't just a possibility – it often happens. There are readers who cannot bring themselves to admit that mysteries exist or that anything that is not fully explained is worth anything – or, most of all, that what is hidden from them has more value than that which is within their reach. Most hidden drawers are overlooked by those who do not need to look for the secret key but who have it ready-made, mass-produced from a model approved by the experts, convinced that it is as universal as the master key used by an experienced burglar, which opens almost all locks. The experts like a lock that succumbs to their key.'

'I'd like to ask something else,' said a young man in a dark-blue uniform, which was not that of a fire-fighter or a soldier or even a police officer.

'Are you a naval officer?' asked the Important Writer.

'I am,' the man replied with a nod. 'My name is Adam. I'm from around here. I was visiting when I heard you'd be the guest speaker. I came here specifically to ask you something – or for us to do so,' he said, squeezing the young woman who sat beside him so tightly that she was almost pulled into his lap.

I was startled to see that the young woman was Eva, Vladimir's former wife. Mum and Dad had probably already noticed her, as they showed no surprise.

'I'd like to know,' said Captain Adam, 'what your view is of the statements of two very well-known people. One is Kant, who said that beautiful art is a beautiful representation of something, and the other is Simone de Beauvoir, who asked whether we can produce a beautiful painting of someone who is a bad person.'

'You are very well read,' acknowledged the Important Writer.

'I grew up among books,' said Adam, almost as if apologizing for his sophistication. 'My father was the doctor in the next village.'

'I don't know how to answer your question,' said the Important Writer with a sigh. 'I don't think it is the job of literature to present things, events, feelings that are not in themselves beautiful in a beautiful way. It is more honest to show them as they are. It's not the job of literature to make people feel better about life by offering them an airbrushed version of reality. Even a bad person can be beautiful, human in his depravity, particularly if he carries inside himself the seeds of transformation, growth, redemption. Certainly one of the functions of literature is to shock but in its own special way – particularly today, when we are so accustomed to shocks that we are startled only when hit by lightning. Why do you ask?'

'I don't know really,' replied Adam in mild confusion. 'Perhaps because I am making notes about my youth and wonder whether to expand them into a book.'

'I can't offer you the definitive response to that,' said the Important Writer. 'Usually the only option is to take the risk.'

'I have a question,' the gypsy with a cruel face suddenly said. 'My name is Janek Hudorovec. I'm Roma by birth – a gypsy, as some around here prefer to call us. I served twenty years in jail for killing someone. I was still a student then. I don't want to pretend it didn't happen. Everyone knows what I did.'

'Ask your question,' said the Important Writer with barely discernible unease.

'I'd like to know,' said the gypsy who half an hour earlier I had decided to kill, 'if you believe in anything or if you are a complete nihilist. And what seems to you to be an appropriate stance in these times when values are false or trampled on?'

The Important Writer poured himself another glass of wine. We all listened attentively. After this question his silence was longer than usual. I could see that even Dad was waiting with interest to hear his response.

'*Credo, quia absurdum*,' he finally said; 'I believe, because it is absurd. An old saying, but everything in this world is old, including that which we haven't heard but which has been heard by others. Some say that the world has shattered into pieces, but I think it was never whole. It was always a swarming mass of fragmented visions, and the most illusory of these is the conviction that the world can ever be whole. We are surrounded only by a cloud of dust, and within it we are all creatures of loneliness. Whatever we do, we do first to ourselves. Values are trampled on only when we have trampled on them ourselves. But then it is too late; then we can no longer ask questions. Then there is only silence and, where it is possible, a dignified movement towards the exit. We have only three loves at our disposal: for ourselves, for others and for God. And there is only one death. If we realize all three loves then perhaps death is less terrible. Certainly life will be less terrible.'

'But all three loves also have their dark side,' said Janek Hudorovec. 'They all conceal countless pitfalls and can be swallowed up, one by the other. Isn't it safer not to love at all?'

'Of course,' said the Important Writer, 'if what we are looking for in life is safety. On the one hand, it's true, but, on the other, we never tell ourselves stories about how safe we felt ten years ago. Love has meaning because it involves risk; it is a training ground where we can practise the skill of giving meaning to our presence.'

'But all three loves,' said Captain Adam, 'must be informed, otherwise they risk becoming a travesty: self-love, possessiveness and religious intolerance. Where is the boundary between the love that gives a man dignity and the abuse of love that mocks and dishonours him?'

'It depends where it seems convenient to draw the line,' replied the

Important Writer, 'for the charm of the three loves is precisely in the fact that the border is a moveable one, otherwise the world would be dead and life would be a parody. The stories we have been telling ourselves for two millennia are precious because between love and its travesty God left such a large space that we need to keep redrawing the boundary. When we get it wrong, it leads to suffering. That's good, because it forces us to try again.'

'You should have talked about this in your speech,' said Janek Hudorovec. His face seemed less cruel than usual. He actually had interesting features, illuminated by experience and insights far exceeding mine. At the thought that I had wanted to kill him half an hour earlier my stomach turned over.

'If I'd spoken about these things', said the Important Writer, 'the jet of water would not have hit me by chance but intentionally and would have stayed on me until it had lifted me up and hurled me to the other end of the village.'

These words were greeted with amiable laughter, but the writer was right. Some people were already wandering off because the conversation had already crossed the boundary of what was interesting or what they could connect with their experience. Some of them gave an amused frown before they withdrew, as if to say 'What a load of old rubbish'.

33

But new ones approached, including Elizabeta, who appeared out of nowhere and pushed her way through to the gypsy with the cruel – but less cruel than it had been – face. She leaned against his back. When he felt the pressure of her stomach and thighs his face softened even more; he reached for his glass of wine and threw it back then wiped his hand across his small moustache in satisfaction.

'Elizabeta,' I suddenly heard Mara's voice, 'come here. I need your help.'

Only now did I notice Mara. She was peering over the shoulders of those standing and recreating the scene at the table with a serious face, as if she was painting the Last Supper.

'I don't have the time,' said Elizabeta. 'I want to hear what the writer is saying. I might ask him for an interview for the school magazine.'

'He has no time for malicious hussies,' said Mara.

'He will for me,' said Elizabeta. 'They say he likes young girls.'

'Don't be impudent,' said her mother, 'and stop embarrassing the poor man.'

From where I was squatting at his elbow it was hard to see the writer's face, but it seemed to me that he hadn't blushed at all. He poured himself another glass of wine, and I began to think that the platitude I'd heard during Slovene classes at school was true: that the typical Slovene writer was resistant to alcohol until the moment it killed him.

'There was something else I wanted to ask you,' said Mum quickly, trying to lighten the atmosphere created by Elizabeta, 'about the hidden drawers in works of literature to which we need to find the key and why the writer cannot leave the key in plain view.'

'And what is the question?' asked the Important Writer with a frown.

'You said that a work of literature must be understandable but it must also remain a kind of puzzle. Because there are such puzzles in your work, where some find a great deal and others see only the surface, I wonder how you would describe what is hidden in your writing.'

'I don't hide anything,' said the writer slightly grumpily. 'Evidently all my metaphors have fallen on deaf ears. I'll try to put it slightly differently. Imagine a device, one which you have no idea what it is for. It is made up of recognizable objects, such as an axe, a wooden spoon, a plough, a toilet bowl, a pickaxe, a shovel, a coffee mill and so on. But imagine that all this has been welded together somehow into a new object, which gives the impression of a whole because the traces of the welding have been erased as if they never existed. You are faced with a puzzle. What is this unknown thing for? Perhaps you *can* use it for something, but use is not its real purpose. Its purpose is to disturb you with its mystery. The recognizable items that make it up are taken from the life that you know, but the whole is given meaning by the author's imagination, which is not his alone but is part of the creative imagination of the universe. You can call it God. I won't object. You can call it a sphinx. For a literary work that is not merely skilful linguistic manipulation is a kind of sphinx that poses questions to the reader for which there are no answers. So each encounter with a work of art is in its way deadly. Illusions plummet into the abyss. I see, madam, that my answer has not exactly made you happy.'

As the Important Writer said this Mum went deathly pale. She exchanged looks with Dad. He, too, looked unwell. Aunt Mara had stopped painting, pushed her way through to the front and was staring at the writer as if he was a monster. Uncle Vinko appeared behind her, and he looked equally alarmed. Elizabeta leaned over and whispered something in Hudorovec's ear.

'But that reminds me of something,' exclaimed Vladimir's former wife Eva, now evidently the lover of the young Captain Adam.

'Be quiet,' said Vladimir, who suddenly appeared out of the crowd. 'You're a thief and a cheat and full of empty promises.'

'Vladimir,' Dad got up to intervene, but Vladimir brusquely said, 'Stop interfering in my affairs.'

'If that's the way you want it,' replied Dad, sitting down.

Vladimir unexpectedly calmed down; he turned, elbowed his way through the crowd and disappeared.

The writer also got up. The inexplicable scene had confused him. 'It's time for me to go to the graveyard and pay my respects to my grandfather and grandmother.'

People stepped back to let him pass. He staggered, and several hands reached out to stop him falling.

'Good heavens,' he said, 'what kind of wine are you serving here?' He cautiously made his way towards the fire station.

'He's certainly had a few too many,' I heard a woman comment smugly.

'And why not?' came a man's voice in defence of the departing guest of honour. 'No one with any sense leaves a fire-brigade do sober.'

34

The Important Writer certainly wasn't leaving sober, as he staggered from one side of the road to the other in the direction of the graveyard, oblivious to his surroundings, and was almost mown down by a car that hurtled past with some drunk behind the wheel. I followed him at a safe distance but close enough to rush to his assistance if he ended up in the roadside ditch.

I wasn't entirely sure why I was following him. My first plan, to ask his advice about Elizabeta, the gypsy and I, seemed absurd after all I had heard. I followed him because I felt an inexplicable need to remain close to him and when the chance arose to ask him what he thought about my idea of becoming a writer. Part of me hoped he would try to dissuade me but the other wanted to tell him Švejk's story so that he might write a novel about him.

I wasn't clear where Švejk had disappeared to. It was only later I learned that he had been drinking with the Austrian fire-fighters, becoming great friends with them, and they had insisted that he visit them. But staying close to the writer, whom I had seen close up for the first time and in a condition where he was not completely sure what was happening to him, seemed more important than finding out where my relatives were.

At the graveyard he was in such a state that he had to lean on gravestones. Then he collapsed between the graves and lay on the grass. But before I ran to him he courageously picked himself up and marched boldly forward. Actually, he went down the slope more through the pull of gravity than intention. How he managed to find the right grave is still not clear to me, but when I came to the cross before which he finally sat down he was raking the neglected grave with his fingers and sighing, 'Granddad, Granny, Granddad, Granny.'

The plaque on the modest wooden cross bore two names: Jožef Gomboc and Ana Gomboc. They had evidently been his mother's parents.

Suddenly, he jerked forward and began vomiting. From his stomach emerged remnants of goulash, sausage, bread, wine and greenish bile. The grave where he had come to pay his respects was soon a mess – as was he, since during the convulsions, in between which his body shook uncontrollably, he rolled in his vomit like a pig in shit. The convulsions showed no sign of ending.

'Oh,' he gasped, while retching, 'oh God, let me die.'

Fearing that he might really die like a sick animal, I rushed back to the fire station. I knew I needed to get help. Among the cars parked by the roadside I noticed Vinko's battered Nissan; it was by far the oldest car there. It wasn't locked, but the key wasn't in the ignition. I rushed into the crowd looking for familiar faces.

First, I came across a scene that took my breath away. At a table beneath a tree Aranka the Fortune-Teller was holding sway. And who was sitting on the bench in front of her with her hand open other than Aunt Mara!

'Aunt Mara,' I shouted. 'Where's Švejk? I need help.'

'Why are you shouting?' she rebuked me. 'Švejk is drinking with the nice son of this nice lady who has returned all my paintings. Look,' she indicated the stack of canvases beneath the table. 'And she has apologized, and Švejk has got his tools back. She has just told me that people often become closer because of a conflict of interests. Isn't that wise of her? Sit down and she'll tell you your fortune.'

'Aunt Mara,' I said, 'you're losing it.'

Once more I began to push my way through the throng of drunken guests. I spotted Peter, Elizabeta, Adam and Eva standing in the shadow of a tree chatting as if they'd known each other for years. Peter was making fun of the 'stupid utterances' of the guest speaker. Eva was laughing, but Adam seemed rather reserved.

'Quick,' I panted, grabbing Peter's shirt sleeve, 'find Vinko, we have to go to the graveyard. Someone's dying. We've got to take him home.'

'What's got into you?' Peter pushed me away in irritation. 'No one's dying at the graveyard. People end up there only after they're dead.'

'The writer's been taken ill at the graveyard,' I explained.

'I'll go,' said Adam and ran towards his car. Elizabeta ran after him. I followed her, and Eva ran after us all shouting 'Wait!'

We squashed into an Alfa Romeo – one suspiciously like Vladimir's in which Eva had disappeared eighteen months earlier – and drove to the graveyard gates. The unfortunate writer was still lying on the grave of his grandparents vomiting, although now only a greenish liquid was emerging from his mouth.

'Oh my God,' said Eva at the sight of him. 'After all his fine words.'

'Not *his* fine words,' said Adam, 'but sulphurized wine. Quite a few villagers have already been taken ill.'

I still don't know how we managed to get the limp body of the illustrious guest to the top of the graveyard and into the car, but fifteen minutes later we were already at our house, dragging him up the steps and placing him on the bed in Švejk's room. He was still retching, so Elizabeta ran to get a plastic bowl and put it beside the bed.

'You throw up, traveller, who has drowned in the kingdom of shadows,' she said.

When Adam and Eva left Elizabeta said we had to get the writer out of his water-and-vomit-smeared clothes and bathe him.

'Are you mad?' I said. 'That would be a gross intrusion on his privacy.'

'What will Švejk say when he finds this mess on his bed?' she replied angrily. 'You dragged him here. Now be gracious and help me drag him to the bathroom.'

Although Mum's favourite writer kept jerking every few minutes as if he were about to produce more from his empty stomach, he was only semi-conscious and didn't know what was going on. I've never seen anyone so drunk. He had no doubt been bowled over by a combination of sun and wine and an empty stomach, as well as the jet of water that Švejk had contributed from the fire-fighters' hosepipe.

Elizabeta and I pulled him from the bed and dragged him into the bathroom, where we leaned him against the bath.

'Let's lift him in,' said Elizabeta, 'or he'll mess up the floor.'

With great effort we rolled the semi-conscious author into the bath.

'There,' said Elizabeta, 'now go about your business, as I'm sure you don't want to see a naked man.' She pushed me out into the hallway and locked the door.

'Hey,' I shouted, banging the door with my fists. 'What are you planning to do with him? I'm going to fetch Mum and Dad.'

'Go,' she replied. 'The writer and I will follow a thousand and one paths to madness.'

'I'll smash the door down,' I yelled, totally beside myself.

'Try doing it with your head,' she said.

I squatted in front of the bathroom door and listened to the emerging sounds. First I heard dragging, sliding, moving and Elizabeta's heavy breathing as she tried to remove the guest's shoes and undress him. Then the sound of running water and of splashing, soaping, rubbing and wringing, then more splashing. Then the shower was turned on, and it flowed evenly for some time. Then silence.

'Elizabeta,' I shouted, 'what are you doing?'

I moved forward and looked through the keyhole. I saw part of Elizabeta's back. Naked! It looked as if she was leaning over the bath, making rhythmic movements. I was filled with horror.

I banged on the door and yelled, 'Elizabeta, God will punish you for this.'

'Really?' she laughed. 'He's more likely to receive me in heaven – God likes young girls who do good works.'

'Get out of there,' I shouted, banging on the door again. 'Come out.'

The door opened. Elizabeta stood before me, a smile on her face, wearing a white T-shirt.

'What were you doing?' I demanded

'Let that remain a mystery. Have you forgotten what the writer said? Mysteries give us the will to live. When everything is explained there's no more reason to do anything.'

'When did he say that?' I asked.

'To me, privately.' She gave an enigmatic smile.

'Liar,' I put my tongue out at her.

35

The writer had dozed off beneath the running water and was slumped in the bath with his head on his chest. He was wearing Dad's dark-blue dressing-gown. His clothes were in a heap behind the door.

'Why were you naked?' I asked Elizabeta. 'I saw you through the keyhole.'

'I've already been soaked to the skin once today,' she said, 'I didn't fancy it happening twice. Are you worried I was sucking off your mum's favourite writer?'

'What if you were?' I said with a shrug. 'I hope you enjoyed it.'

'You've got a warped mind,' she replied.

'Who hasn't in this house?'

'Me,' she replied. 'I'm the only one. And you know why? Because I don't ask myself what is real and what isn't the whole time. For me, everything is real, whether it's reality or a made-up story. And, for me, everything is allowed. How else can I learn how to live?'

The writer chose this moment to raise his head, look around groggily and ask, 'Where am I?'

'It's not completely clear,' said Elizabeta. 'One possibility is that you're in our bathroom, where I've just washed you like a concerned mother; the other is that you were careless when writing your novel and have been caught in the web of your own imagination. Yet another puzzle. But you like them, don't you? So do I. Just this one here doesn't.' She punched me. 'He wants everything explained. Come on, help me get him out of the bath.'

But the writer had already recovered enough to lift himself up. We helped him back to Švejk's room where he fell on to the bed. As soon as he stretched out, his gorge started to rise again. 'Oh no,' he groaned. 'Thank you. Whoever you are.'

'Perhaps we are good angels', said Elizabeta, 'or perhaps Lucifer's grand-children. We haven't decided yet. When we have, we'll let you know. Or you can decide for us. I'll go and wash your jeans and shirt.'

I was left alone with the Important Writer. He groaned a few times and said, 'I've never felt so dizzy in my life.'

'It'll be OK,' I said absently, wondering what exactly had happened in the bathroom. Perhaps Elizabeta really had tried to avoid getting wet. Perhaps that was the only reason she had removed her T-shirt. And those rhythmic movements perhaps meant only that she was rubbing him with a towel or dressing him in Dad's dressing-gown. Maybe I was going overboard with my fears and jealousy. But I felt that the doubts would remain and keep tormenting me. I could not even get to the truth by asking the Important Writer, because in his current condition he probably had no idea what Elizabeta had done with him.

But I still had to ask the question that had prompted me to follow him to the graveyard, and that question was becoming ever more relevant.

'Can I ask you something?' I said.

'Do you have to?' he groaned.

'It's quite urgent.'

'I'd rather wait until another time. At the moment I barely know who I am.'

'It's about the puzzle you mentioned. I'd like to know whether an unsolvable mystery can cause someone to lose control of themselves and start acting against their beliefs.'

'Of course,' he replied. 'A mystery is the mother of uncertainty, which is the mother of fear, which is the father of a narrow viewpoint and hasty actions. These are not clichés or elevated phrases but words I heard spoken by an Indian holy man. A mystery can encourage and ennoble, but it can also undermine and destroy. It all depends on the part we let it play in our lives. Every puzzle is a trap set by God to lure us into his embrace. But traps are also set for us by Lucifer, who is extremely cunning and makes sure his puzzles are very similar to God's. We almost never know who is setting the puzzle and into whose trap we are falling. I hope you understand I'm speaking of our inner dynamics. The words God and Lucifer are a metaphor for our leaning towards the good or evil inside us. I'm not speaking in a religious sense.'

'I understand,' I said, although it was increasingly less clear to me what he was getting at and where his words were leading us. 'It began with a single puzzle. Now they are multiplying at such an alarming rate that no one in the family can keep up. It's as if our house was cursed. I'm afraid that in a moment of real desperation I may do something I'm afraid of. Become a murderer, for instance. Or, even worse, discover that I have an attraction towards the same sex. That bothers me, although only in connection with the girl who bathed you.'

'So you're not brother and sister?'

'No,' I replied.

'Be glad that something is happening in your life. You won't become a murderer, and all the rest is human, and the less that is human is foreign to you the more you will get from life.'

'My father says it's the fault of freedom,' I said, 'that there is no room for it in our hearts. Things that were forbidden or suppressed for many years are pouring down on us so quickly that we don't know which way to turn.'

'It's possible,' said the writer, ever more wearily.

'Just one more thing,' I said, afraid that he would pass out at any moment.

'I'd like to sleep a little. Can it wait until later?'

'One last question,' I said quickly. 'For quite some time now I've been thinking about becoming a writer. I make notes, mainly about what is happening in my family. Not as a diary but more in the form of stories where I record not only what actually happened but things I make up. Actually, transferring reality to the imagination is the only thing that stops me going mad.'

'You keep writing,' he advised, only half present. 'But a piece of advice. Hold on to your notes for ten years or even twenty. Then, illuminated by the retrospection of a mature man, they may really become literature.'

These words were followed by the sound of him snoring.

36

So ended my private conversation with the Important Writer. I was rather sorry that I hadn't read any of his books. If I had I'd probably have found it easier to understand what he'd been trying to tell me with words that were somewhat ambiguous and sounded good but were too impractical for someone seeking concrete advice. I had received no usable answers to my questions, and there was no opportunity for just the two of us to talk later as the rest of the family returned – with the exception of Švejk, who had made so many new friends that it had proved impossible to tear him away from them, said Vladimir.

At the news that we had a very drunk writer in our house, Mum and Dad reacted first with doubt, then amazement and finally with unconcealed delight. When they heard that he had thrown up on his grandparents' grave and that his presence in our house was the result of my concern for this health, they both patted me amiably on the shoulder.

They were somewhat less delighted when I told them that Elizabeta had bathed him and washed his jeans and shirt.

'Were you there when she did it?' asked Peter.

'Of course I was. I helped.'

'I hope you're telling the truth,' said Aunt Mara, 'otherwise I'll pull all her hair out, the little slut.'

'Please,' said Dad, 'we have an interesting guest in the house. It's nice that they took care of him as they should. I don't want to hear an unkind word.'

'Regardless of the fact', muttered Peter, 'that at the fire station he spoke about a device, as if he knew our family's greatest secret.'

'I see nothing significant in that,' said Dad dismissively. 'There are universal metaphors that are in harmony with one another although there is no connection between them. American Indians, Ancient Egyptians and Papua New Guineans have similar myths about the creation of the world, although they never encountered each other. Archetypes are not a conspiracy, although it's true that we always think the worst when we encounter such synchronicity.'

'OK, you have fun with your writer,' said Peter, turning and going to his room.

'What's got into him?' asked Mum in surprise.

'I think that he's finally in love,' said Vinko.

'I hope it's not with one of those gypsy girls he was talking to at the fire station,' said Mum.

'What if it is?' said Dad. 'It's high time he dragged himself away from that computer of his and touched something real.'

'I don't want my son touching a gypsy girl,' objected Mum.

'You're drunk,' said Dad. 'We're all drunk. This is no time for serious conversations. Let's wait for our guest to shake off his hangover, and then we can talk to him.'

'Perhaps he'll be so grateful for all the help that he'll stay for supper,' said Mum delightedly. 'I'll start cooking.'

But when the writer finally emerged from Švejk's room he was so alarmed by all the attention that he clammed up and became almost sullen. Dad's dressing-gown was too big for him, and he looked ridiculous in it. He was evidently aware of this, so his unfriendliness became even more marked.

He wanted to know where he'd been found, who had undressed him and where his clothes were. Elizabeta ran outside and fetched his washed and dried socks, jeans, underpants and shirt.

'I should iron them,' she said.

But the Important Writer tore them from her hands. 'What about my jacket?'

'It's hanging on the bathroom door,' said Elizabeta. 'I sponged it a bit, but I didn't dare wash it. I'll bring it straight away.'

'I'll get it myself.' He turned abruptly and went back upstairs.

'I don't think he'll stay for supper,' said Dad.

'How dare you do something like that?' Mara rebuked Elizabeta.

'You're right,' observed Vinko. 'I know I'd feel uncomfortable if someone told me that a young girl had undressed me and bathed me without my knowledge.'

'No, she shouldn't have done it,' added Dad, 'although I'm sure her intentions were good.'

'Oh, I'm sure they were,' said Aunt Mara sarcastically. 'When they next write an essay at school about one of his books she can add a drawing and say, "That's what his prick looks like. I saw it with my own eyes."'

'You're just jealous, Mum,' said Elizabeta with a sweet smile, 'because you didn't get the chance to paint it and add it to your rich collection.'

Aunt Mara gasped and turned red.

'Please,' Mum intervened, 'no vulgarity.'

Dad and Vinko jumped up and rushed to help Mara, who looked sick and on the point of collapse.

'We've all drunk too much today,' said Vladimir.

'Except for me,' said Elizabeta with satisfaction, 'because I haven't drunk anything at all and have been a good girl in every respect. Nosy but good. Although it's not worth being well behaved. It's boring, and you don't get any credit for it.'

'I'll give you praise,' said Aunt Mara, half rising from her chair, but Vinko and Dad pulled her back down. She tried once more to free herself from their grasp, but just then the Important Writer reappeared.

He stood in the doorway and smiled in embarrassment. He was looking terribly crumpled; I don't know why he wouldn't let anyone iron his jeans and shirt. His jacket was rolled up under his arm.

'Please, come in,' said Mum after a few moments in a sickly sweet voice. 'We're about to have supper.'

'Oh,' said the writer, looking at his watch. 'I think I'd better be going, thanks. But before I go there's something I'd like to ask.'

'Please, please,' said Dad, offering him a chair. 'We're glad you're here and it's an honour to finally meet you.'

The writer sat down without replying and for some time stared into space. He cradled his jacket, still probably covered in vomit, in his lap.

'It's not my first visit to this house,' he said. 'In fact, I grew up here. Thirty years ago my father sold it to the people you later bought it from.'

'Oh,' enthused Mum, 'that's such amazing news that I don't know what to say.'

'Very interesting,' said Dad, with a shadow of concern on his face.

'Did you start writing here?' asked Mum.

'Only a diary. From the age of eleven. Every day. I even illustrated it.'

'That must be interesting reading,' said Mum.

The Important Writer smiled. He suddenly became pleasant, human; I hadn't realized he had so much warmth inside him.

'Interesting for me,' he said, 'especially because I never saw that diary again. It remained here. You haven't found it in the house, by any chance . . . ?' He looked at each of us in turn. In the case of Elizabeta his eyes quickly passed on; clearly he was embarrassed by the bath incident.

'We found many things but not a diary,' said Dad.

'Why didn't you take it with you?' asked Mum.

The Important Writer explained that when his parents moved he had been in Australia and he used to hide the diary in various places around the house to keep it from the prying eyes of his sister. Then he simply forgot about it. When he returned he wanted to try to retrieve it, but the previous owner wasn't keen on the idea of someone poking around the cellars, attics and hidden corners, so he gave up and accepted that he would never see his boyhood writings again.

'But you have renovated the house,' he said. 'You might have come across a diary during the renovation work.'

'Regrettably not,' replied Dad. 'Do you remember where you hid it?'

'That's the problem,' said the Important Writer. 'There were a number of notebooks, at least five, and I hid each in a different location so that my sister, who was always searching for them, would not find them all in one go. I vaguely recall that I stuffed some behind the roofbeams, others behind barrels in the cellar and behind the tool cupboard in Dad's workshop, and other places as well. A shame,' he added. 'I'd love to see what I wrote.'

'If anything turns up we'll let you know immediately,' said Dad.

'They're probably worth quite a bit, those early diaries,' said Elizabeta. 'A lot of people would want to read them.'

'I certainly would,' said the Important Writer. 'I'd like to read them. As far as others are concerned, I doubt it. But I'm prepared to consider a reward should you find them.'

Mum and Dad looked highly embarrassed.

'Elizabeta expressed herself awkwardly,' said Mum quickly. 'There's no question of our wanting any kind of reward.'

'Well, whatever,' said the writer, getting up and putting his business card on the table. 'If anything turns up, call me and we'll sort something out.'

With these words he moved towards the door and headed for the fire station.

'You little bitch,' said Mum to Elizabeta with tears in her eyes. 'Why did you have to do that? You drove him away.'

For the first time I could ever remember Aunt Mara took her daughter's side. 'Oh-ho,' she said, 'someone has fallen in love with the little writer.'

'You shut up,' snapped Mum. 'Have you ever read any of his books?'

'I don't have time even for useful pastimes,' replied Mara.

'Instead of his books we can read something else,' observed Elizabeta enigmatically. She now held up a piece of folded paper. I had no idea where it had appeared from. She unfolded it and triumphantly showed it off.

'I hope it's not your school report,' said Mum, still in a hostile tone, 'because that would make rather depressing reading.'

'This,' said Elizabeta, showing the paper to Peter, who had just come back in the room, 'is the speech that the Important Writer was searching for so desperately as he stood in front of the microphone.'

'It can't be,' said Peter, tearing it from her grasp. 'I'm sure that was a ploy.'

'No, it wasn't,' said Elizabeta, snatching it back with a rapid movement. 'I found it in his jacket pocket.'

'We all saw him searching through his pockets,' objected Peter, more heatedly. Recently he had become increasingly stubborn when it came to defending his theories.

'He evidently forgot that he has two inside pockets,' said Elizabeta, 'and in his panic he forgot to check.'

'Then this is the real speech,' said Mum in delight, 'not what he was forced to improvise. *Now* we will feel the real power of his words.'

'I've experienced stronger,' said Elizabeta, and she began to read. At first, she read nicely, as if reading for her teacher in a Slovene class, but towards the end she began to act the fool.

'"As a child, I wished to see the world. I saw it, lived in many countries, travelled through more than ninety, became accustomed to being abroad. But now, as I look from these hills at the lower ground in Austria and across that to the Pohorje Hills and beyond, to where I yearned to go as a young boy, it seems to me that I travelled a different world, not the one I longed for. As a child I wanted to be successful and well known. I have also achieved that. But it brings me no real joy. If anything it is a burden to me, and I would almost prefer to be anonymous, the child that longed one day to become something. In longing there is more freedom, more hope, more energy than in fulfilment. Now, as I stand before you, fifty years old, I do not wish to be a child again, but I would like once more to have a child's sense of longing; I would like the world once again to be unknown, full of secrets."'

'That's nice. That's wise,' said Mum enthusiastically, when Elizabeta paused for a moment. 'Why are you trying to spoil it? You should be reading it with feeling.'

'What feeling?' said Peter with a frown. 'This is worse than what he came up with at the celebration. Probably he realized at the last moment that he'd written a dud and so he pretended that he'd lost the speech. A collection of sentimental clichés with self-praise oozing from every pore, and his so-called insights are so shallow that even a frog would crack its skull open if it dived in head first.'

'Why do you hate him so?' Mum asked Peter. 'Why can't you find one good thing to say about him?'

'Should I have to?' asked Peter in surprise. 'Who is he? Another lost uncle?'

'Out of respect for literature –' Mum began, but Peter interrupted her.

'What literature, for God's sake? "I would like once more to have a child's sense of longing; I would like the world once again to be unknown, full of secrets." Is that literature? Wake up, Mum. We're on the threshold of the twenty-first century when only science will retain any value. That's where the secrets are, not in shallow words.'

'Sometimes I'm really worried about the world you live in,' replied Mum. 'Of course, you have every right to do so, but I'm your mother and don't want you to live a sterile life.'

'You should be asking what kind of life we are living in this family', said Peter, 'and who should take the blame.'

With these words he turned and stormed off. We saw him running towards the woods.

'Anyway,' said Elizabeta, 'to continue. "Memory is alive, and the memory of the village where I spent my childhood –"'

'Stop, please,' Mum interrupted and began to cry again.

'Put that away,' said Dad, taking control. 'You had no right to steal it. You must return it to him. Here's the address.' He held out the business card.

'No,' said Mara, getting up, 'not his address. God knows what she'd write to him.'

Dad hesitated for a moment and then put the card in his pocket. 'I'll do it.' He held out his hand.

'That will be difficult,' said Elizabeta with a bright smile, 'because it no longer exists.'

With these words she ripped the Important Writer's planned speech to shreds and let them fall to the floor.

'Sorry, Mara,' said Dad as he stepped closer to Elizabeta. He slapped her with such force that she was thrown against the door frame and then slowly slid to the floor. A drop of blood trickled from the corner of her mouth.

'What are you doing?' yelled Mum.

'I don't know,' replied Dad calmly. 'You tell me.' He looked around and asked, 'Does anyone know what I'm doing?'

He turned and, head down, went to his room.

37

The next day I began an intensive search for the writer's lost diaries. I wasn't clear why I was doing this. One of the reasons was certainly curiosity; another was the hope that if I found the diaries it would give me an excuse to visit the Important Writer and continue our discussion about my future.

But curiosity was the most powerful reason. This was connected with a feeling for which I could find neither a name nor a source, as if I were hoping (or fearing) that by discovering the diaries I would get to the bottom of an important secret. While rummaging in the cellars, the attic, outbuildings and other parts of the house where a dusty notebook might be hiding I came across things which had not been hidden by the Important Writer. It soon became evident that members of my family also liked to hide things.

Poking around in private things is, of course, not a nice thing to do, but my excuse was that I did not uncover the items intentionally but came across them by chance. Perhaps I misinterpreted or misconnected a number of things, but the image of my family created by my chance finds disturbed and depressed me. For the first time in my life it occurred to me that in interpersonal contacts we may see at most only 10 per cent of who we really are.

In the end I was forced to acknowledge that I, too, concealed what I really thought from others, mainly because I feared they would see me in the 'wrong' light. I wanted to create the light by which they saw me myself. The absolute right to privacy, which Dad during his 'ethical lectures' had always cited as the primary characteristic of responsible freedom, was a double-edged sword. In defence of our privacy we had become false and hypocritical; behind smiles and politeness there often lurked something completely different.

When I had thoroughly searched every nook and cranny in which the Important Writer's diaries might have been concealed I asked myself where I would hide writings I didn't want anyone else to find. The answer was to hand: I had hidden the draft of my story 'The Thing' and notes on other events in the family beneath the wooden floor in my room, under a floorboard that was cut off in the corner beneath the window and which was therefore easy to lift. For a long time I had kept the story under my mattress, but after I discovered the floorboard the space beneath it seemed safer, especially when I heard Mum say that mattresses should be aired regularly. I covered the board with a heap of books and magazines. It seemed almost impossible that anyone would find what I had written.

I began to wonder whether there were other similar hiding places in other rooms; maybe there were and no one knew about them, since when the house was renovated some rooms were only repainted. The writer's diaries could be concealed in some such hidey-hole.

But searching the rooms and bedrooms of other family members was not easy, for, in spite of the fine summer, we all spent most of the time lurking indoors.

The only one who went to work was Vinko, who locked his room each time and took the key with him. It was easiest to get into Mara's studio, the former pigsty, in which she had also made a bedroom for herself, for since Švejk's spectacular appearance at the fire-fighting event they had once more set up business down by the road. Švejk was hammering at the fire engine, transforming it for the third time into God knows what, and this attracted walkers on their way to the tourist farm on the hill to whom Mara could sell portraits and already completed paintings of Švejk at work.

Mara would lock the studio door but always left the window open, and it wasn't difficult to climb in. To avoid being caught, I searched quickly and systematically: first the floor, then the walls and finally the ceiling. The studio was in a real mess, and before I could be sure I had searched thoroughly I had to move quite a number of canvases, frames, boxes and pieces of furniture. In the corner where she slept, the greatest problem was the wooden bed, which for some reason was fastened to the wall. Much could be hidden there, but before I could investigate I had to remove the heap of paintings that Mara had stuffed under the bed.

I was just about to move these 'works of art' when I heard a key in the lock.

I left the paintings and threw myself through the window just before the door opened; I ran around the outbuilding into the house and shut myself in my room. I was breathing deeply. For some reason I was suddenly overcome by a terrible sense of fear and began to cry out loud. I felt that something incomprehensible was happening to me. What fate did the device have in store for me?

One by one, I got into the other rooms. In all of them I searched for hidden corners, drawers, cracks, holes, depressions, anywhere that something might be concealed. And in each room my methodical persistence, instead of the diaries, led me to things that I wasn't looking for (but which were, when I later thought about it, looking for me).

In Vinko's room, which I climbed into through a partly open window, for he locked the door even when he went out for a short walk, I found a large brown envelope beneath the mattress. At first I wanted to leave it where it was, as it was obviously not the diaries, but curiosity got the better of me. I pulled out from it a sheaf of X-rays of various organs and limbs: lungs, stomach, kidneys, bladder, spine, arms and legs. There were also some cranial scans. On each slide someone had circled with a red marker pen something reminiscent of a dark walnut. On some it was round, on others elongated, in other cases furrowed and on some it had excrescences that protruded like claws in every direction. In every case it was obvious that it was a growth rather than normal brain tissue.

Among the test results I found a bunch of hospital notes on Vinko's health. To judge from the dates it seemed he had been to see one specialist or another on a weekly basis. Although all the diagnoses bore his name, they were so diverse that they might have belonged to twenty different patients. 'A typical papilloma on the right of the floor of the mouth. A granuloma above tooth 5 in the upper-right quadrant, an apical process? The throat irritated, the mucosa thin. With regard to all the tests the patient has undergone, it is worth mentioning fatty liver.'

And the following: 'Numerous soft fibromas under the arms and on the neck, small fibromas on the forehead, a flat soft fibroma the size of a bean on the left side of the chest, a seborrheic verruca and a smallish erythema with a small scab on the left wrist. Diagnosis: *Fibromata mollia colli et axilae bill, Fibromata faciei, Verruca seborrhoica thoracis.*'

As well as: 'Multiple tumorous growths of various sizes in the gallbladder, spleen, liver, stomach, oesophagus, lungs, bladder, duodenum and in the small and large intestine. Similar growths appear also in the lumbar part of the back and two on the neck. A particularly large growth in the brain. Smaller growths in all the joints and one in the nasal cavity. All the tumours are primary and malignant but in a dormant state and with no secondary growths. Blood count normal. The condition is astonishing and completely incompatible with current medical knowledge. According to all the rules, the patient should be dead. The patient urgently needs further tests but refuses them. He claims to be feeling good, better than ever. He does not take any alternative medicines or herbal concoctions, eats and drinks normally, sleeps well, has no mental problems and a positive outlook. IQ normal.'

I put the test results back in the envelope, replaced the envelope under the mattress and climbed back out of the window. The device did not have merely a negative influence, it also caused miracles to happen. However, the unbelievable number of tumours in Uncle Vinko's body must also have been the result of its influence. It was toying with Vinko in the cruellest fashion: destroying him with one hand and preserving his health with the other, in spite of the death it had sowed inside him.

As well as looking for the writer's diaries I began to be increasingly interested how the sphinx was affecting other members of the family.

38

In Elizabeta's room I looked through the schoolbooks and exercise books. In the one for English grammar I found a folded sheet of paper on which was written 'Plan for eliminating the family'. This manifesto was written in a very careful hand and included details under the heading 'Method of execution'.

Vladimir, with his own pistol in the left ear; Vinko, a hundred blows to the head with a large cabbage; Peter, a large piece of meteorite hammered into his arse; his younger brother, to whom I gave my virginity because of the gypsy dogs, the same dogs should bite off his prick and rip his insides out; Švejk, shut him in the water tank on the fire engine and slowly fill it with water; *capo di banda*, Švejk and Vladimir impale him on the lightning conductor, where he remains like a scarecrow until he falls apart; both exemplary mothers, Švejk runs over them in the fire engine and the others collect their remains and roast them with onion and garlic for a last supper . . .

Our Father which art in heaven,
Hallowed be thy name.
Thy kingdom come.
Thy will be done in earth, as it is in heaven.
Give us this day our daily bread.
And forgive us our trespasses, as we forgive those
who trespass against us.
And lead us not into temptation . . .

The unexpected prayer flowed into something that sounded like a love letter:

> Prince of my dreams, you probably don't know you are the prince of my dreams and that I dream of you also when I'm thinking of other things, although the things I think about are so terrible that I'd rather my brain dissolved. Within me there is such a desire for the good, the beautiful, the compassionate, the self-sacrificing, such a desire to love purely everything around me, this whole world, which you created perfect but for one flaw – me. Why did you get it so wrong in my case? Was it intentional, in the hope that I would love you even more unconditionally as a result? Or was it a mistake, a single exception in your career of making perfect worlds? I'm not blaming you at all, even you must have your fun, but why didn't you endow me with some other mistake than that I am afraid to declare my love for you, to acknowledge it to others, to myself and even to you? Why did you make me in such a way that you had to share me with the devil? Was it for fun? Because for me it isn't: I have to tell you that our *ménage à trois* is terribly tiring, and sooner or later I'll have to choose between the two of you, and because I don't know which of you needs me most the decision will be a difficult one. But even if I decide for your competitor, whom I feel ever closer to, I will always miss you and always love you, even when he impales me on his horns . . . Help me, my love. Help me. There's still time. But the clock is ticking, the minutes are passing . . .

In Vladimir's room I found nothing special, just some pages of memoir of his Partisan years crossed out and beside it the draft of a confession that he had taken part in some post-war massacres and later he was responsible for putting hundreds of innocent people behind bars. This was hard for me to understand; it was so distant in time and didn't really interest me; these were stories from a time that had not only passed but which no longer existed.

Only one sentence stuck in my mind from Vladimir's 'confession', which was intended to be found only after his death: 'Loyalty to an idea is as misguided as fidelity to a woman; both are whores that drink your blood and then discard you.'

I thought that something like that could not happen to me; I was without ideas or a woman, nor did I know how to be faithful. The confession, which he described as his 'last piece of heroism', passed me by like most things connected with Vladimir. I didn't find the diaries in his room.

Nor did I in Peter's room, although there I hoped to find at least personal secrets that would overshadow all the rest. Peter was not a person to use paper. He kept most things on diskettes and CD-ROMs; his room was as clean, tidy and functional as an estate agent's office – almost sterile. Whatever secrets he was hiding were certainly on the computer, but they could not be accessed without a password, which recently he had taken to changing on almost a daily basis. And so Peter remained the only one that I found out nothing new about; he remained an enigma, the elder brother to whom I had never been close.

The greatest surprises awaited me in Mum's and Dad's rooms. Ever since they had converted their shared bedroom into a guest room, in which Švejk was now sleeping, they had lived on different floors – Dad on the first, Mum on the ground floor – each with bookshelves on all four walls, each in his or her own world. These worlds occasionally met in the dining-room or on their rare shared walks.

Whether they ever visited each other at night remained an open question that no one worried about too much. Although love was probably no longer the foundation of the relationship they kept on building, with effort and not without success, there was much they shared, including concern for the family and its future. And although they weren't as solid as they had once been, on the chessboard of our fates they still played the king and queen. It had not yet happened that any other figure had had them in check, let alone checkmate. Their authority, albeit weakened, remained the only thing that could be relied on when things got bad.

This they knew, and so they maintained the appearance of authority, even when it was clear to other family members that it represented form without content. The form worked as long the rest of us provided it with content in the belief that we had no other choice. And even Švejk did not provide an alternative, even though the most naïve among us hoped that he would.

Mum did not lock her room. As her morning marathon usually lasted a good hour, I could search not only her hidden corners but also her drawers and shelves. Mum liked order and regularly placed her numerous jottings, records, notes and newspaper cuttings in a folder marked from A to Z. This contained everything imaginable: from recipes to meditation and massage techniques; from yoga to healing herbs to tables of the positive effects of aerobic exercise. And much more besides.

Of least interest were the recipes for cakes, rolls, fruit salads and other sweet dishes. But it was while flicking through them that I found an item that had been placed there so that it would disappear among things that Mum knew no one else was interested in. At first sight it looked like a recipe for an exotic cake. Even the heading was written in such a way that a potentially interested eye might pass over it.

'RECIPE', was written in capital letters and then, 'for a life of guilt, remorse and missed opportunities.' And then:

My dearest Švejk, this recipe is for you. Use it to prepare a sweet mixture of memories of the event which led me to deny your existence for all those years. Try to understand me, try to forgive me. When you fled from our mother, who wanted you to be something exceptional, and sought refuge with me, your younger half-sister who knew you were not exceptional and knew how to convince you of that, we were certainly too young to know what close relatives may and may not do. You believed that angels constantly watched us from above, collecting data regarding who would go to heaven and who to hell. Do you remember what you asked me? What if we only pretended to be kissing? If the angels see we are only pretending they won't be angry, they'll think we are playing and whoever is playing cannot be sinning, for play is God's gift. Even then it was clear to me that there was something wrong with you and that your whole life you would remain a likeable oddball. We can't pretend, said I, thinking myself cleverer than you; it would be too hard. But if there's no other choice we'll just have to grit our teeth, you said. And I said that we couldn't kiss with gritted teeth, that would be even harder. In any case, the angels are not so naïve that they'd fail to recognize cheating. If we have to pretend, let's do so convincingly.

And we did.

I read on:

Do you remember how we pretended with all our hearts and without effort? The angels didn't even suspect what we were doing. The only one to suspect was Mum. And you, always honest and open because you didn't know how to be any other way, told her everything. Nothing happened to you, her pet. But I was forced into an abortion and spent two years in a reformatory. Do you remember, Švejk? I swore then I never wanted to see you again. But now that you have reappeared in my life and act as if you never betrayed me, after the first wave of anger, even hatred, I have been overtaken by a new, unfamiliar feeling: a sense of obligation that, to the best of my ability, I must take care of my idiot half-brother, who I am sure does everything, even the worst things, with the best intentions. There are few people like that – perhaps you are the only one. But you can't help it, and it is my duty to protect you in so far as I am able. I will probably never send you this letter. It will stay among these recipes until my death. In any case, why should I write to you about something you already know? I wrote it for myself, and now I feel easier. Now I know that there is no one who can understand you as I do. You have become the child I was not allowed to bear. When I take care of you, its father, I have the feeling that I am also taking care of that child, no less than I care for my sons, my husband and other members of the family. My life is now complete. Thank you, my little Švejk, for making this possible.

I recalled Elizabeta's words in the circle of dogs by the stream. 'Will it be enough if we just pretend to be kissing?' Elizabeta had been in Mum's room before me! But that was *before* the arrival of the Important Writer. What had she been looking for if not his diaries? Was she driven only by curiosity? Or was she looking for something specific?

I hoped I would find the answer in Dad's room, which was always unlocked, as Mum, who was responsible for the housework, regularly cleaned it. Not only that, Dad's room was an informal family library where we all went to borrow books, usually with Dad's permission but also when he was not there. It didn't bother him if we went in uninvited. However, no one abused this privilege. Dad's privacy was one thing that even the nosiest among us respected.

So when I entered his room, when he and Mum had gone on one of their rare walks together, I had a bad conscience, which I hadn't had when looking through the other rooms. I knew there would be no secrets hidden in the books, since they were accessible to everyone. If Dad did have anything to hide, he would put it elsewhere, maybe in one of the drawers of the large writing desk. It would not be like him to hide things under the mattress or the bed.

After all my discoveries the writer's diaries had become so marginal that I was no longer actively looking for them. It was more than clear that any secret of a retired secondary-school history teacher would be in written form and that it would be among his papers. There were so many of these that I lost hope before I even started. I rummaged through drawers, the folders that lay on the desk and the floor and through the heaps of paper in the cupboard. If I wanted to examine each sheet of paper carefully I would need ten hours.

I had already decided to abandon the whole enterprise when my eye was drawn to a metal container on the desk containing pencils, pens, a letter-opener and so on. Among the various coloured pens I could see a rolled-up piece of paper, seemingly ordinary and uninteresting, with numbers scribbled on the outside. But when I pulled it out and unrolled it, there was a densely typed text on the inside, entitled 'To all those it concerns'. I read on:

The recent encounter with a respected writer whose work I have never read (I'm more interested in essays and history) presented me with the painful truth that I was like an engine driver who, weary of the demands and monotony of the timetable, and wanting only peace and quiet, drives his train on to an overgrown sidetrack and leaves it there to rust slowly. Perhaps I did this because of a sense of helplessness at the Great Mystery, convinced that it was better not to do anything than to make a wrong step. But the writer's observations about three loves and one death, although it sounded like an off-the-cuff statement of the kind that probably represents more of a burden to a writer than a blessing, wormed its way into my head and burrowed its way through all my defences.

I realized that of the three loves he mentioned – for ourselves, for others and for God – I had not realized even one, at least not in such a way that I could be satisfied with the results. To love oneself without contempt and with understanding, which stops before it becomes self-regard, is probably the hardest of all. Here, I have failed in every way. I didn't even know that we were supposed to love ourselves let alone that true love towards others and God arose from settled relations between the ego and the self, as Jung would have said. My love towards the Other, for others, for all those who have come into my life and become my family, is more reminiscent of responsible leadership of an organization than commitment. As if the family were a secondary school of which I was the head.

And so it's not unusual that I don't understand anything that is happening around me and that I don't want to be concerned with the traumas of the other members of the family. Even the signs of sexual maturity I notice in my sons and Elizabeta, although natural and harmless, fill me with revulsion. I am incapable of feeling what others feel. I am convinced that my standards are the only valid ones; everything else is pathological deviation. Even though the unresolved relationship between my wife and her half-brother Švejk is a matter for the two of them, I can't help despising the mother of my children and life companion through good times and bad for her inability to share the secret with myself and other members of the family.

I won't waste any words on what I think about the habits and foibles of the interloper Mara and her so-called art. Of all of them, the one I dislike the least is Vinko, probably because he's so wishy-washy that I barely notice him. I feel sorry for Vladimir because he is a victim of the history that he helped to create, and it has come back to strike him like a boomerang. That I understand, and I can sympathize with his trauma to some extent. The only one who evokes within me a hint of what a very generous person would call warmth is the family fool Švejk, but even that feeling is marred by occasional doubts about how genuine he is, by the suspicion that he is an excellent fraud and that he came to us with impure intentions. That is my relationship with the family I am supposed to love. None at all.

And love of God? It has always been easy for me to say I am an atheist. That gave me automatic access to the club of progressive, superior people. Perhaps I was even ashamed to clarify my relationship with the fundamental dimension of existence. My life reminds me of the shapeless mystery we locked in the garden shed and stopped talking about because it demanded too much of us. Individual parts are recognizable, but as a whole it is unlike anything, and the purpose of the life that I have ruined with a high degree of clear and decisive rational judgement remains a mystery. All that is left to me is this death.

I am writing this because I want all those who I disappointed to understand at least some of the reasons for my decision to quit the game in which I am not needed. I apologize to Vladimir because I will use his gun to achieve my goal. Considering that he used it to kill so many innocent people, he'll probably be happy that the last bullet will kill someone who sentenced himself to death after careful consideration and was convinced beyond any doubt of his own guilt. Although only of not knowing why he came into this world. Why he is here. Why he is what he is.

I rolled up Dad's 'last testament' and pushed it back among the pens and pencils. My first thought was that I must quickly find Vladimir's pistol and bury it somewhere in the woods. But Vladimir was in his room, so I decided to sneak into Švejk's to see if I could find anything interesting there. It was empty, since he had been spending more and more time with his friends at the gypsy settlement latterly. I wasn't at all surprised that he felt better there than with us.

Death had moved into our house, while with the gypsies there was life. Švejk could feel that and was slowly leaving us. I didn't expect any earth-shattering discoveries in his room, at best a bunch of photographs of the newly appointed fire-fighter in his badly tailored uniform, which I duly found, and photographs of his tour with Aranka the Fortune-Teller, which I also found. And it did not seem impossible that beneath the bed I would find at least one of Mara's depictions of Švejk repairing the fire engine. After all, he had also kept a sheaf of newspaper cuttings about his historic battle with a column of tanks.

But when I reached under the bed, instead of photographs I found a bundle of exercise books. I pulled them out and saw what I had been looking for from the very beginning. I put them under my arm and hurried to my room.

And locked the door.

39

Leafing through the childhood diaries of the Important Writer became a kind of compulsion. I didn't read them from beginning to end but turned the pages and stopped when a word or two caught my eye. They covered the period from the age of eleven to fifteen and had the collective title *On the Waves of Life*. This didn't seem very original, and the writing showed anything but literary talent.

> Mum was making lunch. I was bored. I didn't feel like working. I was longing for something . . . but I don't know what. In the afternoon I looked through the window at the sun shining and watched two sweet little birds hopping around the branches of the apricot tree in front of my window.

And elsewhere:

> Today we had a maths test. Yesterday I bet Jožek a bottle of lemonade that I would get a 10. I didn't manage and almost made a complete mess of it. I answered the first question, but the others filled me with fear. I eventually managed two more. I'll get a 7 or at best an 8. Terrible!

The style didn't change much over the years, and once or twice I got the feeling that the early entries were more interesting than the later ones. This, for instance, did not particularly inspire me:

> Today is my birthday. I'm fourteen, which is a lot. I can hardly believe it. I wish that from today onwards I will be the kind of person who never gives up.

This seemed more interesting:

As usual, Mum was late with breakfast and Dad was complaining. That made her angry, and in the end she had a real attack of nerves. She said that Dad and I wanted to do nothing but eat, that she would go somewhere and we could cook for ourselves. Dad said that we were already cooking for ourselves anyway. Of course, lunch was now out of the question again. Dad and I teased her, and she got so angry that I thought she was going to pour the leftover soup from yesterday all over us.

Actually, I soon got fed up with looking through the writer's diary. I still don't know what I expected to find there. I then opened a fatter notebook with the title *Sketches, Poems, Plays and Reports*. At the age of eleven Mum's favourite writer produced poems such as this:

> Cold winter has hurried in
> And covered all the ground.
> Nothing green remains,
> There is snow all around.

Even at that age he was assailed by fears of ageing:

> Youth rushes by like a shadow
> And is lost beyond the hills.
> Icy tears my heart fills.
> Oh, happy youth, why have you left?
> Youth does not listen, because it is deaf.

The sketches were more interesting, where among other things I found the following:

About a kilometre from our house is a small wood where there is a gypsy settlement made up of three modest cottages. They were built by the gypsies themselves. Because they are not good at building their homes are rather sad. One wall is higher than the other, another leans, the third bulges and the fourth is cracked. The roof is torn in a number of places, and smoke comes from the holes. It can't come through the chimney because there isn't one. But on the whole gypsies have modest requirements and so they are satisfied with what they have.

And so on.

Among the short stories, which had simple titles – 'My Sister Saved Me', 'April Fool', 'My Little Pigeon', 'The Earth Is Tired', 'Ghosts', etc. – my eye was caught by the last one in the notebook entitled 'The Object'. When I read it my heart, as the author wrote in his poem, was filled with 'icy tears'.

> This afternoon Dad found a strange object in the orchard. It was unlike anything that any of us had ever seen before. It had no flat surface on which it could stand. From the central mass there stuck out in all directions without any order or symmetry all kinds of iron, aluminium and even wooden things. Among them you could recognize the twisted forms of a shovel, a pick, a hoe, perhaps a scythe or sickle, perhaps a rake and other tools, but these were only the beginning or perhaps the end of what the object might be. Mum said it was a bad joke by a drunken village blacksmith and that we should bury it and forget about it. Dad disagreed. He said that every unknown thing should first be researched and given a name and a meaning. No, Mum insisted, secrets should be left alone because they are dangerous. This object had been sent by the devil to test us. We must get rid of it as soon as possible, otherwise it could destroy our lives and hang over our house like an eternal curse . . .

I couldn't read on. I felt dizzy, and the notebook fell to the floor. I had an urgent need for fresh air. I rushed from the house and headed for the woods. I staggered from tree to tree as long as my legs would carry me. But soon I could no longer feel the ground beneath my feet, and I lay on the moss among the spruces. I gathered up enough strength to drag myself to the nearest tree and leaned against its trunk.

From the host of ideas that swarmed in my head like hornets, two questions slowly crystallized. Was the device in the writer's story real, and had it appeared when he grew up in this house? Or had he thought it up and (perhaps with the power of its symbolism through some strange energy channels) so infected the house that years later it became our family hallucination?

The dilemma I had posed to Švejk came back to smack me in the face. Does only that which can be touched exist or can that which merely pretends to be real also exist? Can both exist at the same time? And, if so, which has the most influence, the greater presence? That the device, whether it was real or merely a hallucination, was influencing us all was beyond doubt. We were gradually becoming strangers not only to each other but to ourselves. We were being transformed, as Elizabeta had correctly deduced, into the opposite of what we wanted to be. The device had concealed God from us, and Lucifer had supplanted him as our third love.

A hallucination is hard to destroy, but if the device was real we could easily melt or break it down or take it apart using Švejk's welding equipment. It might perhaps then lose its hellish power, and the curse would be over.

At that moment I knew what needed to be done. The device had to be dragged from the shed and destroyed. If the others refused to help, I would do it alone. This would become my sacred duty. It struck me that I shouldn't mention the writer's story or my fears to the rest of the family. I should destroy the thing myself without telling anyone. I suddenly saw myself in the role of the family's saviour. That gave me new energy. I ran back to the house.

Mara and Švejk were no longer beside the road. Švejk had had to take the fire engine back to the fire station and park it next to the other one. The weather forecast predicted thunder and lightning. The head of the fire brigade wanted both vehicles full of water and available to the fire-fighters as quickly as possible. Švejk had not objected, particularly since soon after the celebration he had been accepted into the brigade as a fully fledged member. When and how he had completed the necessary examinations, he was reluctant to tell us.

But he brushed his dress uniform thoroughly every day. He put it on a number of times and paraded around the house in it. He gave the impression that he could hardly wait for the first fire; he was eager to show that he did know how to direct his jet of water where it was actually needed. At the same time he could not conceal the fact that he missed his vehicle, which had given his life meaning. With the vehicle (as well as Švejk) gone the bait that had encouraged passing visitors to buy Mara's paintings had also disappeared. When, for two days in a row, she had not sold a single one she packed away her things and retreated to her studio. She became solitary and tetchy.

And so there was no one by the road to see how I ran towards the shed in which we had shut the device eighteen months earlier. Vinko was at work; Peter had gone off somewhere, Elizabeta, too; Mum and Dad were both in their rooms; and Švejk was with the gypsies. I peered through the dirty window of the shed. When my eyes had become accustomed to the gloom I could make out only indistinct shadows. It looked as if someone had moved the object from its usual place. I went around the corner to check the padlock. I discovered that the door was ajar and that someone had cut through the shank of the padlock.

I took hold of the door and opened it.

The shed contained nothing but two shovels, a pickaxe and a rake. On the ground in the corner was a crate of rotten potatoes.

Of the mysterious object there was no trace.

40

I don't know how long I stared inside in the stubborn hope that there would be a flash of light and the device would stand once more where it had been for the past eighteen months. I was overcome by fear and agitation. But this changed in waves to unlimited relief. I rushed to tell Dad that the sphinx had disappeared and that we were finally freed from the curse.

But after a few steps I stopped. It struck me that with its unexplained disappearance the Great Mystery had become even more mysterious. The feeling of relief dissipated, and I collapsed in the shade of an apple tree to weigh up the possibilities. It did not seem likely that the imaginary creation of an underage author would later become a ghost that would haunt the house long after the author had departed. That the device had appeared only after our arrival was almost in no doubt. And it was real. After all, we had touched it, measured it and photographed it at least a hundred times. The newspapers had written about it, and it had appeared on television – and Dad had archived all this.

There were only two possibilities: either someone had stolen it or it had vanished. The broken padlock spoke in favour of the first of these options. But who would do such a thing and why? Had someone realized that we could not continue to live in the shadow of the sphinx and decided to rescue us?

The questions coalesced into a mass of speculation and uncertainty which, in their relations with each other, were reminiscent of the thing itself – just as, increasingly, it reminded me of our family, composed of potentially normal souls but welded into something weirdly unrecognizable, also a kind of sphinx incapable of answering its own questions.

I didn't rush to tell Dad what had happened. I decided to see first whether it brought any changes.

But of what kind? I could no longer remember what we had been like before the device appeared. We must have been different, but all the changes we had undergone could not be ascribed to its power. At least some had been natural consequences of living in the village, growing up, ageing, new desires and new opportunities. And, of course, Švejk's arrival, the books we had read, maybe even meeting the Important Writer, which Dad had even mentioned in his 'last testament'. Vinko's mass of tumours were certainly not a natural phenomenon, nor was Dad's decision to shoot himself with Vladimir's pistol, although I wasn't completely sure about that. Elizabeta's obsession with evil went beyond natural boundaries, especially her behaviour inside the fire engine when Švejk had used us as an excuse to flee from the gypsies.

'Speculate,' she had said to me then with devilish pleasure. I was still speculating and still hadn't reached a conclusion.

Of all the members of the family Elizabeta had most obviously succumbed to the power of the device. And so any kind of change would appear first and be most reliably observable with her. Or, it suddenly struck me, with Švejk. He visited the gypsies every day, and he had already slept there a number of times. But that bothered no one. We realized that he was gradually moving back to them only when his fire-fighter's uniform disappeared from his room. But nobody commented on this; we pretended we did not see what was happening. Just once at supper Mum asked, 'And what are you doing now, Jaro, without your vehicle?'

Before Švejk could answer, Peter said curtly, 'Does he not have the right to enjoy the freedom he fought for?'

'I'm afraid he likes the gypsies more than us,' observed Vladimir, which annoyed Peter even more.

'Me, too,' he hissed. 'I like them more than this family, which has completely broken down.'

No one commented on this accusation, so Švejk got the chance to say a few words. With a gentle voice, almost timidly, he explained that the gypsy settlement was nearer the fire station; in the event of a fire he could get there much quicker than if he stayed here. In the interests of fire safety it was better if he spent most of his time there in future. And almost every other day he took his fire engine for a short drive to try it out, so that if there were an emergency it would not let him down.

'I'm also going to go and live with the gypsies,' said Peter.

'I'm not going to live with the gypsies,' said Elizabeta, 'but it's possible I may go to live with *a* gypsy.'

'As far as I'm concerned', said Mum, 'you can all go.'

Aunt Mara said nothing to this (she had been silent for days), nor did Vinko; Dad cleared his throat as if he had something to say, but then thought better of it.

The next day Švejk finally moved out. He probably did it during the night, since no one saw him leave. It was only around midday that we discovered that he had taken all his things.

'Did he say goodbye to anyone?' Mum wanted to know.

We all shook our heads. Aunt Mara surreptitiously wiped away her tears.

'Well, that's nice.' Mum began to cry, too. 'He didn't even see the point of saying goodbye to the sister who took him under her roof. What's happened to him? It's not like him at all.'

'Typical,' Peter exploded. 'Why do you never ask what's happening to you? To all of us. It's always others who are acting in a mystifying way. He obviously didn't think it worth saying goodbye. I won't when I leave.'

'Is that so?' Mum's tears suddenly became anger. 'And where are you thinking of going, if I may ask as the mother of a son who's still living at his parents' expense?'

Peter turned without replying and ran off towards the woods.

'That last comment was unnecessary,' said Dad quietly.

'Does anyone else intend to leave?' Mum's merciless glance went to each of us in turn.

'I've nowhere to go,' said Mara with a shrug.

'The question seems uncalled for,' said Vinko.

'Uncalled for and insulting,' added Vladimir. 'My loyalty to the family has never been in doubt.'

'I am going,' said Elizabeta, 'but I don't know whether to heaven or to hell.'

'The same goes for me,' said Dad as if speaking to himself, stunning us all.

'And what's that supposed to mean?' asked Mum, who had collected herself. It was clear that Dad's words had shocked her.

'That's supposed to mean', said Dad, 'that we all pass our time not knowing whether we'll end up in heaven or in hell. The question as to why Švejk left without saying goodbye would most easily be answered by you, for I'm sure his decision is not unconnected with your shared secret.'

'What secret?' Mum's voice broke.

'The one', Dad continued relentlessly, 'that you don't consider worth sharing with those who you say are your family.'

With these words he turned and, with head raised, went to his room. It was the first time he had ever criticized Mum in front of others. Mum collapsed into a chair and sobbed convulsively.

One by one we all left.

41

There were more and more paths leading to the gypsy settlement. I discovered this when I followed Peter and then Elizabeta.

Peter no longer communicated with us except through outbreaks of flushed anger, and these were relatively infrequent. Most of the time he was inaccessible and completely, almost fiercely, lost in his thoughts. He spent most of the nights at his telescope and the days, as in the past, on long walks in the woods. I thought that he was perhaps going to spy again on the young gypsy girls who liked to sunbathe naked in a clearing.

One day, when he had wandered off after lunch like a dog with no particular destination, I secretly followed him. As soon as he reached the first trees he began to walk with the step of someone who knew exactly where he was going and who wanted to get there by the shortest possible route. Soon it became clear that he was not going towards the school but to the stream in the valley, beyond which, on the hillside, lay the settlement to which Švejk had moved.

I thought he was going to visit the eccentric uncle with whom, in recent weeks, he had evidently become friends. But I was wrong. In the midst of the bushes by the stream there waited for him the two young gypsy girls that I had first seen as bait for Švejk, when Aranka the Fortune-Teller had come to demand the return of her business partner. I had seen them for a second time at the fire-brigade celebration talking to Peter. Both were stunningly beautiful, certainly sisters, perhaps even twins, black-haired and dark-skinned like Indians with eyes that mocked and sweetly invited at the same time and with long, slender limbs and feline movements.

When they saw Peter they rushed over and began to kiss him. They pulled him to the ground and began to undress him. Peter surrendered to their eager hands without objection – almost, it seemed to me, impatiently. Clearly this wasn't the first time they had done this, as the two girls were giggling the whole time and Peter didn't seem at all embarrassed. All their movements looked practised. It wasn't long before the two girls were also without a scrap of clothing on their shining brown bodies.

But before anything could happen, not far from the oak tree from behind which I was observing them, a shot rang out. A hunter had evidently shot a deer. Peter and the girls were so startled that they threw their clothes back on twice as fast as they had removed them. The girls rushed back towards the settlement and Peter through the woods back in the direction of the house.

The next day I followed Elizabeta. She had also been wandering around a lot recently, and I suspected that, one way or another, this was connected with the gypsy with the cruel face.

But Elizabeta went towards the village church beside the graveyard. The local priest held a mass there only on church holidays, but it was open, and anyone could go inside at any time, kneel before the altar and chat quietly with God. Elizabeta had decided to chat with God out loud; probably because she didn't know that I had sneaked in after her and climbed the narrow staircase to the pulpit.

She kneeled with hands clasped on the steps in front of the wooden statue of Jesus with his crown of thorns. And she spoke.

'Listen, dear Saviour. Dear God who, according to the writer that you have probably never heard of, is my third love. I am Elizabeta, fifteen years old but in body and mind much older. Maybe not in spirit but in intellectual capabilities. At school I am by far the most intelligent, more so even than the teachers. As evidence, let me cite the fact that our art teacher didn't know that Aubrey Beardsley was a man. He insisted that he knew English better than I did and that Aubrey was a woman's name. But I'm not here to boast. I need advice. Actually, that's not true. I came because it seems to me that you, too, could benefit from a bit of advice. Above all, I'd like to advise you what to advise me. I wouldn't even have come to you if someone hadn't said that as far as advice goes you're still better than any fortune-teller or psychologist and, especially, any teacher. That's why I didn't go to see the priest but wanted to speak to you in person. Maybe you'll think me too bold, but that's the way I am. And, after all, I didn't make myself. It was you who supposedly made me.

'My problem is that I want to be a good girl. But, equally strongly, I want to do everything that comes into my head without having to answer for it. For that's how I see freedom, which they say is good not only for the soul but also the body. But it seems to me that often freedom also has serious consequences, so I want you to tell me how far I can sink into evil without drowning and becoming possessed by the one you evicted from Paradise. And, please don't say that I need to find that boundary myself, because I don't know how to. Except for you I have no one to give me the kind of advice I would want to follow.

'I'm so lost. I really don't know what's right and what's wrong. I know what is and what isn't enjoyable, but that can't be a yardstick, whatever my schoolmates say. Tell me, please. Give me a sign. Raise your left eyebrow, or whatever, just so I know I'm not talking to myself. I'm in a real fix. There's no one at home I can trust. Please. Are you even listening to me, or are you dealing with more important matters than a lost soul of a girl without a father and a mother who everyone laughs at? Nothing? Not a word? You'll regret it.'

She got up, wiped away her tears and ran outside. I followed her from a safe distance. She ran past the fire station.

I went to the window and peered inside. Švejk's 800-litre fire engine stood proudly beside the newer one. It was undoubtedly full of water and ready for immediate action should a fire break out. But there was no sign of the thunderstorms that had been forecast and no sign of Švejk, who could hardly wait for his first fire and was probably growing impatient.

I hurried to catch up with Elizabeta, but I had evidently wasted too much time at the fire-station window, and she had disappeared without trace. For some time I ran on aimlessly in the hope that I would catch sight of her. I pushed through the brambles and low bushes and went down towards the clearing beside the stream. I felt certain that she must be heading for the gypsy settlement on the opposite side. I also felt certain that she was not hurrying to see Uncle Švejk. She was heading for the gypsy with the cruel face. But she probably wouldn't dare enter the village. If she were seeing him, they must be doing it on the sly; somewhere by the stream. There, where it all began. Where we lost our virginity. Where I saw Peter with the gypsy girls. I was almost convinced that something else would happen there – and that in this way the sphinx would conclude its business.

I found them near the clearing where two days earlier I had seen Peter and the girls. They were a bit lower down, beneath a sweet chestnut tree, its heavy branches leaning across the stream. I slowed down and crept nearer. They were sitting on the ground, leaning towards each other, doing something. My view was obscured by a bush, so I crawled on all fours a little to the left.

At that moment the gypsy with the cruel face stood up and reached for the lowest branch of the chestnut tree. He pulled it towards him and tore off some leaves. He sat once more and they continued whatever it was they were doing. I saw that they were piercing each leaf with the stem of another leaf and making what looked like a necklace. Eventually, they joined both end leaves together to make a wreath, which the gypsy put on his head. He got to his feet.

'A chestnut-leaf crown,' he said, 'woven on the fifth day after the fall of the chestnut tree, the felling of which demanded five hours of sweat.'

'That's not true,' said Elizabeta. 'If you lie it won't work.'

'Be quiet,' said the gypsy with the chestnut-leaf crown. 'What do you know? If you want me to help you keep still and watch.'

He removed the crown and then fastened it to his head once more. He straightened up and closed his eyes. Then he began to march on the spot. He did that for almost a minute. Then he shouted, 'One, two, one, two, no one knows who goes here. The black devil, who everyone fears. A chestnut-leaf crown. Woven on the fifth day after the fall of the chestnut tree that demanded five hours of sweat.'

He straightened up again. Now he spoke more quietly, and I could barely understand what he was saying. 'In my pockets five medium-sized toads. I'll throw them over my head into the stream behind me.'

Five times in a row he reached into his pocket and pretended to throw something over his shoulder, while counting, 'One, two, three, four, five.' Then he bent over, cupped his hands in front of his mouth and yelled into the woods, directly at me, 'Hoooy! Melalo. All the toads in the stream. Two on the left, two on the right, one in the middle. Now the crown.'

He removed the crown and placed it on Elizabeta's head as she kneeled in the grass. He straightened up.

'I will dance three devilish dances, Melalo,' he announced. 'If you're a hundred-headed worm, I know you. If you're a magpie, I know you. If you're a bark beetle, I know you. I know you, even if you are air. I know you in every form.'

He took a step towards the tree and yelled so loud it echoed, 'Melalo! Here's your daughter who has lost her mind. Ready. I'll dance for her. Play!'

The gypsy spun in a powerful dance, flinging his arms and legs around as if he wished to be rid of them. He stopped and spun in the other direction; and then once more, again changing direction. Out of breath, he stopped and collapsed in a heap in front of Elizabeta.

'What was that?' she asked.

For some time he breathed heavily, looking at her. Then he said, 'An old gypsy curse. The chestnut-leaf crown draws poison from your brain. It kills the worms that burrow through your skull.'

'Will I be normal now?' asked Elizabeta. 'Will I no longer want to die with you?'

'No,' he said.

'And if I do?' she persisted. 'You'll kill me first and then yourself? Or both at once?'

The gypsy with the cruel face slowly got to his feet. 'I'm sorry,' he said. 'I'm trying to help you, but you're not even interested.'

'How can I be if I'm only interested in one thing?' she said on the verge of tears. 'You don't understand me at all. You don't want to understand me.'

'The Devil himself would steer clear of you,' he said, heading for the stream.

'He does,' yelled Elizabeta. 'God doesn't hear me, the Devil avoids me, at home they don't even see me. As if I'm not there. Come back! Notice me!'

The gypsy stopped, slowly turned and looked at her. With a sudden gesture, she lifted her T-shirt and showed him her breasts. He shook his head and continued looking at her as if he had no idea what to do. She pulled her T-shirt off, then her skirt and then her panties. She lay back on her elbows and opened her legs.

'Do you dare?' she asked.

'No,' he said.

'What about yesterday?' she opened her legs even wider. 'And the day before? And the day before that? How is it that sometimes you dare and sometimes not? Today we could try some new position.'

'Come on then,' he said, slowly approaching, 'although everything you've just said is the result of your sick imagination.'

'Do you like what you see?'

'No,' he said. 'But maybe you'll like this.' He leaned over and hit her hard across the face. I thought the blow would separate her head from her neck. Then he hit her from the other direction. This time her elbows gave way and she lay on the grass.

The gypsy with the cruel face went towards the wooden footbridge over the stream. He was soon on the other side. With long strides he headed for the settlement in the woods. I looked at Elizabeta, who was lying naked, legs apart beneath the chestnut tree. Her head had fallen back, and her hair was spread across the grass. Even a month before this sight would have brought a lump to my throat. Not because of the lascivious pose, which was in such contrast to her humility in the chapel, but because of the provocative wantonness, offering her concealed vulnerability with such aggression that violence seemed almost the natural response. Now I remained strangely untouched. What is more, her nakedness seemed excessive. Slightly ridiculous.

I followed the gypsy with my eyes. He was now near the edge of the woods where the settlement was. The dogs were running towards him. I noticed that Elizabeta was getting dressed. Not only that, I clearly heard her sobbing. When she was fully dressed she raised her tearful face to the sky. And a convulsive shout arose from her lips.

'Now do you see what you've done? Why don't you send me a sign? Why are you silent? You can't give me life and then forget about me!'

42

She leaped to her feet and ran through the trees towards home. I hurried after her but at a safe distance so she would not see me. As she ran she kept sniffing and wiping away her tears. It was only when she got near the house that she calmed down a little. She ran into her room and locked the door.

'What's wrong?' asked Mum.

'I've no idea,' I replied. 'I wasn't with her.'

I saw that no one believed me, but in the dining-room, in spite of the unusual hour (two in the afternoon), the whole family was present, and there was an atmosphere you could have cut with a knife. Obviously something had happened. They were all agitated but at the same time looked depressed. Dad was restlessly pacing from one door to the other. Vladimir was restlessly drumming his middle finger on the table. Vinko was supporting his head with his hand and staring into space. Aunt Mara was keenly examining her toes. Peter was standing with his arms crossed, thoughtfully staring at the ceiling. Mum was nervously toying with a lock of hair.

'Has someone died?' I asked.

'We've all died,' said Dad. 'Have you been near the garden shed?'

'No,' I shook my head.

'Are you sure?' He looked at me once more.

'I swear.' I raised two fingers.

'Stop suspecting your own son,' said Vladimir suddenly. 'I know exactly who stole the device.'

He marched out of the door and headed for the road. For his age he walked surprisingly quickly. He held his head high, and he was swinging his arms as if going off to battle.

'I hope he hasn't got his pistol with him,' said Vinko.

'Oh my God.' Mum jumped up. 'Go after him. Stop him before he does something stupid.'

The whole family rushed after Vladimir, apart from Elizabeta, who was in her room, and Peter, who decided to stay at home. But when I looked back from the edge of the trees I saw that he was now following us. Vladimir was taking such long strides that I could barely catch up with him, and the others could barely keep up with me. There was a short cut to the gypsy settlement, with which Vladimir was evidently familiar. When we got to the stream I was right behind him, but he was so focused on his goal that he didn't notice. The others were far behind; perhaps they'd got lost or taken the longer path.

The gypsies obviously knew we were coming, for the entire village was gathered together. They were standing, looking towards us as if posing for a group photograph: in the foreground eight dogs and a group of kids squatting in the dust; behind them Švejk in his fire-fighter's uniform, Aranka the Fortune-Teller, her son with the cruel face and, on either side, the two in leather jackets; behind them a row of girls, ripe for marriage, including Peter's two lovers; and behind them, in a wide semi-circle, all the other boys, men, women, old folk and children. Some small boys had climbed trees and were looking down from the branches like curious chimpanzees.

Vladimir stopped ten metres in front of them; I two metres behind him. He still hadn't noticed me.

'Švejk,' he said, 'come here a minute. I want to ask you something.'

Švejk began to respond obediently, but the gypsy with the cruel face stopped him.

'Ask him from there,' he said.

Vladimir shifted nervously, trying to keep calm. 'I can't,' he said. 'It's something confidential. We only need two minutes, that's all.'

'Send him the question by post,' said Aranka the Fortune-Teller.

Her words were received with general laughter. The gypsies were on home turf and felt confident.

'I'll count to five,' said Vladimir.

'No need,' said Aranka. 'We'll count to one.'

Once again they all laughed, except Švejk and Hudorovec who remained deadly serious. The two in leather jackets were grinning.

'One,' Vladimir raised the thumb of his left hand.

'Two,' Aranka raised the thumb and index finger of her right hand.

'Two,' said Vladimir, adding his index finger.

He didn't carry on, since one of the leather-jacketed guys gave a sharp whistle and the dogs jumped up, growled and rushed towards Vladimir. They were only halfway when a pistol appeared in Vladimir's hand. It exploded, and the biggest of the dogs, one of the Alsatians, emitted a brief noise, a cross between a bark and a howl. An unseen force threw it into the air, and then it fell lifeless on the ground. The other dogs squealed and ran back towards the gypsies, their tails between their legs. They returned to their former places and shrank as if they wished to become invisible.

'Three,' continued Vladimir, pistol in hand.

Švejk moved, and this time no one restrained him. Nor was there any laughter. He stepped over the kids who were squatting in front of him and then the frightened dogs. He meekly walked towards Vladimir, carefully avoiding the dead Alsatian. He stopped in front of Vladimir, kneading his hands together like an embarrassed schoolboy.

'Švejk,' said Vladimir, 'tell me where you're hiding the device.'

'What device?' replied Švejk in surprise. 'I took it with me. It's mine.'

'It's not yours,' said Vladimir, 'so tell me, now, where you've hidden it, otherwise there'll be unpleasant consequences.'

'Of course it's mine.' Švejk slightly raised his voice. 'It's true that you bought a few things – a hammer, a drill and three screwdrivers – but you said they were mine. I didn't know you wanted them back.'

'Švejk,' Vladimir waved the pistol, 'stop pretending to be even more stupid than you are. You know damn well which device I'm talking about, and if you don't tell me *right now* where you've hidden it I'll be compelled to forget we are friends.'

'I've no idea what you're talking about,' replied Švejk with a shrug.

The old Partisan raised his hand and with a sharp blow knocked the hero of the war for independence to the ground. The gypsy with the cruel face and the guys in leather jackets moved to help him, but they took only one step before Vladimir aimed the pistol at them and said, 'Keep going. One cur has already got what it deserves.'

At that moment we heard a rustling noise; the other members of the family were finally making their way through the trees and bushes.

'Vladimir,' yelled Dad, 'put your weapon away.'

'Unfortunately, I can't,' said Vladimir. 'We're in the middle of a war.'

'It's not a war,' said Dad, when he got to him; 'it's a dispute. The old way of settling disagreements is no longer permitted. The world has moved on. Give me the gun.' He reached out his hand.

'No,' I wanted to shout when I remembered Dad's 'last testament', but it was too late, for Vladimir had already handed it over.

Dad put it in his trouser pocket and said, 'From now on I'll take care of it.' He turned to Švejk, who had just got to his feet.

'What did he do to you?' Dad asked.

'Nothing,' said Švejk, taking hold of his lower jaw to see if he could still move it. 'I tripped and fell. Can I go back now?'

Dad looked at him in perplexity. 'Where to, if I may ask?'

'To where I belong,' Švejk jerked his head towards the gypsies.

'But you belong with us,' said Mum, taking a step towards him. 'Since when do you belong with them?'

'Sorry,' said Švejk and with drooping shoulders walked towards the gypsies. He resumed his place beside Aranka.

Then we saw Peter follow him.

'And where do you think you're going?' Mum demanded.

'Also where I belong,' said Peter without turning around.

He joined his two beauties. They put their arms around his waist and each kissed him on the cheek.

'Oh God,' sighed Mum and crossed herself.

'It's a little late to be doing that,' said Dad. He straightened up to give at least the appearance of authority, but it was obvious that even he no longer believed in it. 'Let's talk like reasonable people –' he began, but Aranka cut him short.

'We can't while there's a dead dog lying there.'

Dad looked at Vladimir, who shrugged and said, 'It had a stroke because of the heat. It's very humid. I think there's a storm coming on.'

'You don't even see us as people,' Aranka continued. 'You see us only as gypsies.'

'That's not true,' objected Dad. 'No one ever said you're any different from us.'

'That's precisely the problem,' said Janek Hudorovec. 'We are different from you, but you're incapable of accepting that.'

'But we are,' said Dad. 'After all, two members of our family have joined you, including my son.'

'This son of yours is going to cost you dear,' said Aranka smugly. 'He's got two of our naughtiest ones pregnant. How do you like the idea of gypsy grandchildren?'

Once again there was a wave of laughter.

'Oh no,' stammered Mum, 'I think I'm going to pass out.'

'I wouldn't recommend it,' said Aunt Mara. 'Someone will have to wash nappies and watch the little bastards while the two bitches are having fun.'

'You know what,' Mum twisted towards her, 'you look to your own daughter first before gloating over the misfortunes of others.'

'Please, please,' Dad pleaded. 'Vinko, can you make them see sense?'

But Vinko merely shrugged, surprised that Dad had turned to him.

'Švejk,' Dad made an effort to sound more official, 'let's get to the bottom of this like the friends we still are. If I recall your own words: the only true goal of all of us is inner peace. Let us find it. Ever since the mysterious device that all the papers were writing about eighteen months ago disappeared from the shed at the bottom of the orchard we have felt wrong. We all feel as one that the device is ours. I'm not saying it brings us any kind of benefit, but its value is deeply symbolic. It represents a great family mystery that we can deal with only if it is with us and under lock and key. Something that influences us much more than we realize has escaped our supervision and fallen into the hands of someone who might not be well disposed towards us. Can you imagine how dangerous that is? Be a good man and tell us what you know about it.'

43

Silence followed. All eyes were turned on Švejk. He shifted slightly and said, 'Oh, that? All I know about that is what the boy told me,' and he pointed to me. 'He said it wasn't even real, that he'd made it all up. I believed him. Why shouldn't I? After all, such a thing can't be real. Where could it have come from?'

'All the papers wrote about it,' said Dad.

Švejk shrugged. 'I don't read newspapers. Recently I've read only the *Fire-Fighters' Bulletin*.'

'He's lying,' muttered Vladimir. 'He's lying through his teeth.'

'Perhaps he doesn't know anything,' commented Mum.

'Of course he does.' Vladimir got worked up. 'He stole it, and the gypsies helped him. They probably already have a buyer for it. People collect all sorts of things these days.'

'It's true some American offered me a quarter of a million dollars,' Dad recalled.

'You see?' added Vladimir. 'Švejk maybe wouldn't do this off his own bat, but the gypsy witch has enchanted him. And it's quite possible that Peter is involved.'

'Oh no he isn't,' Mum protested.

'Peter,' Dad turned back towards the gypsies, 'do you know anything about this?'

'Nothing,' said Peter. 'It's the first I've heard of this device. I don't remember ever seeing it let alone reading about it in the papers.'

'I knew it,' muttered Vladimir. 'He's been caught by the lowest form of trick. Those two were first offered to Švejk, do you remember?'

'But, if that's true,' said Vinko, 'we'll never see the device again.'

'Of course we will,' said Vladimir. 'But we have to fight a war first. We must be prepared for casualties.'

'Before you declare war on anyone,' said Dad, 'don't forget that your pistol is in my pocket, where it's going to stay.'

'So are we supposed to sue them?' replied Vladimir, agitated.

'Švejk.' Dad turned once more towards the gypsies.

This time he was interrupted by thunder rumbling above the nearby hill. Only then did we notice that during our confrontation the sky had become covered with threatening black clouds. The first of the forecast storms was evidently on its way.

On Švejk's face I saw relief; he did not try to hide how delighted he would be if lightning were to hit one of the village houses and he could finally prove himself in the role of fire-fighter.

'There's going to be a downpour,' said Mum, 'and we've no umbrellas.'

'Then we'll get wet,' said Dad dismissively. 'Perhaps the water will wash some of our sins away. We're not going anywhere until we get to the bottom of this. Švejk,' he turned back to our lost uncle, 'I'm appealing to you, to the good I know you have within you, to tell us the truth. We're willing to negotiate for the device. Just tell us where it is.'

'I can't right now,' said Švejk, 'because the siren may go off and I'll have to rush to the fire station.'

'Then you admit that you know what I'm talking about.'

'I'll have to think about it. At the moment, I need to be completely focused.'

At that very moment, his and our concentration was destroyed by what sounded like half the sky falling down.

Lightning struck the neighbouring hill.

'Fire!' yelled one of the gypsy boys from high in a tree. He pointed towards our village.

Švejk disappeared among the trees, and the gypsies rushed after him, except for the oldest, who scattered to their homes. Large drops began to fall, and a wind blew through the treetops.

The family also headed for the stream and followed the crowd led by Švejk. Vladimir and Aunt Mara were left far behind. Beyond the woods on the hill we could already see flames.

'Thank God it's not our house,' panted Mum who, as an experienced marathon runner, was leading the family.

'Poor comfort for those whose house really is burning,' observed Dad.

'Švejk will save what can be saved,' said Mum. 'When he puts out his first fire he will change – he'll even move back to us. And return the device. If it really was him who took it.'

'Of that there's no doubt,' said Dad.

Peter wasn't with us; he had caught up with the crowd of gypsies that had already disappeared into the trees on the opposite slope.

When we finally struggled up the slope and out of the woods into the open we were stunned to see that it wasn't one of the village houses on fire but the fire station. A crowd of people stood in front of it, helplessly watching the flames consuming not only the building but also the two fire engines. The fire-fighters stood in a semi-circle, shaking their heads and patting each other on the shoulders in consolation.

The most visibly upset was Švejk. Several times he tried to rush into the flames, but strong hands restrained him.

'My fire engine,' he lamented. 'My fire engine.'

The fire had brought almost the whole village out. Some rushed up with buckets of water, but they did nothing to diminish the speed with which the fire consumed the building and equipment in which the villagers had invested so much money and effort. Rain would probably have helped, but only a few drops were falling from the dark clouds. The centre of the storm had moved on to the neighbouring hill; lightning was dancing somewhere over the gypsy settlement.

Finally Vladimir and Mara caught up with us.

'Poor Švejk,' panted Mara. 'If he'd left his vehicle at our place he would have been able to use it to save the other.'

'How could lightning hit the fire station?' said Vladimir, annoyed. 'Didn't they have a lightning conductor?'

'Perhaps this is a metaphor for our efforts to understand things that cannot be understood,' commented Dad.

'Oh, go easy on the metaphors,' said Peter, who had left the gypsies and returned to us.

'Nice that you're here,' said Mum. 'You'll be forgiven everything if only you'll stay with us.'

'I'm convinced that the sphinx is involved in this incident, too,' said Vinko.

'Don't overdo it,' Mum rebuked him.

Then there was a terrible explosion, and from the centre of the fire an unbelievable number of things flew into the air, including pieces of brick and charred roof beams but mainly metal fragments, which were evidently from the two fire engines in which the fuel had exploded. They slowly fell to earth, and we heard them landing on the concrete, which was the only thing the fire had left untouched.

When the flames had subsided and the smoke cleared we saw something unusual in the middle of the fire station. At first, we thought it was the remains of one of the vehicles, which had been mangled by the fire into an unusual form, but when we moved closer there was no longer any doubt that it was the mysterious device, which had somehow disappeared from our shed and ended up there. We looked at Švejk, who was slowly walking towards us.

'Švejk?' said Dad.

The fire-fighter manqué and hero of the war for independence hung his head and said, 'I put the device in the water tank, which I made air-tight and filled with water. Peter and Janek Hudorovec helped me. I did it for you. I saw that you were sick. I wanted to save you from this cursed object.'

But the device was no longer quite as we remembered it. The relations between the component parts were changed. The toilet bowl was no longer fused with the rake but with the pickaxe, the pan with the chain rather than the cogs, and everything else was rearranged in a different but equally incomprehensible pattern.

The shortwave radio in the centre suddenly crackled and started to broadcast, but it was no longer the Arabic-sounding voice commenting on something. The tone of voice was the same, but it was repeating incessantly a string of syllables: dan dan dan dan dan din din din din don don don don dun dun dun dun den den den din din din don don don dan dan dan . . .

I remembered how the Important Writer had ended the story about the mysterious object in the school exercise book entitled *Sketches, Poems, Plays and Reports*. I hope you won't mind if I use his ending, slightly adapted:

> With lowered arms and eyes we stood around the diabolical thing and listened to the voice coming from God knows where... maybe from space, maybe from the centre of the thing itself or from our defeated imaginations, which, under the weight of the event, had become – like the object in front of us – a mass of uncertainty and disorder.

It began to rain.

When we got home, we found in the living-room, on the blood-soaked couch, Elizabeta's body.

She had cut her wrists. Her wide-open eyes stared motionless at the ceiling, through the ceiling, through the roof, into the depths of the sky.

She had left a message on the table:

> Now do you see what you've done? You can't give me life and then forget about me!

Also by Evald Flisar

MY FATHER'S DREAMS

978-1-908236-22-7 • paperback • 192pp • £9.99

'Evald Flisar, Slovene man of letters extraordinaire, undertakes fearless forays into the bizarre ways in which the mind works. *My Father's Dreams*, a deadpan, slow-burning cautionary tale, requires patience yet ultimately delivers . . . It is a book about how a child is influenced and undermined and betrayed.'
– Eileen Battersby, *Irish Times*

'A masterful and disturbing novel . . . At the heart of *My Father's Dreams* is a brilliant interplay of human deception and the unsettling lies and obsessions of which humans are capable.' – A.M. Bakalar, *Words Without Borders*

My Father's Dreams: A Tale of Innocence Abused, is a controversial and shocking novel by Slovenia's best-selling author Evald Flisar and is regarded by many critics as one of his best. The book tells the story of fourteen-year-old Adam, the only son of a village doctor and his rather estranged wife, living in apparent rural harmony. But this is a topsy-turvy world of illusions and hopes, in which the author plays with the function of dreaming and story-telling. The story reveals an insidious deception, in which the unsuspecting son and his mother are the apparent victims; and yet who can tell whether the gruesome ending is reality or just another dream . . .

My Father's Dreams can be read as an off-beat crime story, a psychological horror tale, a dream-like morality fable or as a dark and ironic account of one man's belief that his personality and his actions are two different things. It can also be read as a story about a boy who has been robbed of his childhood in the cruellest way. It is a book that has the force of myth, revealing the fundamentals without drawing any particular attention to them. It is a story about good and evil and our inclination to be drawn to the latter.